The
Sand Dancer

ROSIE GOODWIN

The Sand Dancer

headline

First published in Great Britain in 2008
by HEADLINE PUBLISHING GROUP

1

Cataloguing in Publication Data is available from the British Library

ISBN 978 0 7553 4373 7

Typeset in Bembo by Avon DataSet Ltd,
Bidford-on-Avon, Warwickshire

Printed and bound in Great Britain by
Mackays of Chatham plc, Chatham, Kent

Headline's policy is to use papers that are natural, renewable and
recyclable products and made from wood grown in sustainable forests.
The logging and manufacturing processes are expected to conform to the
environmental regulations of the country of origin.

HEADLINE PUBLISHING GROUP
An Hachette Livre UK Company
338 Euston Road
London NW1 3BH

www.headline.co.uk

The
Sand Dancer

Chapter One

IT WAS ON OUR third wedding anniversary that Hamilton suddenly put in an appearance. I had not seen him for a number of years and so it was something of a shock, to say the least, when I saw him over Tommy's shoulder.

Tommy, my husband, was preparing to leave for a weekend on his boat and I was feeling ashamed, for I found that I was looking forward to him going. Tommy Balfour was my third husband, which still seemed incredible to me, to think that three men could have wished to marry *me*, who Gran Carter had once referred to as plain as a pikestaff. Three very different men, I may add. The first, Howard Stickle, had married me for the house and the money that my mother had left me in her will when she died. He had made my life a misery, but had finally met his comeuppance when he died, still a comparatively young man.

My second husband, Leonard Leviston, or Nardy, as I had always affectionately called him, had left me a broken-hearted widow. I had met Nardy, who was a publisher, when I submitted my first book to him, a book about the very creature that was staring across Tommy's shoulder right now. I had expected him to reject it out of hand. After all, I had reasoned, who would

1

want to read about a girl with a wizened arm who was so lonely that she had invented an imaginary horse to talk to? But Nardy had not rejected it, he had published it, and it had become the first of many bestsellers, which just went to show how wrong I could be. It was whilst we were working on the first draft of that very book that Nardy and I had fallen in love and he had shown me that not all men were the same. But our happiness was to be short-lived, for Nardy and I had enjoyed precious little time together before his untimely death. And now here I was married to Tommy, who had been a close friend and colleague of Nardy's. I had never loved him with the unswerving devotion I had felt for Nardy, but even so I had expected our marriage to be a happy one, and it had been for all of six months. From then on it had been downhill all the way, although I hadn't immediately realised it, of course. The change in our relationship had been a gradual one until I had suddenly woken up one morning some months ago and realised that I was happier when we were apart and I could spend time alone with Harold, the child I had adopted almost four years ago.

I started when Tommy's exasperated voice brought my thoughts back to the present.

'Maisie, are you listening to me?' he said. 'You always go off into a world of your own when you're at that blasted typewriter. I was asking – have you got everything you need until I get back?'

'Oh yes,' I assured him. 'And anything I haven't got, Janet will get for me.'

Mrs Janet Flood, to give her her correct title, was my housekeeper and Harold's grandmother as well as being a true friend. Until I adopted him, Janet had cared for Harold after her daughter, Maggie, had abandoned him to go off with one of her numerous boyfriends.

2

'Good.' Tommy paused. I knew he was feeling guilty for going off and leaving me on our anniversary, although I had assured him that I really didn't mind. I also knew that he would be fretting about me leaving the house without him, for Tommy could be very jealous and often accused me of falling in love with every man that I spoke to. His jealousy had become worse during the three years we had been married, until now I had resigned myself to rarely venturing from the house unless he was at my side. Even then he would imagine that I was making cow eyes at every man I met. In actual fact I enjoyed the sanctuary of my apartment. Nardy had left it to me when he died, and strangely, Tommy was happy to stay there.

'You could always change your mind and come with me,' he told me now, but I shook my head.

'I know I could, dear. But with the weather as it is I would really much rather stay here. And I do have this deadline to meet. Go on, you go off and enjoy yourself. Harold and I will be perfectly all right.'

'Very well then, I shall be back tomorrow evening. Goodbye, my dear. Goodbye, Harold.'

Harold, whose head was buried in a comic, nodded as Tommy quietly left the room.

I found myself smiling as I stared at the child's bowed head. Harold was now almost eleven years old and, to use a term his grandmother was fond of, was growing like a weed. He seemed to be all arms and legs. Sandy, our poodle, was curled up on the sofa at his side, but that was no surprise, for the two of them were inseparable.

I waited until I heard Tommy enter the lift in the outer hall outside our flat, then turning back to Harold I asked him, 'Would you like a drink? I think I'll have a cup of coffee before I get started on this again.'

'Ner,' he replied, and then as he saw my eyebrows rise, he quickly changed it to 'No thank you.'

I stood up and hurried away to the kitchen, trying hard not to let him see me smile. It was a constant battle with Harold, trying to get him to speak correctly, that was. Tommy often told me that I was fighting a losing battle, and that I would never make a silk purse out of what he termed a cow's ear. But still I continued to try; after all, I considered that adopting Harold was one of the best things that I had ever done and not a day went by when I did not thank God for him.

It was as I was filling the kettle that I heard a key in the lock and seconds later Janet appeared and dropped her umbrella into the sink.

'Goodness me, it's grand weather for ducks,' she commented, nodding towards the rain that was lashing against the windows. 'His nibs gone off on one of his jaunts on the boat again, has he?'

'If you mean Tommy, yes he has,' I replied, feeling the need to defend him.

Janet sniffed. I had never uttered so much as a single word to her about our marriage not being quite as it should be, but Janet was no fool and as she often said, she had an uncanny knack of knowing when things were not right.

'And what about his Lordship? Got his head buried in a book as usual, has he?'

I grinned now as I spooned coffee into two mugs. 'Yes he has, though he's off to play football for the school this afternoon.'

Janet smiled back. Although Harold was now legally mine by adoption, she was still very much his grandmother and took a great interest in him, especially since she had been widowed the year before.

'Well, that's another string to his bow then, ain't it?' she stated proudly as she hung her wet coat over the back of a kitchen chair. 'A voice like an angel an' good at sports into the bargain, eh?'

I nodded in agreement, trying hard to ignore Hamilton. He was standing behind Janet now, wagging his head at me over her shoulder. I quickly looked away as I felt colour flood into my cheeks. Why had he decided to come back now? I wondered. Normally he only showed up when I was deeply unsettled about something.

'I, er . . . I'm just going to my room to get a handkerchief,' I told Janet as I placed her coffee down in front of her. To my consternation I saw Hamilton start to follow me as I hastily left the room.

Once in the privacy of my bedroom I rounded on him and in a low voice hissed, 'So, what brings you back then?'

Hamilton put his head to one side as he observed me, his glorious white mane spilling down his broad back.

I just thought it was time for a visit, he said gravely. I thought you were looking a little peaky. But then, I suppose it's to be expected seeing as you rarely venture out nowadays. This place might be nice but you should be careful it doesn't become a prison. He spread his front legs as if to add emphasis to his words as I ran a hand distractedly across my eyes.

'Rubbish. I *like* staying in. I have a book I need to finish and it won't get done if I'm out gallivanting off all over the place, will it?'

His head now moved to the other side as he silently stared at me before saying, Are you *quite* sure that's the only reason you stay in?

'Of *course* it is.' I would have said more but at that moment Janet's voice wafted through the closed door.

'Who are you talkin' to in there?' she asked. 'They reckon it's a sign of madness to talk to yourself, you know.'

I glared at Hamilton as I turned to snatch a handkerchief from the drawer. 'Oh, I wasn't talking,' I shouted back. 'I was singing actually.'

When I turned back Hamilton was gone, and for no reason that I could explain a great sense of loneliness engulfed me. But then I pulled myself together, and after blowing my nose I headed for the door again.

By now Janet was flicking a duster about with one eye on Harold. 'So, I hear you're off playin' football this afternoon then,' she remarked.

He grinned as he dragged his eyes away from his comic. 'Yes I am, Gag. Mr Trent reckons I might make the school team if I carry on as I am doin'.'

'*Doing!*' I corrected him, and he rolled his eyes at his gran as he rose from the chair.

'It's a wonder you didn't go with Mr Tommy, ain't it?' she now asked, and Harold glanced at me before shrugging.

'Oh, I thought I'd give it a miss this week.' He looked vaguely uncomfortable so I hastily changed the subject.

'Well, just make sure that you wrap up warmly. It's very cold out there from what I can see of it.'

'Makes no difference once you're on the field,' he pointed out, and I nodded in agreement. He did have a point, though personally I had never been able to understand how anyone could find pleasure in kicking a ball about a wet field. But then I wasn't a boy.

As he passed me on his way to his room I watched him go affectionately. Sometimes lately I felt that it was only Harold and my writing that kept me going, although I would rather have died than admit it to anyone else, of course.

His door had scarcely closed behind him when I became aware that Janet had paused in her dusting and was watching me closely.

'Is everything all right?' she asked softly.

Forcing my brightest smile to my face I replied, 'Of course, why wouldn't it be?'

'Oh, I don't know . . . it's just you've seemed . . . a little preoccupied lately. You're not feeling ill, are you?'

'I'm as fit as a fiddle,' I assured her, but she wasn't ready to close the subject yet.

'It just seems strange that you've stopped goin' on the boat of a sudden, that's all.' She was bending over the coffee table again now with the duster flying in all directions, but I knew that she was watching me from the corner of her eye.

'Well if truth be told, now that Tommy has taken to sailing her across the Channel I can't say that I'm too keen on it.' That was not altogether an untruth. Tommy had bought the boat, *Spring Fever*, just before our marriage and for the first couple of years had been happy to go no further than up and down the canal in her, but lately he had become more adventurous and had started to take her across to France. I had never felt happy about leaving the still waters of the canal and so it had given me the perfect opportunity to decline his invitations.

'And Captain Lee still sails it for him, does he?' she asked.

'Not always. Tommy is very good at sailing himself now.'

'Mm, strange that Harold doesn't want go any more either, ain't it?'

'Now, Janet,' I told her sternly. 'Don't go reading things into it. Harold is at that age where he wants to spend time with his friends after being at school all week.' I was keen to get away from her now, for Hamilton had appeared again, this time standing in the kitchen doorway, and he wasn't alone: an old donkey was standing beside him.

I almost choked on my coffee, and as I dabbed at my chin with my handkerchief I told her, 'I, er . . . Think I'll just go and have a lie down for half an hour if you'll excuse me, Janet. I could do with a break from all this typing. I have a slight headache coming on.'

'All right, I'll call you when Harold is ready for the off, shall I?' she replied good-naturedly.

I nodded as I swung about and headed for the bedroom where, just as I had expected, I found Hamilton and his new friend waiting for me.

'So who is this then?' I asked the second I had closed the door behind me.

Hamilton glanced across at his mate before replying. It's Dusty. He used to live in an animal sanctuary but he came to join me and Begonia a while ago.

How strange, I found myself thinking; the book I was writing at present had a donkey in it.

'And where is Begonia?' I forced myself to ask. Hamilton had turned up some years ago when I married Nardy with a beautiful thoroughbred mare who he had introduced as Begonia.

Oh, she's busy at the moment. He tossed his mane as Dusty watched him with a bored expression on his face. We are going to have a foal, you know, he went on to inform me. She's really looking forward to it, isn't she, Dusty?

I ran my hand across my forehead, wondering what else he was going to spring on me, but words temporarily failed me and I made no comment. Instead I crossed to the window and looked out at the rain-drenched street beyond.

'I sometimes wonder why you suddenly just turn up out of

the blue,' I told him wearily, and when there was no answer I turned around to find myself alone again.

I sighed before lying on the bed, where I soon slipped into an uneasy doze.

As promised, Janet roused me some time later, in time to see Harold off to his football match. He was warmly wrapped in a thick coat and a scarf and gloves that Janet had knitted him the previous Christmas.

'Are you sure you wouldn't like to come and watch me, Mrs Nardy?' he asked me hopefully.

I tucked his scarf into his lapels, avoiding his eyes. It was funny how he always reverted to calling me Mrs Nardy when Tommy was not present. When he was here, his term for me was Mrs Tommy, or sometimes Mum.

'No, I won't today, dear,' I told him. 'I really do have to get on with this book or I shall have the publishers screaming at me.'

He eyed me with far more wisdom than his years warranted. 'Are you sure it ain't . . . isn't 'cos Mr Tommy don't like you going out without him?'

A little shock coursed through me as I realised with a jolt that Harold was noticing Tommy's obsessive behaviour. I really shall have to put my foot down, I thought, but to him I said brightly, 'No, Harold, I would have loved to come and watch you, but as I said I really am working to a very tight deadline.'

As he slouched towards the door I knew that he hadn't believed a word I had said. Taking up the bag with his football boots and his kit in he shouted towards the kitchen, 'Bye, Gag,' and then flashed me a smile and was gone as I stood there watching the door he had just closed behind him.

There were delicious smells issuing from the kitchen, and

when I walked in I found Janet just placing a steaming dish on the table.

'I've done you an' Harold a shepherd's pie for your tea,' she informed me. 'You can warm it up whenever you want. I was hopin' to get off to bingo if there was nothin' else you wanted doin'. There's a grand up for grabs at the Palace at this afternoon's sittin', an' who knows? It just might be me lucky day.'

'It might indeed,' I agreed with a warm smile. 'Go on, you get off and enjoy yourself. Harold and I will be just fine.'

'Mm, well that's a matter of opinion.' Sniffing loudly, she took her coat from the back of the chair. 'I'll see you on Monday then, eh?'

'You certainly will,' I told her brightly, and then she too was gone, and as I sank down at the table, loneliness wrapped itself around me like a blanket. Only now could I admit just how much Hamilton's appearance had shocked me. It made me realise how low I must be, for Hamilton was rarely there when I was truly happy.

Looking back over my life, it seemed that I had never really been destined to know happiness for any length of time. The few years I had spent with Nardy, my beloved second husband, still stood out as the best time, closely followed by my adopting Harold, who continued to be the light in my life. I realised now that marrying Tommy had been a mistake although I couldn't say that he was a bad man, at least not in the way Howard Stickle had been bad. Tommy had never so much as raised a finger to me, or his voice for that matter, and that was part of the problem. He wanted to wrap me in cotton wool and keep me exclusively to himself, which had seemed nice for a while, but the novelty had long since worn off and now I was beginning to feel stifled.

'What should I do?' I asked as I looked around the empty room for a glimpse of Hamilton. He could usually point me in the right direction, but there was no sign of him now, so slowly I returned to my typewriter, which was a poor second to being allowed to go and watch Harold play football.

Chapter Two

'**Y**OU BEAT ST Joseph's! Why that's wonderful, dear.' I smiled as I helped Harold shrug his wet coat off, but there was no answering smile; in fact, he looked decidedly dejected.

'Willy Smith's mum an' dad *an'* his grandad were there to watch *him* play,' he announced with a note of resentment loud in his voice.

Shame cut through me like a knife. What Harold was really saying was, and no one bothered to come and watch me!

I placed my hand on his shoulder but he shrugged it away as he bent to stroke Sandy, whose tail was wagging furiously.

'Well, that was nice for him,' I said lightly. 'I shall have to make sure I'm there to watch you the next time you play.'

'*Really?*' His face was brighter than a ray of sunshine now as I solemnly nodded.

'Really,' I assured him. 'But now it's a bath for you, young man. I've no doubt you'll have half of the football pitch smeared across your legs.'

He made for the bathroom without argument, and left alone with my thoughts I crossed to the lounge window and stared down into the street below.

That's freedom out there. Do you remember what it feels

like to be free? a voice asked, and glancing over my shoulder I saw Hamilton standing with his front legs crossed watching me closely.

'Yes, I do remember,' I muttered. 'And I think it's about time I made a stand. Tommy's behaviour is becoming obsessive and the more I give in to it the worse it will become.'

Hamilton nodded in agreement, his black coat gleaming like a seal's in the light from the small lamp standing on a table to the side of him.

'I'll start tomorrow,' I told him. 'I'll take Harold for a walk in the park and then we can go and have lunch somewhere. There's no harm in that, is there?'

At that moment a voice from the bathroom shouted, 'Mrs Nardy, could you get my dressing gown, please? I forgot to bring it in with me.'

I smiled at Hamilton as I hurried towards Harold's bedroom, and when I came out seconds later he was gone. Shrugging my shoulders, I took the dressing gown in to Harold and then went to the kitchen to warm up the pie Janet had left for us.

We spent a pleasant evening watching television and doing a jigsaw, but at nine o'clock Harold started to yawn, so I patted his arm and told him, 'Go on, young man. Get yourself off to bed. I'll tidy this lot up. All that football must have tired you out.'

He flashed me a smile that warmed my heart as his arms snaked around my neck and he kissed me soundly on my cheek.

'You did mean what you said about comin' to watch me the next time I play football, didn't you?' he asked.

I nodded. 'I most certainly did. Now off with you while I put this jigsaw away.'

He scampered away, all arms and legs, as I began to pile the jigsaw back into its box. It was one of the ones I had bought for

Nardy to do while he was confined to bed, and as I thought of him now, tears stung at the back of my eyes. There would never be another Nardy. Only now did I realise that I had married Tommy out of loneliness following Nardy's death. It had been a mistake, but I was forced to admit that not all of the blame lay with him. He was a good husband in many ways and I wanted for nothing. Yet still there was something missing . . . I mentally shook myself. It was no good crying over spilt milk, as Gran Carter would have said. I had made my bed and now I would have to lie on it; try a little harder to love Tommy as he deserved to be loved. Perhaps then his obsessive behaviour would wane. In a more positive frame of mind, I began to turn off the lights and prepare for bed.

All my good intentions flew out of the window the very next evening when Tommy stormed into the flat with a face on him that could have curdled the milk. Harold and I had spent a lovely day together, first walking in the park and then having lunch in a small café in Piccadilly before returning home with glowing cheeks caused by the wind that was whipping up and down the streets.

'Hello, dear,' I greeted Tommy as he yanked his coat off and slung it across the back of a chair. 'Did you have a good weekend?'

'I've had better,' he told me shortly as he dropped on to the settee. 'Is there any tea going?'

'We had lunch in Piccadilly,' Harold informed him, and instantly Tommy's eyes were tight on me as he said, 'Oh yes, and who with?'

'With each other, of course,' I replied calmly as I lifted his coat and headed towards the coat rack.

Harold's face fell a foot as he saw the look in Tommy's eyes.

Keen to change the subject, I asked, 'So what went wrong with your weekend, then?'

'Oh, the skipper just informed me that he's going to retire.' Tommy looked as if the end of the world was about to arrive, and I tried to hide my amusement as I said, 'Surely you can replace him? You don't take him along most weekends now anyway. Do you really need a skipper?'

'Not on every journey,' he admitted. 'But I do when I go across the Channel. I dare say I'll have to start looking around for a replacement. Till then I'll have to stick to the river.'

'Why don't you put an ad up in the boatyard?' I suggested.

'That's not such a bad idea. I just might do that next weekend. Now where's that tea, eh?' Tommy was smiling now as I moved towards the kitchen, leaving him to chat to Harold.

The wind battering against the window the following Saturday morning woke me from a deep sleep. I could hear the sound of the television in the lounge and someone clattering about in the kitchen. Tommy had gone out the evening before and not come home until the early hours of the morning, and now as I felt his side of the bed I found that it was empty. Yawning, I swung my legs to the side of the bed and tugged my dressing gown on before heading for the kitchen.

'Morning, Mrs Tommy.' Harold flashed me a bright smile as I walked through the lounge and I smiled back.

'Morning, dear. What are you watching?'

He waved a hand towards the television set. 'There's been a real hurricane in southern England,' he told me excitedly. 'They reckon it's caused damage all the way from Dorset to East Anglia an' the cost could amount to three hundred million quid. It's been bad in London too, an' a third o' the trees in Kew

Gardens 'ave been blown down. The fire brigade 'ave been out all night dealin' wi' the damage an' all.'

'Oh dear,' I replied, glancing nervously towards the window, then I hurried on to join Tommy in the kitchen. He was standing at the cooker frying bacon and he looked up as I entered the room. A huge bruise covered the whole of one cheek, and when he saw me looking at it he fingered it self-consciously.

'I did it on the boat last night,' he hurried to tell me. 'With the weather being so bad I thought I'd make sure that everything was all right. Captain Lee was still there when I came home early this morning; he didn't want to leave her. *Spring Fever* was bobbing about like something demented and we were worried that she might break free from her moorings. I told him we'd done all we could to make her secure, but he insisted on staying on. Talk about a captain not deserting a sinking ship, eh?'

'That looks quite nasty. You should get it looked at,' I told him as I raised my hand to touch his swollen face, but he brushed me away.

'It's nothing,' he insisted. 'The deck was slippery and I went flying and banged my face, but it's only a bruise. I would like to get back over there this morning and make sure everything's all right, if you don't mind. I was hoping to take her out this weekend but I can't see me managing it with the weather being as it is. I think we must have copped the tail end of the hurricane.'

I nodded in agreement as I took some plates from the cupboard and spread them out on the kitchen table, and for a while the storm was forgotten as we all sat down to breakfast.

It was some half an hour later when we heard the sound of the lift doors opening on our outer landing. Harold had skipped off back to the lounge with the morbid curiosity of youth to watch the update on the hurricane damage, and Tommy and I were enjoying a leisurely cup of tea.

'Who could that be at this time of the morning?' I tied the belt of my dressing gown a little more tightly and rose from the table.

'It's probably Janet,' Tommy replied, but I shook my head.

'No, if it were Janet she would use her key. I gave her the day off today anyway.' I had no sooner said it than the doorbell rang. I hurried to answer it and found two very wet gentlemen standing in the reception hall.

'Mrs Balfour?' one of them enquired.

Glancing down at the puddle of water that was pooling around his feet, I nodded. He instantly produced an identity card from the top pocket of his overcoat and flashed it at me.

'I'm Inspector Beck,' he informed me solemnly. 'I was wondering if I might have a word with your husband. Is he in?'

'Yes he is,' I told him, wondering what on earth he could want with Tommy. 'Won't you come in?'

He looked down apologetically at the water before stepping past me into the hallway, where we were confronted by Tommy and Harold who had come to see who was at the door.

The Inspector frowned before muttering, 'Is there somewhere we could perhaps talk in private?'

I followed his eyes to Harold and said, 'Of course, go through to the dining room. Harold, why don't you go back to your programme?'

Harold sighed heavily, obviously afraid of missing something, but he turned all the same and disappeared back into the drawing room with a deep frown on his face as Tommy ushered the two men into the dining room. Once inside, the man who had introduced himself as Inspector Beck looked round appreciatively until the door closed, when he turned to face Tommy and me, who were standing side by side.

'Mr Balfour,' he began without preamble, 'are you the owner of a boat called *Spring Fever* that is moored on the Regent's Canal?'

When Tommy nodded he went on, 'Then I wonder if you could tell me your whereabouts last night?'

Tommy flushed before saying, 'Actually, I was on the boat trying to secure her against the terrible weather we're having. Why do you ask?'

The two policemen glanced at each other, and then Inspector Beck cleared his throat before saying, 'Before I answer that question, could you tell me if you were alone on the boat?'

'No, I wasn't,' Tommy told him instantly. 'My skipper was there with me and we worked together.'

'And would that skipper happen to be a certain Captain Edward Lee?'

'Yes, it would.' Tommy nodded vigorously as he ran his hand through his hair. The Inspector was eyeing the bruise on his cheek, but before the man could ask him how he had come by the injury, Tommy self-consciously raised his hand to it and told him, 'I slipped on the deck, but could you please tell me what this is all about?'

The Inspector cleared his throat again, and with his eyes tight on Tommy he then told him, 'I'm afraid there has been a rather unfortunate incident involving Captain Lee.'

'What sort of an incident?' Tommy questioned.

'Captain Lee was found floating in the canal early this morning, sir, not far from your boat as it happens. It appears that he had been dead for some hours when he was discovered. I was wondering if you could tell us what time you left him.'

Tommy had paled and groped at the back of a chair for

support as he muttered, 'It must have been around ten thirty.'

I forced myself to fix my eyes on the floor as shock coursed through me. Tommy had not returned until the early hours of the morning. Where had he been since leaving the boat?

'Can you confirm this, madam?' The Inspector's eyes were fixed on me now, and deep in shock I sank on to the chair that Tommy had hastily pulled out for me.

'I . . . I'm not quite sure what time he came in,' I stuttered. 'I was already in bed and asleep.'

The Inspector seemed to accept this, and I blinked back the tears that had started to my eyes.

'W . . . was his death an accident?'

The Inspector shrugged. 'It's too early to say yet, I'm afraid.' He turned back to Tommy. 'Did the Captain leave the boat at the same time as you?'

'No,' Tommy shook his head. 'Captain Lee loved the *Spring Fever* like she was his own. He was still there when I left. He wanted to make sure once more that she was as secure as we could make her. He made me go home after this happened and assured me that he could manage on his own.' He once again pointed to his cheek, and the second policeman, who was scribbling away furiously in a notepad, glanced at his superior.

'Was the Captain well when you left him?'

'Of course he was.'

'And did you happen to see anyone suspicious hanging about the moorings?'

'No, no I didn't.' Tommy dropped his face into his hands, and seeing his deep distress, the Inspector told him, 'Very well, Mr Balfour. That will be all for now. I would of course ask that you keep yourself available to assist us with our inquiries.'

Tommy nodded as the second policeman snapped his notebook shut and followed his superior to the door.

'Good day, Mrs Balfour,' the Inspector said politely. 'I'm sorry to be the bearer of such bad news. Hopefully this will turn out to be nothing more than a tragic accident and we can close the case.'

Forcing myself from my chair, I followed them to the door, where I stood and watched the lift doors close on them before turning and going back into the flat. Harold had reappeared from the drawing room, his eyes as round as saucers, and he instantly asked, 'What's goin' on then?'

I was so distressed that I was tempted to send him back into the drawing room again but realising that he would have to hear sooner or later, I told him, 'I'm afraid something terrible has happened, Harold. The Captain had an awful accident last night and was killed.'

'Cor blimey! Yer mean Captain Lee?'

'Yes I do,' I told him with as much calm as I could muster. 'Now give me a moment, would you? Mr Tommy is in a bit of a state, as you can imagine. Why don't you get wrapped up and take Sandy for a run in the park while I make him a nice cup of tea?'

Harold sniffed but hurried away to do as he was told. Slowly I went back into the dining room to Tommy, who was staring out of the window with a look of great sorrow on his face.

'I can't believe it,' he muttered distractedly. 'The skipper was all fine and dandy when I left him. What do you think could have happened?'

'Probably something similar to what happened to you,' I replied sensibly. 'Think about it, if you slipped he could have done the same. With the boat bobbing about as you say it was, he could quite easily have slipped off, and if he was stunned he wouldn't have stood a chance.' Crossing to him I took his hands in mine and shook them gently. 'Try not to blame yourself, dear.

As you just told the police, he was well when you left him and you weren't to know what would happen.'

Even as I uttered the words, I realised that they didn't ring true. Edward Lee had been sailing for years and it was highly improbable that he would not have been aware of what could have happened. He was too much of an old seadog for that.

'Look, you sit there and I'll go and make you a nice sweet cup of tea, eh?' I was longing to ask Tommy why he had told the police that he had left the captain at ten thirty when he had certainly not come home until around two a.m, but decided that now was not the time. No doubt Tommy would tell me when he was good and ready. And then there was the captain's sister and brother-in-law to think about. Edward had lived with them in a house overlooking the Regent's Canal, and I guessed that they must be devastated at his death. Tommy had moored the boat there since the day he had bought it, and we had spent many happy hours floating up and down on it. He had been happy to leave it on the Regent's Canal because it was part of a network of canals that stretch across the north of London and link up with the Grand Union Canal before connecting with Paddington Arm and going westwards towards Brentford, then to the east of London and Limehouse Basin and the docks. Somehow the canal had managed to remain a haven of beauty even though it ran through one of the largest cities in the world, and I knew that being the owner of *Spring Fever* had never lost its appeal for Tommy, although I wondered if it might now. I myself had thoroughly enjoyed my trips around the canal network; it had only been since Tommy had grown braver and had started venturing further afield that I had abstained from going with him on his jaunts. Meandering along a peaceful canal was one thing, but a choppy sea was quite another as far as I was concerned.

Tommy suddenly turned abruptly and headed towards the bedroom, his lips set in a grim line.

'Where are you going?' I asked. He turned.

'To the boat, of course. I can't just sit about here after what's happened, can I?'

Personally I couldn't see what good going to the boat could do now, but I wisely held my tongue. If it helped Tommy to come to terms with what had happened, then I supposed it could be no bad thing.

'Would you like me to come with you?' I offered, but the only reply was the sound of the bedroom door slamming resoundingly shut behind him. I had a funny feeling it was going to be a very long day.

Chapter Three

'EH, PET, YOU'RE in the papers *again!*' Gran Carter declared the next day when she phoned me.

'Well, it isn't actually *me* that's in there,' I pointed out patiently.

'You've got a mention, though,' she hurried on. 'It says, "Miriam Carter's skipper found dead floating in the water at the side of her boat *Spring Fever.*"'

Miriam Carter was the pseudonym I used for my books, and it seemed that the papers were happy to clutch at any straw to keep me in the headlines.

'Have they found out what happened to him yet?' Gran rushed on, and I had a picture of her standing in her little hallway in Fellburn gleefully gripping the phone.

'No, the investigation is still going on, though at the moment it's looking like nothing more than a tragic accident.'

It was difficult to keep the sarcasm from my voice, and Gran obviously picked up on it because she then said, 'There's no need for that attitude, lass. I'm bound to be concerned about anythin' that concerns you. Just 'cos I'm stuck up here don't mean I don't still worry about you. Trouble seems to follow you about whichever way you look at it.'

'Sorry, Gran,' I muttered, wiping a hand across my weary

eyes. I didn't feel like I had been to bed, for Tommy had tossed and turned all night.

'How is George and the family?' I now asked, hoping to steer the conversation away from the accident.

'Not bad,' she told me. 'Kitty just had what we hope will be the last of the grafts on her leg till she's older, an' it seems to have gone well.'

Once again I felt guilty. Kitty was one of George's step-children, and had been horrifically burned on the night my ex-husband Howard Stickle had tried to kill me by setting fire to the house my mother had left me in Fellburn. It had been nothing more than a burned-out shell after the fire, and for a time I had thought of letting it stay that way. But eventually I had decided to have it restored, and now George and his family were happily living there again, which never ceased to surprise me, for I knew that I could not have stayed there after what had happened.

Thankfully the conversation was stopped from going any further when Harold burst out of the lift on our landing and erupted into the hallway.

'Them two coppers what come the other day are just gettin' out of their car outside,' he gushed breathlessly. 'What do yer reckon they're after?'

'I have no idea, dear,' I told him patiently, then to Gran, 'I'm sorry, but I shall have to go. Can I call you back later?'

I heard her sigh and just had time to say a hasty goodbye before the lift doors opened yet again and Inspector Beck and his colleague stepped on to the landing.

'Ah, Mrs Balfour. Might your husband be in?' the Inspector enquired.

I nodded numbly as I motioned him towards the dining room. This whole thing was turning into a nightmare. The previous evening, Tommy and I had visited Captain Lee's family, who had been almost beside themselves with grief and adamant that his death could have been no accident.

'He was too much of an old seadog to let a boat get the better of him,' his sister-in-law had declared hotly. 'There's foul play afoot, you just take my word for it.'

Her statement had done nothing to help Tommy, who was already beside himself with guilt for leaving the Captain alone in such bad weather conditions. To make things worse, his offer of paying for the Captain's funeral had been met with angry stares.

Harold was hopping from foot to foot and finding the whole thing extremely exciting.

'Go and get Mr Tommy,' I ordered him shortly, wishing with all my heart that the sorry episode might soon be behind us. Harold went haring off in the direction of the bedroom, and minutes later Tommy joined us all in the dining room.

'Mr Balfour, I would like you to accompany us to the police station to help us with our inquiries into the death of Captain Edward Lee,' a grim-faced Inspector Beck told him.

Tommy's mouth gaped open. 'Wh . . . what for?' he stammered. 'I've already told you all I know. When I left the boat, Captain Lee was as right as rain.'

'Even so, I would be grateful if you would come with us, sir. We have reason to believe that the Captain's death might not have been accidental after all. A large bump at the back of his head indicates that there might have been something suspicious about his death.'

My hand flew to my mouth as Tommy asked incredulously, 'Are you arresting me?'

'Not at this stage, sir. As I said, at present we merely wish to question you. Now would you kindly come with us?'

Pulling myself together with an enormous effort, I asked, 'Shall I come too?'

'No, Mrs Balfour. It might be best if you stayed here with young fellow-me-lad.'

Following the Inspector's eyes, I turned to see Harold standing in the dining-room doorway with his mouth gaping open, giving him the appearance of a goldfish. At the same moment the door into the hallway opened and Janet stepped through. I instantly crossed to Harold and, pushing him gently towards her, told him, 'Go into the kitchen with your gran, dear. I shall be with you shortly.'

When the kitchen door had closed behind them I hurried away to fetch Tommy's coat for him, and as he was shoving his arms into it, I asked the Inspector, 'How long will you be keeping him?'

'I'm afraid I can't answer that question at this moment in time, ma'am.' He shrugged.

'Will you ring me when they've finished with you?' I asked, turning back to Tommy.

He shook his head. 'No, dear. Don't worry, I'll hop in a cab and be home before you know it. Now try not to worry. As the Inspector said, I'm only going to help them with inquiries. They're not going to lock me up and throw the key away.'

I watched helplessly as the two men led him from the flat. Once they were gone, I turned and trudged towards the kitchen and the barrage of questions that I knew Harold would throw at me.

They started the second I set foot through the door.

''Ave they arrested Mr Tommy?' Harold's eyes were on stalks. 'Did 'e kill the Captain?'

'Of course they haven't arrested him! And *no*, he didn't kill the Captain,' I snapped. 'How could you even think such a thing, Harold?'

Suitably ashamed, he hung his head, but then it snapped up again and he asked, 'Well why 'ave they carted him off then?'

I was so distressed that for now I didn't even bother to correct his grammar as I informed him firmly, 'Mr Tommy is simply helping them with their inquiries, Harold. They will question everyone who saw the Captain that evening as a matter of routine, so don't go reading things into it. You should know Mr Tommy wouldn't harm a fly.'

Janet, who up to now hadn't muttered so much as a word, crossed to me and took my hand as her head slowly wagged from side to side. 'It's a bad do,' she exclaimed. 'But try not to worry. Everythin' will come out in the wash.'

I blinked back tears as I stared into her kindly face. Over the years Janet had become a true friend and at that moment I was glad of her company.

'Go an' tidy yourself up an' I'll make you a nice cup o' coffee, eh?' she suggested kindly as she nudged me towards the door. Then, turning her attention back to Harold, she told him in a loud voice, 'An' *you*, young man, can go an' straighten that room o' yours up. It looks like a bomb's dropped in there. I can't even swing the hoover round there's so much stuff strewn across the floor.'

'Ah, but Gag . . .' Harold's voice trailed away as he saw the determined glint in his gran's eyes, and knowing when he was beaten, he slowly slouched away as I made my way to my own bedroom.

I had no sooner set foot through the door and closed it quietly behind me when I was confronted by Hamilton, who was standing by the window that overlooked the street with his tail swishing from side to side. Begonia was standing to his right and her soft brown eyes were sad as she looked at me. There was no sign of the old donkey today, which I supposed was one blessing at least.

Hamilton put his head to one side and sighed. *Another fine mess you find yourself in then*, he said.

'This isn't *my* mess,' I hissed. 'It's poor Tommy who's in the mess.'

Poor Tommy?

'Just what is *that* supposed to mean?' I snapped back.

His sleek black shoulders shrugged, setting his snow-white mane dancing. *Are you quite sure he's innocent?*

'Well of course I am,' I told him indignantly. 'Tommy was very fond of the Captain.'

Mm, so why was the Captain talking of retiring all of a sudden then?

My eyes stretched wide in surprise at the question. 'Because of his age, I suppose,' I retorted, swinging around and snatching up my hairbrush from the dressing table. When I turned back, both Hamilton and Begonia had gone, and I chewed on my lip as I stared at the place where they had been standing. What could Hamilton have meant? Had Tommy upset the Captain in some way that I wasn't aware of? The talk of retirement did seem strange now that I came to think of it. The Captain had loved the *Spring Fever* with a vengeance, and although he had just turned sixty he had appeared to be very fit for his age. As I slowly tugged the brush through my hair my mind ran riot. Hamilton had certainly given me something to think about.

Tommy returned at six o' clock that evening and it was clear that he was not in a good mood.

'How did it go?' I asked tentatively, and he almost bit my head off as he replied, 'Well, how do you think it went? I was locked in a room and questioned and made to feel like a criminal.'

'But you are innocent, so you have nothing to worry about,' I pointed out.

'I suppose not,' he admitted as his face slowly relaxed.

'I've got your meal ready for you.' Crossing to the oven, I was in the process of lifting his dinner out when Harold ran into the kitchen and skidded to a halt with a wide smile on his face.

'Gran Carter an' George are here,' he exclaimed, and I was so shocked that I almost dropped the plate.

'Are you quite sure?' I questioned. 'They didn't tell me they were coming.'

'Oh, I'm sure all right.' Harold was beaming. 'I just looked out o' the window in the lounge to see if there were any sign o' the rain slowin' up an' I saw 'em get out o' George's car.' Without waiting for a reply, he went scooting off down the hallway, and sure enough, seconds later the lift doors swished open and there were Gran and George as large as life.

'I wasn't expecting you,' I told Gran as I hurried forward to be gathered to her in a bear hug.

'There were no reason why you should, lass, seein' as I never told you we were comin' like,' Gran declared as I smiled at George over her shoulder. 'But I thought you might be glad of a friendly face wi' all what's goin' on. Me an' our Georgie have been drivin' since early this mornin'. Eeh, I don't mind tellin' you, me stomach thinks me throat's cut an' I'm gaggin' for a cup o' tea, so get that kettle on while you tell me all that's been happenin'.'

Tommy discreetly slipped away, leaving his meal to go cold on the table, while Harold went with George to fetch their bags up from the car.

An hour later, Gran knew all there was to know and was

settled in the chair in the drawing room with her feet stretched out towards the electric fire and her third cup of tea in her hand. George was doing a jigsaw with Harold on the coffee table and Tommy had shut himself away in our room.

'Poor bugger,' Gran sighed. ''E were one o' life's gentlemen were Captain Lee. I don't mind tellin' you, had I been a few years younger I'd 'ave set me cap at 'im. But I'm sure everythin' will come out in the wash. It's more than obvious that what's happened were nowt more than a tragic accident, an' once that's been established you an' Tommy can put all this behind you.'

I nodded absently, hoping that she was right, although nothing could bring the Captain back, of course.

'So what will 'e do wi' the boat now?' Gran asked, nodding towards the bedroom.

'I'm not sure,' I admitted, 'though he has said that if he keeps her he may change her moorings. I think he's considering moving her to the Limehouse moorings to the east of London. Truthfully, it would be much more suitable. There's a good direct connection to the Thames, and *Spring Fever* was always a little large for the Regent's Canal. Tommy only kept her there because Captain Lee's house overlooked the canal and he could keep his eye on her during the winter months. I doubt he'll want her left there now, though. It would be like rubbing salt into the wound for his family to have to keep looking out on her.'

'Aye, there is that in it,' Gran agreed. Looking towards Harold she now asked, 'An' how has his Lordship been behavin'?'

'Perfectly well.' I was instantly on the defensive, as I had always felt that Gran had not totally approved of me adopting Harold. From my point of view it was the best thing I had ever done.

'An' what about your *other* friend, the horse? Put in an appearance lately, has he?'

Thankfully I was saved from having to answer that question because at that moment George rose and yawned loudly. 'Stone the crows, Ma, I'm that tired I reckon I could sleep the clock round,' he declared, flashing me a knowing wink.

I smiled at him gratefully as he hauled Harold to his feet and turned him in the direction of his bedroom. 'Right, that's enough jawin' for one night, Ma,' he told Gran sternly. 'Maisie looks dead on her feet an' I reckon she's ready for a bit o' shut-eye.'

I could have kissed that dear man there and then. I loved Gran Carter dearly but sometimes found her rather hard work, as George was fully aware. George had been married to my mother when I was just a little girl and had been the closest thing to a father I had ever known. Even when he and my mother had split up, he had continued to look out for me, and over the years he and his mother had become my family.

He now pecked me on the cheek as I took Harold's hand and led him towards his bedroom. Once inside, Harold threw off his clothes and yanked his pyjamas on. His face was alight with excitement at the arrival of the unexpected guests and as he scrambled into bed he told me, 'I love Uncle George, I do.'

'So do I, dear.' I stooped to plant a kiss on his flushed cheek. This child was so incredibly precious to me that I couldn't now envisage my life without him, even though he was a constant challenge.

'I wish Mr Tommy would play games wi' me like Uncle George does,' he muttered sadly.

'With me,' I corrected for want of something to say. How could I reply to a statement like that? Tommy had been

31

going out an awful lot lately, leaving Harold and me to entertain ourselves. I hadn't realised until now that Harold had
noticed.

'Good night, my dear.'

'Good night, Mrs Nardy.'

The use of my late husband's name brought tears stinging to
my eyes and memories flooding back as I turned and headed
towards the door. I paused to look back and saw that Harold's
eyes were already closing. Shutting the door softly behind me, I
went to join Tommy in our room.

George and Gran had been staying with us for two days and
Harold was in his element, begrudging the time he had to spend
at school because he was apart from them. It was a gloomy
Tuesday morning. Harold had departed for school and George
was reading the newspaper at the kitchen table when Gran took
me completely by surprise, asking, 'How long's it been since you
got your hair done, lass?'

I touched my hair self-consciously as colour flooded into my
cheeks. It had been so long that I couldn't actually remember
and was shocked to feel it hanging on my shoulders.

'I, er . . . couldn't tell you, to be honest,' I admitted.

'Right then, how about you an' me go an' treat usselves to a
new hair do an' a good old shoppin' trip?' Gran suggested. 'You
didn't have anythin' better planned, did you?'

I had to admit that I hadn't, and seeing as Tommy had gone
out early there was really nothing to stop us.

'I suppose I could do with a trim,' I admitted.

Coming to stand behind me, Gran pointed at a picture of
Princess Diana in the newspaper George was reading. 'I reckon
you should have it cut into that style,' she said. Gran was a great
admirer of the Princess, as she told us all at every opportunity. I

laughed before pointing out, 'I'm hardly a teenager, Gran. Don't you think that style might be a little young for me?'

'Fiddlesticks,' she declared. 'With your small face it would suit you down to the ground. While Nardy was alive you seemed to take a pride in yourself for the first time in your life, but I have to say that since he went, God rest his soul, you've let yourself slip, lass.'

I wanted to argue but found that I couldn't because I was only too well aware that she was right. There didn't seem much point making an effort seeing as I rarely set foot out of the door any more.

'One o' them nice suits wi' the padded shoulders would suit you an' all,' she went on. 'You're straight up an' down an' they'd give you a bit o' shape.'

I didn't bother to argue as she was only stating the truth. I had never been under any illusions where my looks were concerned. I was what could only be described as plain, and no amount of fancy clothes would ever alter that. Even so, the thought of a shopping trip was suddenly appealing, and so glancing at George I asked, 'Would you mind very much if we went out, George?'

'No I wouldn't, lass,' he answered. 'In fact I reckon it could be just what the doctor ordered. An' speakin' o' doctors, Dr Kane asked me to give you his love an' tell you he an' Jane will be down to see you as soon as they can. Jane's been poorly as you know an' he's aware that he's been neglectin' you.'

Thoughts of the kindly doctor with the great hairy face made me smile. Dr Kane had been my doctor ever since I was a child living in Fellburn right until the time I had come to live in London with Nardy. He had helped me out of many a dilemma and I was very fond of both him and his wife.

'That's settled then,' I said brightly. 'I'll go and get ready and we'll be on our way. We can get into London by cab. I know of a very good hairdresser who'll probably be able to fit us in without an appointment.'

In no time at all we were striding into a very chic salon that went under the name of Toffs, where we were instantly leapt on by two eager young assistants.

Once I had had my hair washed, I sat in front of a mirror sipping coffee and watched the hairdresser snip away at my tresses. By the time she was done I could hardly believe the transformation. The Princess Di look really did suit me just as Gran had prophesied, and I felt my spirits begin to lift a little.

'Right,' Gran said when we were finally out on the pavement again after paying the hairdresser and leaving a generous tip. 'Hail a cab, lass. I reckon a couple of hours down Oxford Street would just round the mornin' off nicely now.'

And so I hailed a cab, and within minutes Gran was whipping me into one shop after another until I was laden down with bags.

'That's enough now,' I finally protested mid-afternoon. My withered arm was paining me now with the weight of the bags I was carrying and my feet felt as if they were about to drop off. 'Come on, let's call it a day, eh?'

She grinned as she nodded in agreement. 'All right then. I dare say we've spent enough for one day, an' I must admit I'm gaspin' for a good strong mug o' tea.'

George met us out of the lift when we got back to the flat and laughed as he saw the number of bags we were carrying. 'Talk about shopping for England.' He scratched his head. 'Is there owt left in the shops?'

'Cheeky little bugger,' Gran scolded him with a twinkle in her eye, then turning to me said, 'Go an' try a few o' your new outfits on for us while I put the kettle on, eh?'

Knowing that there would be no point in arguing, I headed for the bedroom as Gran slung her bags at George and made for the kitchen.

I was just trying on the last of my new outfits half an hour later when Tommy strode into the flat with a face like thunder. He stopped short at the sight of my new hair do and asked, 'Been out then, have we?'

I nodded as I self-consciously stroked my hair. 'Yes I have. I went on a bit of a shopping spree with Gran and got my hair done. Do you like it?'

Ignoring my question he scowled. 'I'm glad you can fill your head with things like that when the skipper is lying on a mortuary slab.'

I felt as if he had slapped me in the face as colour stained my cheeks. Gran stepped in.

'Hold up, lad. That were a bit harsh like. The lass only went out for a few hours. Is there a law against enjoyin' yourself in this neck o' the woods?'

Tommy's hands clenched into fists and he slammed away into our room as I turned to Gran and hastily apologised for him. 'He didn't mean it,' I told her. 'He's just strung up about what's happened to the Captain, that's all.'

'Mm . . . Well that's as maybe, but as far as I can see you were long overdue for a bit o' time out,' she muttered. 'From what young Harold's been sayin' you barely set foot out o' the door any more, an' it ain't healthy, you just mark my words. This might be a lovely place but it could turn into a prison if you ain't careful. You just think on what I've said.' With that she flounced along the corridor to her room as I stood there with tears in my eyes. We had had such a lovely day but it had all been spoilt now. Tommy had been barely civil to Gran or George since the moment they arrived, and although I knew he was heartsore about the Captain's death, I could make no excuses for his rudeness.

Seeing my distress George told me tactfully, 'Don't fret about it, lass. Me an' Gran are headin' off home this evenin'. If we travel through the night happen she'll sleep most o' the way an' I won't have her naggin' in me ear. We'll miss most o' the traffic an' all, all bein' well.'

I stared at this dear man, suddenly wishing that I was going with them and then instantly feeling guilty for thinking that way. My home was here with Tommy now. Strangely, the thought brought me no joy.

Chapter Four

'THE VERDICT WAS accidental death.'

'Why Tommy, that's wonderful,' I told him. 'At least now we know there was nothing underhand in his death. It was obviously nothing more than a tragic accident.'

Tommy had just returned from Captain Lee's inquest and looked as white as a ghost himself. He nodded slowly as he strummed his fingers on the table and then suddenly he said, 'Maisie, I'd like us to move.'

I was so shocked that I almost dropped the kettle I had been just about to place on the stove. '*Move!* What do you mean? Do you mean move from here? The flat?'

'Yes, that's exactly what I mean,' he told me. 'I've always felt like I was living in Nardy's shadow here and I think it's time we made a fresh start somewhere else.'

My eyes flitted around the familiar room. I still loved every inch of the place as much as I had on the day Nardy had first brought me here, and the idea of leaving what I considered to be my home was unthinkable.

'But I . . . I thought you liked living here,' I told him tamely.

He shrugged his broad shoulders. 'I thought I did until all this happened,' he said quietly. 'But I realise now I'd like us to start afresh. Let's be honest, as long as we live here the ghost of Nardy will always be between us.'

It was obvious that he had put some thought into this and now there was an edge to my voice as I asked him, 'And just where were you thinking of moving us to?'

'Back up north.'

My eyes almost leapt out of their sockets now, but before I could say anything he hurried on. 'I've been into a few estate agents and they have some lovely properties in Fellburn. Nowhere near where you used to live, of course. There's one in particular up on Brampton Hill that I'm sure you'd love. It's a detached house with twice as many rooms as we have here and a lovely garden. Think how nice it would be to have a garden for Sandy and Harold to play in. It's very close to a lovely marina as well where I could moor *Spring Fever*. At least *think* about it, Maisie, before you turn the idea down. Look, I've brought you the leaflets to look at.' Even as he spoke he was spreading the brochure out on the table and I had to admit that it was a beautiful house. A great rambling building with tall chimneys and a multitude of leaded windows.

'But this must cost *a fortune*,' I exclaimed.

Tommy had obviously thought of everything and assured me, 'We could afford it easily if we sell this place. This flat is in a prime location and would be snapped up.'

'*Wh . . . at?* Sell this place!'

'Well of course. What use would it be to us if we were living in Fellburn?'

I had never defied Tommy in all of our married life but now I stood my ground and told him, 'You'll have to give me some time to think on this, Tommy. It's come as a bit of a shock, to say the very least. There's just so much to think about. I mean . . . what about Harold's schooling? And how will he feel about moving away from all his friends and family?'

'We can't allow some child to decide our future,' Tommy snapped peevishly, and in that moment I glimpsed another side to him.

My chin jutted as I stood up to him. 'As I said . . . I need some time to think. And Harold isn't just some child. He's *my* child!'

Tommy turned on his heel and stormed away without another word. Once I heard the door slam behind him, I leaned heavily against the side of the sink and began to tremble.

'Oh Nardy,' I whispered brokenly to the empty room. 'What am I going to do?'

Twenty minutes later, Janet arrived to find me sobbing uncontrollably at the kitchen table.

'Why, love, whatever's the matter?' she exclaimed as she gathered me into her arms.

'Oh Janet,' I whimpered. 'Everything is *such* a mess. First of all the Captain dying as he did, and now Tommy has informed me that he wants us to move back up north.'

Shock registered on her homely face as she stared down at me. 'And how do you feel about that?' she asked.

I wagged my head from side to side. 'I can't bear the thought of selling this place,' I admitted. 'Somehow when I'm here I still feel close to Nardy. I know it's wrong to say that but I can't help it. I miss him so much, Janet.'

'I know you do,' she said sadly as she rocked me to and fro. 'I do too if truth be told. But life has to go on. Nardy wouldn't want you to feel like this.'

We were silent for a moment as she hugged me to her and I enjoyed her warmth, but then she suddenly said, 'There could be a way around this.'

As I stared up at her enquiringly she went on, 'You don't necessarily have to sell this place. You could rent it out and that way at least it would still be yours.'

I sniffed the tears back as I thought on what she had said. I had to admit it did make sense.

'Do you think I'd be able to rent it out?' I asked tentatively. 'What I mean is, to someone who would look after it properly. Nardy loved this place and I couldn't bear to think of it being neglected.'

'Ah, it just so happens that I might be able to help you out there.' She suddenly looked uncomfortable and I waited for her to clear her throat and go on.

'The thing is, our Hilda informed us last night that she'll be gettin' married next month an' she'll need somewhere to live until they can afford a place of their own.'

'Hilda . . . getting married?' I exclaimed. This certainly was turning out to be a day full of surprises.

Studiously avoiding my eyes, Janet nodded. 'Yes, she's gettin' married, an' you'll never guess who to if you try for a million years.'

I was smiling broadly now, for I had been very fond of Hilda ever since the time she had become entangled with the Mohican, as we had all once known him. The Mohican had turned out to be an undercover policeman in disguise and had once saved my life before professing his love for me. I had turned him down because I had been engaged to Tommy, but I still thought of him from time to time and often wondered how my life might have turned out if I had married him instead.

'She's marrying . . . the Mohican,' Janet said softly, and I felt as if someone had kicked me in the stomach.

'But I . . . I thought it was all over between them,' I stammered. 'He made her have an abortion.'

'Yes, he did,' Janet agreed. 'An' as you know, for a time she was brokenhearted. But then thanks to you she decided to better herself, an' better herself she did. An' then about six months ago their paths crossed again an' . . . Well, the rest you can guess at. I didn't even know about it meself till recently, an' a right gliff it gave me I don't mind tellin' you!'

'But why the rush to get married?' I asked, trying to take it all in.

Janet grinned sheepishly. 'Between you an' me I think there's another little 'un on the way. She ain't said as much, but when you've turned out as many kids as I have you get to know the signs. I weren't too happy when I knew he was back on the scene at first, but our Hilda is so happy that I ain't had the heart to go against her. After all, it's her life at the end o' the day, ain't it? An' we all have to make our own mistakes. I've certainly made a few in me time. So there you have it.'

She sat down opposite me as I tried to take it all in. I remembered back to the time the Mohican had come to see me in hospital. I had tried to persuade him to take Hilda back, but all he had said was, 'She is of a type. All she wants is bed; she's as oversexed as a bloody rabbit.'

Well, the oversexed rabbit must have still held some appeal for him; he was now about to marry her, possibly with another little one already on the way.

'Ain't you goin' to say anythin' then?' Janet asked eventually, and with an effort I forced a smile to my face and told her, 'If Hilda is happy then so am I. I wish them both all the best. But before I can consider renting the flat to her I would have to talk to Tommy. You do understand, don't you?'

She nodded affably. 'O' course I do. Now how about a cuppa before I start work, eh?'

I nodded as I rose from the table and went in the direction

of the bedroom. Inside I was crying and I was ashamed of the fact, for I realised that I was feeling jealous of Hilda as I tried to picture her living here with the Mohican, who I was in fact very fond of. She was finally going to marry James Bainbridge, as his real name was. It was going to take a lot of getting used to.

Tommy arrived home shortly after Harold later in the afternoon, looking very contrite and gripping a large bunch of flowers.

'I'm sorry,' he said as he held the flowers out to me. I took them from him and nodded towards the kitchen. Luckily, Harold was engrossed in a television programme, so I hoped that we might be able to have a private chat. I closed the door softly behind us, placed the flowers in the sink, bent to stroke Sandy, and then motioned Tommy to a chair before saying, 'I think we need to have a little talk, don't you? I might just have found the solution to our problems.' I went on to tell him of the conversation I had had earlier in the day with Janet and her idea of renting the flat out.

'The house in Fellburn costs a hundred and fifty grand,' Tommy pointed out. 'Will we have enough to buy it if we don't sell this place?'

I was mildly surprised, for I had imagined that Tommy was hoping to buy the house himself, but I told him, 'I could afford it if need be, though I had rather thought we might buy it jointly.' I knew that Tommy's mother had left him a very wealthy man when she died, and he now further surprised me when he said, 'Actually, I was hoping to plough my money into a business up there. I shall need to do something when I give up my job at the publisher's, won't I?'

'I suppose you will, but what business did you have in mind?'

He flushed before muttering, 'Actually . . . it's a scrap yard.'

'A *scrap yard*!' No matter how hard I tried, I just couldn't picture Tommy in a scrap yard somehow. He was too fond of his smart suits and collars and ties.

'It's not the sort of scrap yard you're thinking of,' he said quickly. 'I shan't be trawling the streets in a rag and bone cart or anything like that. The people bring the scrap metal to the yard, weigh it in and get paid for it. It's as simple as that, and of course I shall have men working for me who'll do all the dirty work. I've been looking into it and it's a very lucrative business with lots of profit to be made.'

'Well I suppose if you're able to compromise and let me keep the flat, then I should let you have a go at this business,' I told him and was pleased to see relief wash across his face.

'Perhaps we ought to get ourselves up to Fellburn and have a look at the house then?'

I nodded in agreement. 'That sounds fine, but first I need to break the news to Harold. He's very settled here and I don't know how he's going to feel about it yet.'

'He's young and he'll soon adapt,' Tommy assured me, and he then crossed to me and took me in his arms. 'This is going to be a brand-new start for us,' he promised, and as I laid my head against his broad shoulder I prayed that he might be right.

From the corner of my eye I saw Hamilton running backwards and forwards in the confined space of the kitchen. The old donkey that I had seen on the other occasion was with him, and as I looked at him he slowly shook his head from side to side with a look of such sadness in his eyes that I wanted to cry.

'Come along, dear. We'll never get off at this rate.'

With his hands thrust deep in his blazer pockets, Harold scowled at me and clambered ungraciously into the back of the car. He had not taken to the idea of moving at all but had eventually agreed to come and look at the house with us, and so now here we were all ready to go. Gran Carter had offered to put us up for the night at her house once we got to Fellburn, and we were planning to go and visit the house on Brampton Hill the following morning. But first there was a long journey ahead of us. Sandy was already curled up on the back seat with Harold and I hoped that the two of them might fall asleep for part of the journey.

Tommy appeared happier than I had seen him for some time and I wondered if perhaps he hadn't been right after all. It could be that a new house of our own choosing would be just what this family needed. Even so I was apprehensive as he tucked a travel rug across my knees and flashed me a warm smile. Even though Howard Stickle was dead, I could never return to Fellburn without expecting him to pop up from somewhere like magic. Deep inside I had also decided that if I didn't like the house I would refuse to move from the flat and Tommy would just have to deal with my decision.

'We're off then,' Tommy said as he put the car into gear, and soon we were cruising through the streets of London. It was very early but already the streets were teeming with traffic. This was something I would certainly not miss if we moved. I had never been fond of the hustle and bustle of a big city.

The journey passed without event. As I had hoped, Sandy and Harold, curled up on the back seat, slept for most of the way. It was late afternoon when Tommy finally drew the car to a halt outside Gran Carter's little terraced house, and there she was in the window, peeping past the net curtain waiting for us. She ran out in her slippers and crushed me to her in a fierce bear hug as Harold got Sandy out of the back.

'I bet you're just gaggin' for a cup o' tea, ain't you, hinny?'

she gushed as she released me and turned her attentions to Harold. He gave her a wide grin as she ruffled his hair and then led us all into the house that smelt of furniture polish and roast beef.

After a lovely meal, I sent Harold off for a bath and Tommy and I decided to go and have a peep at the outside of the house on Brampton Hill. I wasn't quite sure what to expect, for I had seen many houses that sounded almost palatial in the estate agent's details but that when viewed turned out to be little more than run-down slums. However, our first glimpse of The Chimneys filled me with awe. We approached it along a long tree-lined drive, and then, after turning a bend, there it was, its leaded windows winking into the soft evening light.

'Oh Tommy, it's lovely,' I exclaimed as he helped me from the car. We started to walk around the house, peeping in at the windows. The light was fast fading, but even so we could see that all the rooms appeared to be of large proportions with high ceilings. The front door was enormous, with three rounded concrete steps leading up to it, and my first sight of the enormous garden and the woods beyond at the rear of the property made me gasp. It seemed to go on for ever. The place had obviously stood empty for some time, for many of the flower beds were overgrown, but as Tommy was quick to point out, it was nothing that a good gardener could not put right within a few days.

Down below us the lights of Fellburn winked into the night, and as Tommy slid his arm around my waist I started to feel better about the move. I could hardly believe that I, Maisie Rochester, was really looking at a house on Brampton Hill with a view to buying it. Me, who had come from a small two-up and two-down that was just one step removed from Bog's End.

'Let's just hope the inside lives up to the outside when we

view it properly tomorrow,' he commented, and I nodded in agreement. I was feeling more than a little guilty, for I had almost made my mind up before I had even viewed it that I would not like this house. But up to now there had been nothing not to like about it and I returned to Gran's in a slightly happier frame of mind.

George brought his wife Mary and the children round to see us that evening and the time passed pleasantly as the grown-ups caught up on all the gossip and the children played cards.

I was tired by the time we climbed into the lumpy old bed in Gran's back bedroom, but feeling happier than I had for some time, and within no time at all I was fast asleep and dreaming.

Gran woke us the next morning with a cup of tea and the daily newspaper.

'You're in again, look,' she exclaimed gleefully, and I sighed, wondering what I was supposed to have done this time.

BESTSELLING AUTHOR RETURNS TO HER ROOTS, the headline proclaimed, and I raised my eyebrow. 'How did the papers get to know I was coming back?' I asked Gran.

She flushed and grinned as I pulled myself up on the pillows and took the tea from her.

'Well you know what the jungle drums are like round here. You can't keep owt secret for long, lass. Anyway, you should be chuffed about it. You'll be a celebrity hereabouts now. Just make sure you look your best when you go an' view the house this mornin', 'cos as sure as eggs is eggs they'll be on your tail.'

Tommy laughed as he too took his tea from Gran, and as she pottered out of the room he remarked, 'You don't think she let on to them, do you?'

'I wouldn't be surprised,' I admitted, and we smiled at each other.

The previous night, Mary had offered to take Harold for some of the day to play with her children, and when Tommy and I went downstairs to breakfast he was raring to go.

'I promise I'll drop you off to George's later in the morning,' I told him patiently. 'But first I want you to come and look at the house with us.'

'Ah, do I *'ave* to?'

'Yes you do *have* to!' I corrected him as I tousled his hair. 'You're going to have to live in the house too, so I think you should at least see it and tell us what you think before we make a decision about it.'

He nodded glumly. 'All right then . . . but will yer take me to George's after?'

When I nodded, he tucked into his breakfast as if he hadn't been fed for a month. I looked fondly on. Already I could picture him gambolling in the garden at the back of The Chimneys, with Sandy romping at his side. All I had to do now was hope that the interior of the house lived up to the exterior.

Mr Harper, the estate agent, a pompous little chap with a bulbous red nose, met us at the bottom of the drive leading to The Chimneys.

'Ah, Miss Carter,' he greeted me effusively as he held out a rather sticky hand, and I took an instant dislike to him.

'Mrs Balfour,' I corrected him primly and he smiled.

'Apologies, dear lady. It isn't often I get to show a famous author around one of our properties.'

Ignoring his comment I pointed to Tommy and Harold. 'This is my husband and my son.'

I felt colour creep into my cheeks as Harold flashed him a cheeky grin and swiped his sleeve across his nose.

We all got back into the cars and followed the estate agent

up the drive. Taking the house keys from his pocket with a flourish, he opened the front door and waved us inside. I found myself in a spacious hallway. Three doors led off from each side of it and in the centre a beautiful staircase swept upwards to a galleried landing. A huge chandelier covered in a thick layer of dust hung above us and the original tiles on the floor were grimy, but even so the whole place spoke of grandeur. Mr Harper was gushing as he told us the merits of the many different features, but I cut him short to ask, 'Would you mind very much if we wandered about on our own for a while?'

'I, er . . . Well, no, please do.' He was obviously not too pleased about it but I wasn't in the mood for all his sales talk and wanted to make my own decision about the place. Harold had already scampered off up the stairs and now Tommy and I began to explore the downstairs rooms. The first door we tried led to a large lounge with an original marble fireplace and enormous French windows opening on to the garden. The second led to an equally spacious dining room. The third opened to an enormous kitchen, boasting a range large enough to cook for an army on. On the other side of the hall was another sitting room, a games room and, to my delight, an enormous study, again with French windows overlooking the garden.

'I can just see you writing in here,' Tommy said as he took in the huge bookcase that covered the whole of one wall. Already in my mind's eye I could picture myself sitting at a desk here and I nodded, unable to keep the smile from my face.

The upstairs proved to be just as beautiful; there were four huge bedrooms, each with lovely original fireplaces, and two enormous bathrooms with a great claw-footed bath in the centre of each one.

Our inspection ended with a tour of the garden, which I was

told amounted to a little over one acre and contained its own private woods.

'So . . . what do you think? Can you picture yourself living here?' Tommy sounded anxious as we started back towards the estate agent, who was glancing impatiently at his wristwatch.

'I think it's lovely . . . and yes, I can see myself living here,' I replied.

'Me an' all,' Harold shouted as he ran ahead of us. 'I'll 'ave me own woods to play in.'

'So, shall I put an offer in?'

I glanced at him as a picture of Nardy's flat floated in front of my eyes, but then plastering a smile on to my face I nodded. 'Yes, go ahead.' And so it was decided.

Chapter Five

WE WERE HEADING back to London and the mood in the car was light-hearted. Even Harold seemed happy at the thought of the move now. Our offer on the house had been accepted and now the legalities of the sale had been placed in the hands of a solicitor, who had informed us that because there was no chain we could possibly have the keys within six weeks. Everything had happened so fast that I could barely take it in. The only cloud on the horizon was the fact that I would now have to tell Janet that we were definitely going to move, and I knew that this would not be easy.

'So what school will I be goin' to when we move to us new house?' a little voice from the back seat piped up.

'*Our* new house,' I corrected him, and then, 'I don't know yet. Gran is going to make some enquiries for me.'

Satisfied with that, Harold sat back, fondling Sandy's ears as we cruised along.

It was dark by the time we pulled up in front of our flat in London and I was tired. The journey back had taken longer because we had met a lot of traffic on the way, and now all I wanted was a good strong cup of tea and my bed.

Tommy took Sandy for a fast run in the garden opposite

whilst Harold and I made our way up to the flat in the lift.

'Home sweet home,' I sighed as I pushed the key into the lock.

'But not for much longer, eh?' Harold grinned.

The smiles were instantly wiped off our faces when the door swung inwards. My heart began to hammer. It had been unlocked, which could only mean that someone had been in the flat. Janet was the only other person who had a key, and I knew without doubt that she would never have left without locking up.

Trying not to panic, I looked at Harold and said as calmly as I could, 'Harold, run and fetch Mr Tommy straight away, and mind how you cross the road.'

'I ain't leavin' you here alone,' he said fearfully. 'There might still be someone in there an' they might cosh yer one.'

'Just go and do as you're told.' There was a firm edge to my voice now and Harold picked up on it and scooted away as if the devil himself was chasing him.

Tentatively I pushed the door open and clicked on the light. The sight that met my eyes brought tears smarting to them. The plant pots that had stood at intervals along the long hallway had been overturned and dirt trodden into the carpet. The pictures had been torn from the walls and smashed and there was glass everywhere. Picking my way amongst the debris I headed for the lounge, and once again my heart plummeted. The settee and chairs had been slashed, the cabinets containing Nardy's treasured trinkets overturned and the whole room totally trashed. The same scene greeted me in each room, and by the time Tommy tore in to stand beside me I was in floods of helpless tears.

'Oh Tommy, who could have done this?' I sobbed.

The look on his face was incredulous, but when I made to lift the phone he snapped, 'What are you doing?'

'Phoning the police, of course!'

Snatching the receiver from my hand he slammed it back into the cradle before saying, 'There's no need to do that just yet. We should find out what's been taken first.'

'But . . . surely we should leave everything as it is and let the police deal with it?' I choked. His mouth set in a grim line as his head wagged from side to side. 'No, we can deal with this ourselves.'

Harold had been watching the exchange with fearful eyes, and now I hugged him to me as I said with a cheerfulness I was far from feeling, 'It's not the end of the world, is it? At least no one was hurt. Now why don't you go and get washed and into your pyjamas while Mr Tommy and I tidy up a bit? I'm sure it won't be as bad as it seems once we get cracking.'

For once he didn't argue, just nodded numbly and left the room quietly.

'At least let me phone Janet,' I implored Tommy now that we were on our own again. 'She was the last one here and she might have seen someone hanging about.'

Without waiting for his reply I lifted the phone and dialled the shop at the end of Janet's road. She did not have a phone in her house but the shopkeeper always got a message to her when necessary. I gave the woman on the other end of the phone a garbled account of what had happened, and she assured me that she would let Janet know straight away. I put the receiver down and looked around at the carnage, wondering where I should start.

Tommy meanwhile had poured us both a generous measure of whisky and handed one to me. I had never been a great one for spirits but at that moment I was glad of it.

'Here, get that down you,' he ordered. 'It will do you good, you've had a nasty shock.'

I gulped at it, coughing and spluttering as it burned its way down to my stomach, but I had to admit I did feel better when I had drained the glass. We then took off our coats and began to lift the overturned furniture back into place.

By the time Janet arrived with her son Max half an hour later, the room looked fractionally better, but even so her mouth gaped open at the sight of so much destruction.

'Good God above!' Her mouth was stretched so far open that the wrinkles temporarily disappeared. 'What the bloody hell's been goin' on here!'

'I was rather hoping you would tell me that,' I replied ruefully. 'Did you come in today, Janet?'

'Yes, I did.' She nodded vigorously. 'I left at lunchtime an' I can tell you the place were like a new pin when I went, *an*' I locked up after me.'

'Oh Janet, I never thought for one moment that you wouldn't,' I hastily assured her. 'But did you notice anyone you didn't know hanging around? Inside the building or outside?'

She chewed on her lip as she cast her mind back but then sadly shook her head. 'Can't say as I did to be honest. I'd have noticed anyone strange. Where's Harold?'

'It's all right,' I assured her. 'I've sent him to get changed and told him to go to bed.'

As she nodded she was stripping off her coat and now she set to to help us put the place back to rights. Max meanwhile hurried into the kitchen and emerged clutching a dustpan and brush before attacking the dirt on the hall floor. When it was all swept up and the plants back in position he asked, 'Have you called the police? Seems to me like whoever did this were lookin' for somethin'.'

'Such as what?'

He shrugged his shoulders. 'Can't rightly say, but they ain't done all this for fun, have they? Have you noticed anythin' gone missin' yet?'

'No I haven't,' I told him as I lifted another of Nardy's trinkets. 'Everything appears to be here though there are quite a few pieces broken.' I was choking back the tears as I fingered Nardy's treasures. Each and every one of them had been collected over the years by him and his mother and had been very precious to him.

'Ain't much we can do about this,' Janet piped up regretfully as she placed a cushion back on the slashed settee. 'Looks like they used a Stanley knife or summat on it. I reckon you'll have to get it re-covered or treat yourself to a new suite.'

'I'll get it re-covered.' Once again the suite had been chosen by Nardy and the thought of getting rid of it was painful.

Two hours later, apart from the damage that was irreparable, the flat was tidy again, though I still personally thought that we should have left it as it was and called the police. When I went into the kitchen to put the kettle on and said as much, Janet agreed with me.

'Why is he so against you callin' the coppers in?' she questioned.

I shook my head. 'I don't know. He seems to think it was probably just some vandals broke in and trashed the place for the fun of it. If it had been burglars they would have taken something, wouldn't they?'

Janet sniffed. 'Well I still think you should have called 'em.' And with that she bustled about getting the tea things ready.

Max and Tommy were still in the lounge when the phone rang. Tommy lifted the receiver. He seemed to pale in front of my very eyes as I stared at him through the open doorway, but ignoring my raised eyebrow he looked at Max and asked, 'Would you mind giving me a minute, Max? This is, er . . . private.' He pushed a cut-glass tumbler full of whisky into Max's hand, and as Max walked through the door to join Janet and me in the kitchen, Tommy closed it behind him, shutting off his conversation.

Janet clucked her disapproval. 'What a night this is turnin' out to be,' she remarked. Then, seeing that I was still deeply distressed, she asked, 'But how did you get on in Fellburn? I forgot to ask with all this goin' on. Was the house suitable?'

'It was more than suitable. In fact we've put in an offer on it and it's been accepted, so you can tell Hilda and James that they can rent the flat if they wish to.'

'Oh!' Janet's voice was flat-sounding. 'So you'll really be goin' then? An' takin' his Nibs through there with you?' As she thumbed towards Harold's room I nodded, feeling like a total traitor. None of this would be easy for Janet, for even though I had legally adopted Harold, he was still her grandson.

'How long till you go?'

I gulped deep in my throat before replying, 'Hopefully within six weeks. Seeing as there's no chain it's simply a matter of waiting for the solicitors.' Half of my mind was on the conversation that Tommy was having on the phone beyond the closed door, for I couldn't help but notice from the snatches I could hear that he sounded highly agitated. And then there was Hamilton, pounding on the door leading into the lounge with his front hooves and snorting at me.

'As soon as that, eh?'

I forced myself to look at Janet. I could see that she was fighting back tears, and my guilt intensified as I wondered if I was doing the right thing. I was happy here, or I had been, and

Harold was happy here too, but there was no guarantee that I would be happy living back in Fellburn.

'You'll be able to come and see us whenever you like,' I promised Janet, forcing a brightness into my voice, and then suddenly I blurted out, 'Better still . . . you could come with us!'

It was hard to say who was the more astonished of the two of us as she gasped, 'What do you mean? I could come with you! *To live*, do you mean?'

I nodded vigorously. I had no idea where the idea had sprung from, but now that it was there it seemed to make more and more sense with every second that passed.

'But I . . . I can't up sticks an' move just like that!' Janet muttered.

'Why not, Mum?' This was from Max, who had been silent up to now. Max was the clown of Janet's family, always into scrapes of some sort or another and always cracking jokes. But at this moment he looked deadly serious as Janet stared at him open-mouthed.

'What do you mean – *why not*? An' who would look out for you lot if I were to go?'

'I think we're all quite old enough to look after ourselves now, Mum.' As Max smiled at her I saw Janet's lip tremble. 'Let's face it, you've been an unpaid skivvy to us all since the second we drew breath. Over the years we've each of us flown the nest in turn but we've always come back to where our bread was buttered, an' I reckon it's time you thought o' yourself now. You've always got on with Mrs Nardy here an' you'd be close to Harold. An' don't tell me that ain't important to you 'cos I happen to bloody know otherwise. He might be a little tyke but I know you love him, so don't bother denyin' it.'

'But if I *were* to go . . . and I say *if* . . . what would I live on?'

'I'd give you wages,' I hurriedly told her. 'The house we're buying is lovely but it needs a lot of TLC putting into it to turn it into a home, and I can't think of anyone who's better at that than you. *Please* think about it, Janet. You've got Gran there and you both get on like a house on fire, so you'd have someone to go out with whenever you felt like it, and I wouldn't treat you like a maid, I swear. You could have as much time off as you liked.'

'Mm, I reckon I'll have to give it some thought.' Janet sniffed. 'It ain't every day someone offers me the chance to go off an' live in a completely different part o' the country, you know.'

'Of course you need time to think about it.' I gave her a little hug. 'But now why don't you both get yourselves off home and get some rest. And thank you for tonight. I really don't know what I would have done without you.'

I followed them through the lounge and kissed them both as they slipped into their coats, noticing that Tommy had disappeared. He's probably in the bedroom, I thought to myself, but when I went through there was no sign of him. Shrugging, I went to run myself a bath and half an hour later fell into an exhausted sleep as I lay in bed waiting for him.

The sound of the shower woke me the next morning, and as I glanced towards the door I saw Tommy heading for the kitchen with a huge bath sheet wrapped around his bottom half. I dragged myself out of bed and followed him. He was at the sink filling the kettle when I walked in, and when I spoke he almost jumped out of his skin.

'Where did you disappear to last night?'

'Oh, er . . . that phone call was from a chap that lives down the road. He thought he'd seen someone loitering about outside yesterday afternoon and he just wanted to know if everything was all right, so I went round to have a word with him.'

Tommy seemed nervy and on edge but I put that down to

what we had come home to the night before. He was saved from having to answer any questions when Harold appeared in the doorway knuckling the sleep from his eyes.

'Morning, champ,' Tommy greeted him, and my mind instantly moved on to other things. I would have a lot to do today. First of all I would call an upholsterer and then I would get someone in to properly clean the carpets. Until it was back to normal I knew that I would not feel that the flat was mine. Not that it would be for much longer, only on paper. Strangely, I felt slightly better about moving now. I felt as if someone had invaded what had been my own private space and wondered if I would ever feel truly safe there again. Who was it that had come uninvited into my home, and would they try to come back again? It was a daunting thought.

After I had got a loudly protesting Harold off to school, Tommy rang a locksmith at my request before leaving for work. The man arrived within the hour and changed the lock on the front door, but even when it was done I still felt strangely vulnerable and on edge. I had intended to work on my book this morning but found that I was unable to concentrate. I rang an upholsterer, who arrived within the hour to take my suite away to be re-covered, and then a firm of steam cleaners, who came during the afternoon to deal with the carpets. Now all I could do was try not to think about what had happened and put the incident behind me. It was time to look ahead.

The next three weeks passed in a blur. I saw little of Tommy, for he was constantly going backwards and forwards to Fellburn, and as I did not want Harold to miss too much school I opted to stay at home and leave him to it.

I had made numerous calls to schools in Fellburn and had found a small but select private one that I thought would be just right for Harold. I had also ordered a large amount of new furniture for The Chimneys that would be delivered when we eventually moved in. Tommy was deep in negotiation with the person who owned the scrap yard he was hoping to buy and had also found a new mooring in a marina in Newcastle for *Spring Fever*, which he seemed very excited about.

Janet came and went just as she always had, but had given me no indication as to whether she would be coming with us to Fellburn. I had not pushed her, for I felt that it was a decision she should be allowed to make on her own, though I hoped and prayed that she would decide to join us. And so now it seemed there was very little left to do but wait for the solicitors to tell us when we could sign the contracts that would make The Chimneys ours.

On a grey late October morning I was working when the doorbell rang. Janet was polishing the lounge, humming softly to herself, but she hurried away to answer it, and after a muttered exchange she came back into the room alone.

'Who was it?' I asked as I glanced across her shoulder. Since the night the flat had been broken into I still felt very nervous every time I heard the lift doors open.

'Oh it weren't nobody for you,' she informed me airily as she squirted some polish on to the long sideboard. 'It were two Irish blokes lookin' for Mr Tommy. Between you an' me I didn't like the look of 'em. They looked shifty.'

I laughed aloud for the first time since the night of the break-in. 'Oh Janet, I really don't know what I'd do without you,' I exclaimed. 'I sometimes think with your imagination it should be you that's the author. And speaking of being without you, have you given any more thought to the suggestion I put to you?'

'Between you an' me I ain't thought of much else,' she

admitted. 'But it's a big wrench to just up sticks an' move to another part o' the country at my age, you know!'

I nodded. I knew that she was right and could only give her space now to make up her mind without putting pressure on her.

Two days later my suite was delivered back to me as good as new. I had taken four hundred pounds out of my bank account the previous day to pay the upholsterer, and now I hurried away to fetch my purse from the bedroom. I opened it and then stared into it in dismay. The money had gone, and yet I knew it had been there in the morning because I had seen it when I opened it to give Harold his dinner money before he set off for school.

'Oh dear.' I could feel my cheeks flaming with embarrassment. 'I did get the cash out to pay you but I think my husband must have borrowed it. Could I pay you by cheque?'

'Of course, Mrs Balfour,' the man said gallantly. Hurrying away again I hastily got my chequebook and scribbled one out for him. Once he was gone, I stood there staring about. The only person who had been in the flat that morning other than myself and Tommy was Janet, and I would have staked my life that she would never steal from me. Shrugging, I decided to question Tommy when and if he came home for lunch. With his constant trips backwards and forwards to Fellburn we were seeing little of each other lately, but of course all that would change once we moved into our new home. Or at least I hoped it would. This was to be a new start for all of us.

Chapter Six

I WAS SITTING WORKING at my typewriter when I heard the lift doors open. Janet had been and gone and I wondered who it might be. I opened the door to find Hilda standing there, but not the Hilda I remembered. Gone were the garish clothes and outlandish haircut she used to sport; standing before me was a very attractive young woman.

'Hilda.' I was so genuinely pleased to see her that I gave her a hug and she returned it as I ushered her into the flat. I quickly took her coat, trying hard not to let my eyes rest on the small mound of her stomach. So Janet had been right then, she was going to have a child. I could only pray that this time the father would let her keep it. I felt a slight pang of envy as I thought of James, but then pushed it away. Hilda had worked hard to better herself and deserved a little happiness.

'Sit yourself down and I'll make us some tea,' I told her as I headed off to the kitchen. When I returned with a tray some minutes later I found her staring around the room in awe.

'It's a beautiful flat.'

I nodded in agreement. 'Yes it is, and Janet tells me you might be interested in renting it.'

'I was hoping to,' she admitted as she took the cup of tea I had just poured out for her. 'But now that I've seen it I think it might be a little beyond what we can afford to pay.'

I waved my hand dismissively. 'Oh, don't worry about that, dear. To be honest, I'm more interested in getting someone in who will look after it than the amount of rent I can charge. I'm sure we'll be able to come up with a figure that is mutually agreeable to us both.'

'Oh, I would look after it like it was my own,' she said quickly, then, placing her cup down on the table, she said quietly, 'I suppose Mum told you that I was back with James and that we're going to be married.'

I nodded, suddenly very glad that Hilda had come alone although I couldn't explain why. 'Yes she did and I couldn't be more pleased for you.' I meant every word I said.

She flushed shyly and dropping her hands into her lap told me sincerely, 'I can't believe how lucky I've been, Mrs Nardy.' I found it strange that she should still call me that when I had been married to Tommy for over three years, but I chose not to comment on it as she went on. 'When he left me before I thought my world had ended, but as I told you at the time, I was going to better myself, and I did. And then one day we just bumped into each other again and it all started from there. I can't believe how lucky I've been. There's never been anyone but James for me, but then I don't think I need to tell you that, do I?'

As I gazed across at this lovely girl my heart swelled. She so deserved a little happiness and I prayed that this time James would give it to her. She too had had her hair cut in the fashion of Lady Diana's and it suited her. She was dressed in a pretty flowered Laura Ashley dress with softly padded shoulders and her skin was glowing.

'So when is the big day to be?' I asked.

'In December. We're not having a big splash do, though. Just close friends and family at the register office. I, er . . . was rather hoping you would come along.'

'I would have loved to,' I told her truthfully. 'But I believe we shall have moved by then and no doubt we'll be busy settling into our new house in time for Christmas. I do hope you understand.'

'Of course.'

'So do you think you could be happy here, dear?' I now asked, and as her eyes once again travelled the room she nodded vigorously.

'Oh yes. It's lovely; and so central for James and me to get to work. I'm not too keen on having to take the underground since that flash fire at King's Cross last week. I think everyone thought it was the IRA again for a start-off. All those poor people that were killed; how must their poor families be feeling so close to Christmas?'

I could see that she was getting upset so I then quickly mentioned a sum of money for the rent that made her eyes pop.

'But you could get much more for this place than that,' she gasped.

I shrugged as I picked up my cup and sipped at my tea. 'I dare say I could, but as I told you earlier I'm much more concerned about having someone in here that will look after it. You see . . . this place is very special to me. Nardy lived here all his life and I can't bear the thought of selling it. So, do we have a deal?'

Her smile lit up the room as she held out her hand and we shook on it.

'Right then, I shall leave the keys downstairs with the caretaker and you can pick them up whenever you like after we have moved. Shall we say a six-month lease to start off with?'

Again she smiled, and so the deal was struck.

I felt restless when Hilda had gone so I wandered around the flat. There seemed to be boxes in every corner full of the things that I wanted to take with me to our new home. I had decided to leave all the furniture, so we would only need one small van to follow us with our possessions when we moved. Tommy had decided that he would sail *Spring Fever* to her new moorings in Newcastle and George had offered to come to London on the train and drive myself, Harold and Sandy back to Fellburn in our car. The solicitor had rung only the previous day to say that the contracts were almost ready to be exchanged, and I could hardly take it in. Everything seemed to have happened so fast. The time I had spent in this flat had been the happiest time of my life, particularly, I was forced to admit, the too short time I had lived there with Nardy. But as Gran was fond of saying, life has to go on, and I wondered what this new chapter in my life would hold for me.

I was still wandering about when I again heard the lift doors swish open and I walked into the hallway as someone rang the bell. When I opened the door I found two men standing there and I smiled at them politely.

'May I help you?'

'Is Tommy in?' the taller of the two enquired in a broad Irish accent.

'No, I'm afraid he isn't. Can I help?'

The two men exchanged a glance before the one who had spoken shook his head with a look of annoyance on his face. I wondered if he had been a boxer at some point, for his nose seemed to be spread across his face, and although both men were well dressed they appeared to be coarse individuals, or as Gran would have termed it, common as muck.

'Tell him Paddy was here,' the man now said, and his face was straight and unsmiling. 'An' tell him we'll be needin' to speak to him . . . an' soon.'

With that they swung about and went back into the lift. As I heard it descend to the ground floor I clutched my short arm into my waist and chewed on my lip. What could men like that want with Tommy? I wondered. They had reminded me of gangsters I had seen in films on the television. I went back into the flat and hastily locked and bolted the door, suddenly feeling very vulnerable again, and there was Hamilton with his full menagerie waiting for me in the drawing room with his head to one side.

You do know something funny is going on, don't you? he said as I gazed back at him.

'Nonsense!' I retorted.

Then why is Tommy always out just lately and what do you think he's up to? Why is he always so on edge?

I was at a loss as to how to answer him, so I looked at Begonia and Dusty, who were nodding their heads in agreement with him. For the first time I noticed that Begonia was heavily pregnant and I found myself thinking, she has the same glow about her that Hilda has.

Where is Tommy right now? was Hamilton's next question, and I stuck my chin out as I told him, 'Why, he's at work at the publisher's, of course!'

Quite sure of that, are you?

I was getting annoyed now. 'Well of course he is. Where else would he be?'

Hamilton tossed his mane as he waved a hoof in my direction. There's been a lot of funny things going on though, hasn't there? Captain Ned dying. The flat being trashed. Tommy's urgent need to get out of London all of a sudden. Money missing from your purse. Hasn't any of that set alarm bells off for you?

'Tommy is a good honest man,' I snapped more sharply than I had meant to. Then I turned my back on all three of them and with a sullen expression on my face looked out of the window into the street below.

I was just in time to see Tommy's car pull up and him climb out of it. He was about to enter the building when the two Irishmen who had just visited stepped out of the foyer and walked up to him. From where I was standing it looked as if the three were having heated words. Tommy was highly agitated and his arms were flying in all directions as he spoke to them. And then to my horror I saw one of them push him roughly against the car. My heart leapt into my throat, but then they were striding away and I saw Tommy straighten his tie and pull himself up to his full height before entering the building.

You see, I told you there was something not right, I heard Hamilton say.

I swung around to answer him but he and his friends were gone and now all I could do was wait for Tommy to find out what was going on.

Minutes later he strode into the flat as if he hadn't a care in the world, although I noted that he was deathly pale and his hands were shaking.

'Hello, dear.'

I inclined my head in answer as he headed straight for the whisky decanter and poured himself a stiff measure. 'Isn't it a little early in the day for that?' I enquired.

'Oh, I just fancied one.'

A silence stretched between us for some moments until I forced myself to say, 'Would you like to tell me what's going on, Tommy?'

He almost choked on the mouthful of whisky before saying, 'What do you mean? Going on?'

I sighed as I clasped my hands together. 'I'm not entirely stupid, you know. You haven't seemed yourself for some time. I know there's something troubling you. We are man and wife, so shouldn't we be sharing whatever it is?'

His shoulders suddenly seemed to sag as he sank on to the nearest chair and buried his face in his hands.

'Oh Maisie, I'm afraid I've got myself into rather a mess,' he muttered.

'What sort of a mess?'

For a moment I thought he was not going to answer me, but then he said quietly, 'I've been gambling and I owe those men who just left a great deal of money.'

'So why haven't you paid them?'

'Because I . . .' He hung his head in shame. 'I haven't got anything to pay them with.'

'*What?*' I was so shocked that I was rendered speechless and my mouth gaped as I stared at the top of his bowed head.

Eventually he looked back up at me and spread his hands in a helpless gesture. 'All I have left is *Spring Fever*. The money my mother left me went months ago.'

It was so unbelievable that all I could do was stare at him. He was talking about thousands and thousands of pounds. 'But . . . but what about the properties she left you?' I managed to stammer.

'I lost them too.'

'Oh, *Tommy*.' As I sank down on to the chair next to him I was trying to take in what he had told me. It was inconceivable.

As well as the house they had lived in and seventy-five thousand pounds, she had also left him four office properties spread across London, each worth at least a hundred thousand pounds. And here he was telling me that he was without a penny to his name.

'Those men that just left . . . if I don't get the money to pay them soon, there's no telling what they might do. They're ruthless, Maisie.'

'How much money are we talking about?'

He gulped deep in his throat before saying softly, 'Ten thousand pounds.'

'*Ten thousand pounds!*' I could feel my eyes popping as I stared at him in utter disbelief.

He nodded miserably. 'I'm so sorry, Maisie. I was hoping that if we could get away from London they would lose track of me and we could start again, but after what they did to the flat . . .'

Everything began to make sense. 'So it was them that trashed it, as a threat to you? And you that took the four hundred pounds from my purse?'

Shamefaced, he nodded again. I stood up and began to pace up and down, willing my heart to slow into a steadier rhythm. If these men were capable of that, what else might they be capable of? The thought was terrifying.

As another thought occurred to me, I slowed my steps to ask, 'If all your money is gone, how were you hoping to buy the scrap yard in Newcastle?'

The flush that sprang into his cheeks was my answer.

'You want me to buy it for you, don't you?'

He nodded as I shook my head from side to side. I could hardly believe this was the man I had married. The man I had thought was so thoughtful and steady.

'I . . . I'll change once we've moved,' he told me urgently.

'You just see if I don't. I'll make you proud of me. Work every hour of the day to make it up to you, as sure as God is my judge.'

The shock was wearing off now and in its place was a great sadness. I almost felt as if I had been living with a stranger, for all this had been going on right under my nose and I had been blind to it.

'Right, I suppose the first thing we need to do is get that money to them,' I told him, unable to keep the chill from my voice. 'And then I think after what's happened the sooner we get away from London the better.'

He smiled with relief but I found in that moment that I could hardly bear to look at him. 'I'll go and get ready and you can take me to the bank,' I informed him shortly, and turning on my heel I walked into our bedroom and closed the door behind me, wondering how I would ever be able to have him near me again.

It was now evening. Tommy had gone off with the money I had withdrawn from the bank in a briefcase and Harold, Sandy and I were watching the television in the drawing room. At least Harold was. My mind was so full of the day's happenings that I found I couldn't concentrate on anything. I felt utterly betrayed and found I was looking at Tommy through different eyes. We had barely spoken since he had told me what was going on, and the way I felt right now, that suited me down to the ground. I could barely look at him let alone speak to him at the moment.

Harold was totally engrossed in *The Dame Edna Everage Experience* and his laughter was bouncing off the walls, so I slipped away to the sanctuary of the kitchen, softly closing the door behind me. I somehow felt that the last few years I had spent with Tommy had been a lie, and I wondered if I would ever feel anything for him again.

I thought of making myself a hot drink but decided against it. I had drunk so much tea during the day that I felt as if I could drown in it. Thankfully, Harold was blissfully unaware of what had gone on, and when he joined me in the kitchen some time later his face was bright.

'They're havin' a leavin' do for me next week at school,' he told me brightly. Forcing a smile to my face, I put his milk on the stove to warm as I placed some biscuits on a plate. 'I can't wait to see Gran an' George again,' he gabbled on, but then he stopped and his face became solemn as he asked, 'Is somethin' wrong, Mrs Nardy?'

'No, dear. Of course there isn't,' I assured him with a false smile. 'I think my head is just a little full of the move and everything I have to do before we go, that's all.'

Sliding on to a kitchen chair, he began to fiddle with his fingers as he told me in a low voice, 'I ain't 'arf goin' to miss me gag an' me uncles.'

Crossing to him, I held him to me and planted a kiss on his springy hair. 'You'll still get to see them,' I told him cheerily. 'And don't forget, once we're there you'll have Uncle George's brood to play with.'

Slightly happier, he smiled again. 'There is that. An' it'll be right grand to be close to the sea. I'll be able to practise me swimmin' whenever I like.'

'Only if you have an adult with you,' I warned. 'You must never go into the sea on your own. There are tides and under-currents that will pull you out before you know it.'

He sighed as I poured his milk into a glass and placed it in front of him, and I smiled back before hurrying away to turn his blankets back for him.

Long after I had tucked Harold in and retired myself, I heard Tommy's key in the lock, but I turned on my side and pretended to be asleep until at last his gentle snores echoed around the room. One of Gran's favourite sayings had been 'Everything will look better come morning', and tonight I could only pray that it was true.

'Cor blimey! 'Ow did you get that?' Harold exclaimed the next morning as he stared at Tommy across the breakfast table.

Tommy tentatively raised his hand to the bruise that was spreading across his left eye before answering, 'Oh, I, er . . . slipped on the frost on the pavement last night when I got out of the car.'

Harold's eyes were as round as saucers. 'I ain't seen a shiner like that since the last time me Uncle Max walked into somebody's fist,' he declared.

Hoping to change the subject, I hastily passed him his satchel. 'Come on, young man, or you'll be late for the school bus,' I told him.

He sighed heavily but slid down from the table and took his bag from me. At the door he paused to ask, 'You two are goin' to the cinema tonight to see *Dirty Dancin'*, ain't you?'

'Oh, I'm not sure yet, dear. We do have the tickets but I think I have a slight headache coming on, so we'll see.'

'But I thought Gag was comin' to babysit me?'

'Harold, I told you – we'll see. Now get off with you.'

He rolled his eyes and headed for the door, humming as he went. We listened to him leave, then Tommy asked, 'How are you feeling?'

'How *should* I be feeling?' My voice was uncharacteristically sharp but I didn't care and Tommy had the grace to flush.

'I've been on to the chap that's selling the scrap yard,' he told me. 'And he says he's prepared to rent it to me until we can afford to buy it, so that will be a help at least, won't it?'

I flashed him the dirtiest look I could muster before flouncing out of the room. I was nowhere near ready to forgive him yet for all the lies and betrayal.

Chapter Seven

'SO, THIS IS it then?'
I blinked back the tears as I stared into Janet's eyes. Her own were swimming with tears too.

'Won't you please change your mind and come with us, Janet?' I begged.

She looked away and slowly shook her head. 'I can't, love. Our Hilda is gettin' wed on Saturday, an' what would the lads be like without me to keep 'em in order, eh?'

'Well, you know there will always be a place for you in our home if you change your mind.'

She nodded and now the tears came, rolling down her cheeks in torrents. 'I shall miss you, love,' she sobbed. '*An'* that little bugger there.'

'I shall miss you too,' I answered, then I pressed an envelope into her hand. 'Give this to Hilda and James for me on Saturday, would you? There's a little bit in there for them to get anything they might need.'

'Ah, ma'am.' Janet sniffed and mopped at her face with a large white hankie. 'Thanks. I'll be sure an' see they get it. Now you take care of yourself, do you hear me?'

I nodded numbly, too choked to speak as she turned her attention to Harold. 'An' you, young fellow-me-lad. You just watch your manners, eh? You're goin' to live in the nobs' part of Fellburn on Brampton Hill, so don't go lettin' Mrs Nardy down now.'

'I won't, Gag,' he answered as she caught him to her in a bear hug. But then George took my elbow and steered me towards the door, saying, 'Come on now. Let's be having you. All this blubbin, you'll have me at it in a minute, woman. Anyone would think you were emigratin' to the other side o' the world instead of up north.'

I paused to look around Nardy's flat for one last time. And it was still his flat; it would always be his in my eyes, even though it was now my name that was on the deeds. I had shared the happiest years of my life with him here and now the memories were locked away in a little corner of my heart to be treasured for all time.

In a few minutes I was sitting in the front of the car with George. Harold and Sandy were in the back and the boot was full of suitcases containing our clothes. The removal van containing the things we were taking with us had left some half an hour ago.

Janet was standing on the pavement waving a handkerchief and Harold was waving back as we pulled away from the kerb.

'Right, we're off then,' George said cheerfully.

'So we are,' I agreed. 'But do you think we could make just one very short stop on the way?'

'I don't see why not, lass. Where did you want to go?'

'To the chapel,' I told him, and at the corner of the street he steered the car in that direction.

In no time at all he drew to a halt again, and as he stared at the lych gate he asked, 'Do you want me to come with you, lass?'

'No thank you, George, I'd like to go alone.'

He squeezed my hand and I climbed out of the car and hurried up the path through the churchyard. Some way along it, I stepped on to the grass, which was heavy with hoar frost, and approached a smart marble headstone beneath the barren branches of a large oak tree. This was where my beloved Nardy's ashes had been scattered, and as I looked down on his resting place the sadness that was never far from the surface flooded through me. It was here that I always felt close to him, for it was here that I had had my last glimpse of him on the day of his funeral. I could remember it clearly. We had stepped out of the chapel following the funeral service and I had suddenly felt his presence so tangibly that I had looked up, and there he was standing with Hamilton and Begonia and, strangely, my mother.

It was hard to believe that here we were almost in the heart of the city, for the place was quiet and peaceful and the heavy traffic seemed a million miles away. I stood for some seconds letting the tranquillity wash over me, then bending down I whispered, 'I have to go now, Nardy. Another part of my life is about to begin. Tommy has been very foolish, but he's my husband and so I must try to forgive him and start again. I know that's what you would want me to do. Goodbye, my love . . . sleep tight.'

Then I straightened and strode away to begin the next part of my life without looking back.

As George pulled on to the tree-lined drive leading to The Chimneys, I saw the lights of the house blazing through the darkness ahead. I knew that Gran and Mary had spent the last two days there, waiting for the new furniture to be delivered and sprucing the place up for me, and I was more grateful than I could say.

'Here we are then, lass. Home, eh? Who would ever have

thought little Maisie Rochester would end up living in a grand house on Brampton Hill, eh? You should be proud of yourself; you've come a long way.'

I smiled at George. I didn't know quite how I felt at that moment. Everything seemed so strange, but I didn't have time to ponder, for soon we were pulling up at the door and Gran came hobbling out to meet us wrapped in a voluminous flowered apron that had seen better days. Mary was close behind her and they both hugged me as I stepped from the car. My short arm was paining me, usually a sign that snow was on the way, and my legs had gone to sleep from sitting in one position for so long.

Harold had been fast asleep for the last part of the journey, but now he spilled out of the back of the car and hopped from foot to foot in his excitement as he stared up at the house, which looked absolutely enormous.

There was a thick frost on the ground and it was so cold that our breath hung on the air like steam from a kettle.

'Come on, lass. Let's get inside, eh? It's too bloody cold to be standin' out here,' Gran said in her own inimitable way. George was manhandling the suitcases out of the boot with Mary's help as I followed Gran inside. And then I was in the hallway and I stopped and stared about in amazement. The whole place was sparkling and I had the sensation of entering a mansion. High above, the chandelier sparkled down on me, and the tiles on the floor shone. The banisters had been polished and the smell of wax and something delicious was floating on the air.

Seeing my surprise, Gran grinned broadly. 'It's lookin' nice, ain't it?' she said. 'I don't mind tellin' you, me an' our Mary have scrubbed till us hands are red raw.' She held them out for my inspection but I was speechless and could only shake my head while she chattered on. 'I've had all the new furniture set out. I just hope as I've had it put in the right rooms for you.' She flung open the door to the dining room, and again I was shocked. The new mahogany table and six matching chairs were in pride of place in the centre of the room and all laid out for a meal. There was a huge fire roaring in the ornate marble fireplace and the heavy brocade curtains I had ordered had been hung at the windows and drawn tight against the freezing night.

'Why, Gran,' I gasped in delight. 'I can't believe it, it looks absolutely wonderful.'

Her chest puffed with pride at the praise, and she ushered me towards the living room, where again the new furniture was set out and the whole room was gleaming.

'I . . . I can't believe you've done all this. I don't know how I'll ever be able to thank you.' I was so choked at her kindness that a large lump had formed in my throat, but she waved my thanks aside.

'Eeh, there were nowt wrong wi' the place that a bit of elbow grease an' spit an' polish wouldn't put right,' she assured me.

I ran my hand along the back of the rich brocade settee and stared in awe at the heavy matching curtains. She had laid my lovely Chinese rug in front of the fireplace and the whole place looked warm and inviting.

'I've had a go at the two main bedrooms an' all,' she now informed me. 'I'm afraid we ain't had time to tackle the other rooms yet, but at least you'll be able to sleep comfortable tonight. Still, first things first. I've got a meal prepared an' I've no doubt you'll be gaggin' for a cuppa, so come on through to the kitchen; the kettle's on.'

I entered the hallway just in time to catch Harold slithering down the highly polished banister rail. I stared at him sternly. He slithered off the end and grinned at me sheepishly before following me into the kitchen with Sandy hot on his heels.

This room too was sparkling. The scrubbed pine table and chairs I had ordered had been placed in the middle of the room and the old cooking range I had admired when Tommy and I had viewed the house now shone to such an extent that I could see my face in it.

George joined us at that moment with a wide smile on his face. 'Bye, this is some pad,' he exclaimed as he stared around him. 'It's like walkin' into a fancy hotel. Not that I've been in that many, mind.'

We all laughed and the atmosphere was light as we sat down together to enjoy a much-needed cup of tea. Then Gran served up the meal in the formal dining room and I found that I couldn't stop smiling. There was a delicious shoulder of lamb, crispy roast potatoes and a selection of vegetables, followed by a home-made apple pie and a jug of thick creamy custard that had Harold's mouth watering.

After dinner I followed Gran upstairs, where she showed me the room that Tommy and I had decided to claim as ours. The new bed was all made up, there was a bright fire burning in the grate and the new curtains were hanging at the windows.

'Oh, this is so much cosier than the electric fire I had in the flat,' I sighed contentedly.

Gran chuckled. 'Aye, well let's hope you still think that when you've had to make 'em all up an' empty the ash trays a few times.'

I hadn't thought of that.

'I reckon you're goin' to have to get somebody in from down in the village to help you out,' Gran pointed out. 'This is a great ramblin' place to keep clean on your own. You'll never have any time to write if you don't get somebody in to lend a hand. Truth is, lass, I'd volunteer but I ain't as sprightly on me old pins as I used to be an' I don't reckon I'd manage the climb up that hill every day.'

'Oh Gran, I wouldn't hear of it,' I assured her. 'But I think you're right. Once I've settled in I'll see about getting a daily.' I thought of Janet regretfully. She would have loved to have this place to potter about in. Still, she had made her decision and I was happy to abide by it.

We went along the landing to Harold's room to find him already there unpacking his toys. 'This bedroom is twice as big as the one I had back at the flat,' he told us gleefully. 'An' I can see the woods at the back from my window.'

Seeing that he was content, Gran and I left him to it and went back downstairs to join Mary and George, who were washing up the dinner pots in the kitchen.

'Thank you so much for all the hard work, Mary,' I told her. 'And you too, George, for coming all that way to fetch us.'

'It was a pleasure,' Mary assured me, but then wiping her hands on the tea towel she glanced at the clock and told George, 'We really ought to be getting off now. Lord knows what the bairns will have been up to while we've been gone.'

'You're right, lass.' George hurried away to fetch their coats as Gran frowned and asked, 'So when is Tommy due to arrive then?'

'He should be here tomorrow morning when he's moored *Spring Fever*.'

'An' are you quite sure you'll be all right here on your own tonight?'

'Of course we will,' I told her brightly. 'Once Harold's gone to bed I'll have time to have a proper nose round and get a feel for the place. I've still got a lot of unpacking to do too.'

'All right then, if you're sure, we'll get off. Me feet feel as if they don't belong to me an' I want a quiet hour by the fire wi' a bottle o' Guinness an' a packet o' Woodbine.'

I kissed them and thanked them again before walking to the door, where I waved them off. As I was standing there on the step, the first flakes of snow began to gently flutter down and I pulled my cardigan more tightly about me. It wasn't until the car had disappeared from sight that I realised how very quiet it was. I was used to the hustle and bustle of London, but here there was not a sound to be heard and the silence was deafening. Even the wind had died away, and the trees surrounding the house stood stiffly to attention like silent sentinels. As I gazed down on the lights of Fellburn twinkling in the night and beyond to the sea that was as still as a millpond, tears pricked at the back of my eyes. How my mother would have loved this house. All of her life she had strived to be a lady, which was why I had been such a grave disappointment to her. A plain child with a deformed arm, with no self-confidence and not guts enough to say boo to a goose. Yet it was I that had ended up on Brampton Hill, and she that had died a lonely, unhappy woman.

Shaking my head, I slowly turned about and went back into my palace.

Chapter Eight

TOMMY ARRIVED AT eleven o'clock the next morning and like me was shocked at how much work Mary and Gran had done on the place.

'I hadn't realised how big it was,' he exclaimed as he strutted from one room to another like the lord of the manor. I was trying desperately hard to be normal with him but still felt resentment at his betrayal.

'What does Harold think of it?'

'He loves it. He went off into the woods with Sandy about half an hour ago and I haven't seen them since. He wondered if we might take him down into the town later on to buy him a sledge. The way this snow is coming down, he'll need one soon.'

Tommy nodded as he glanced towards the window. The snow was still falling thick and fast.

'Did you manage to get *Spring Fever* into her new mooring?'

'Yes, I did,' he replied with a smile. 'And I have to say it will be so much easier to get her out to sea from here. I've got to go and see the guy that owns the scrap yard too this afternoon . . . if it's still all right with you, of course.'

I avoided his eyes as I asked, 'Are you quite sure this is a lucrative business to go into, Tommy? I mean . . . you know very little about scrap metal. Will the people hereabouts be able to bring you enough to make it profitable?'

'Oh Maisie, it doesn't work like that, you silly goose,' he chuckled. 'The main money in scrap metal is from imports. You watch the price of metal abroad and when you can buy it at a cheaper rate than you can get it here, you have a container load delivered via sea passage and sell it on.'

'Oh, I see.' I was feeling very foolish. He obviously had his heart set on doing this, so I went on, 'Of course you must go ahead with it if it's what you really want to do.' I was hoping that a new business venture would keep his mind off gambling, so my decision was not purely unselfish. 'Although,' I went on, 'I'm afraid you're going to have to rent the yard for now. Our funds are a little depleted after paying for the house and the ten thousand . . .'

He flushed with shame and stared down at the floor as he nodded. 'Of course.'

I stared out of the window then just in time to see Harold and Sandy bound out of the woods. The child looked so happy that it did my heart good to see him. 'Well, there's one person who I think will settle here,' I muttered.

Tommy looked at me closely before asking, 'Don't you think you will then?'

I shrugged. 'It's too early to tell. At the moment I feel like I'm rattling about the place like a pea in a pod,' I admitted.

'Well, as you say, it's very early days.' With his mouth set in a straight line, he walked out of the room, leaving me alone to watch the antics of the pair gambolling in the snow outside.

A week later I was already beginning to wonder if moving into this house had been such a good idea after all. The local newspapers had cottoned on to where I lived and so I almost dreaded going down the drive, for there was always someone hovering there. On top of that, I realised that Gran had been right when she had told me that the house would take a lot of keeping up. I seemed to be forever putting coal on one fire or another or emptying ash cans. Now I fully understood just how much Janet had done for me, for she had kept the flat like a new pin, giving me time to write my books. I hadn't typed a single word since moving in; I had been too busy keeping on top of the cleaning and unpacking. Tommy had been very little help, as he was already busy with his new business and seemingly enjoying every minute of it, which was something at least. Another blessing was the way Harold had settled into his new school. He was full of it and had already made friends, some of whom he had brought home for tea. So all in all, things were going well, but I was lonely. I missed Janet's company and her cheerful chatter. My relationship with Tommy seemed to have undergone a subtle change and I couldn't decide whether this was on his part or mine. He was no longer possessive as he had been in London and didn't seem to mind me going out alone any more, which was a huge relief. He was still considerate and polite, but when he came home each evening he would retire to our room, and when I joined him he was always asleep. Christmas was creeping up on us and I knew that I should be thinking of getting a tree and some decorations, but up to now I hadn't managed to find the time.

I had visited Tommy's new scrap yard just the once and was not keen to hurry back. It was much bigger than I had expected it to be and was a dirty, dismal place with a huge weighbridge and piles of scrap metal on seemingly every inch of floor space. Tommy now had four men working for him. One of them was simply referred to as the Sand Dancer, the nickname given to people who had been born in South Shields. Tommy had set the lad on the first week he had been there and found him highly amusing, for he was never seen without a balaclava that completely covered his face, leaving only his eyes on show. I found him a surly lad, for when I said hello to him he merely grunted and moved on, ignoring my outstretched hand. When I mentioned this to Tommy, he threw back his head and laughed. 'I don't care if he never utters a word,' he told me. 'I've hired him to work, and as long as he does his job I'm not much bothered about niceties.'

I supposed he was right but hadn't taken to the young man all the same. On a happier note, I had some visitors that I was definitely happy to see. First of all Dr Kane turned up with his wife Jane. I had missed them during the time I had spent in London and seeing them again made me feel more at home.

'It's been a long time since you used to visit my surgery every Monday morning, isn't it, miss?' Mike's eyes were twinkling and I giggled. 'Do you remember what you used to say when I spoke to you?' he went on, and before I could answer he put his head to one side and said, '*Wh . . . at?*' and we all burst out laughing. He then became serious and taking my hand said softly, 'You've come a long way, Maisie. I am very proud of you. But are you happy now?'

Happy. The word bounced around in my head. What was happy? Happy was the times I had spent with Nardy. But how could I be *un*happy? I had a beautiful house, the like of which I had never thought to own. I was a bestselling author, and I had a husband, a son and a dog. So why was there this little empty space still inside me?

Forcing a brightness to my voice I told him, 'Of course I'm happy. What do I have to be unhappy about?'

Mike peered at me under his bushy eyebrows and I felt myself blushing. I always felt when he looked at me that way that he could see right into my very soul.

My second unexpected but very welcome visitor was Father Makin, who huffed and puffed his way up the drive as if he was climbing a mountain.

'Eeh, it's a long way up that hill, so it is,' he told me as I opened the door to him. 'And enough to freeze the hairs off a brass monkey. I'm thinkin' a sup o' the hard stuff is what I'm needin' to warm me up, so it is.'

Almost choking on my laughter, I ushered him into the living room and poured him a stiff measure of whisky, which he tossed off in one go.

'Ah, now that warmed the cockles o' me old heart, so it did,' he told me as he held his glass out for a refill. 'An' where's this new husband o' yours then, Maisie?'

'He's had to go back to London with a container full of metal,' I told him. 'But he should be home tomorrow. And he's not that new, Father. We've been married for over three years now.'

'Ah, you must have been. And I heard he had taken over the old scrap yard. So . . . can I hope to see you both in church on Sunday?'

I gulped before saying, 'I doubt that you'll see Tommy there, Father. He isn't a Catholic.'

'Mm . . . an' what about you, Maisie? How long has it been since you set foot inside a church or went to confession?'

'I, er . . .' Thankfully, Harold burst into the room at that moment, and although I hadn't entered a church since I lost Nardy, I offered up a silent prayer of thanks.

'Look, I got a star for . . .' Harold skidded to a halt and hung his head as he saw our visitor.

Going to his side, I took his hand and told Father Makin, 'This is my son, Harold.'

'Ah, I heard you'd adopted a child,' the priest said with a smile at Harold. 'An' a fine little laddie he is an' all. How do you do, young Harold?'

Harold shyly shook the proffered hand as Father Makin lurched a little unsteadily out of the chair. 'Well now. I must be on me way. I have a call to make down in Bog's End. Old Arthur Scafferty is about due to meet our maker, so he is.' He quickly crossed himself as Harold and I followed him to the door, doing our best to keep our mirth subdued until we had seen him on his way.

'I have to admit it was a lovely surprise to see you, Father,' I told him. 'I thought you would have retired by now.'

'Well, Maisie, let's just say I'm semi-retired.' His eyes were twinkling as I raised a questioning eyebrow. 'The thing is, you see, the new priest, Father Will, is a little young, so I've stayed on in the vicarage for a time to show him the ropes. Can you believe he roars about on a motorbike an' wears denim jeans beneath his cassock? May the Holy Mother bless us – whoever heard of a priest on a motorbike indeed! But then it's a sign of the times, an' he has a heart as big as a bucket, so he does. He's started a youth club down in the village hall; you'll have to come and join it, lad, when you've settled in.'

He tucked his scrawny neck into his chest now as he leaned towards me and whispered, 'An' that little friend o' yours, Maisie – the horse. The one that only you can see . . . Is he still about?'

When I nodded, his head wagged from side to side. 'An' his wife?'

Again I nodded, and now he said, 'I don't know, Maisie. I have to say, you're a strange girl. Always have been if it comes to that, but strange in the nicest possible way, of course. Anyway, goodbye, Maisie. Goodbye, Harold.' His voice floated back to us through the snow as he strode away, his long black cassock flapping about his legs.

'Goodbye, Father.' I quickly closed the door, and as Harold and I looked at each other, we fell together laughing.

I felt slightly happier after Father Makin's visit. Some people never changed.

'Seven more days to go!' Harold was almost jumping up and down in his excitement as we both stood back to survey the Christmas tree we had just decorated. We had gone into Newcastle that morning to buy it, and now, dressed in its lights and baubles, it looked beautiful.

'When will Mr Tommy be 'ome to see it?' he asked, and glancing towards the window I stifled a sigh. Tommy seemed to be working all the hours God sent, and even when he was home he seemed preoccupied and edgy. I supposed it was because he was trying so hard to get his business going and so up until now I had said nothing. I would tonight, though; I wanted us all to spend our first Christmas in our new home together.

'I'm not sure, but don't worry. I dare say he'll be closing the yard down soon until after the New Year.'

Harold nodded as he called Sandy to him and headed towards the coat closet. 'Me an' Sandy are goin' to take me sledge out for a while,' he informed me over his shoulder.

I went to the window and watched them both crossing the snow-covered lawn, Sandy leaping high and Harold towing his sledge behind him. Eventually they disappeared into the woods and I turned back to the empty room, suddenly feeling lonely. I noticed that the fire was burning low, and it was as I was throwing some more coal on it that I heard a car come along the drive and pull up outside. Rubbing my hands together I hurried into the hall. Through the frosted glass in the front door I could just make out the shape of someone standing on the step. I flung open the door and then my sooty hand flew to my mouth as I saw who it was standing on the step.

'*Janet!*' I hardly dared blink in case I opened my eyes to find I'd imagined it. But I did blink, and when I looked back she was still there, smiling at me sheepishly as a taxi driver carried a suitcase up the steps.

'Hello, ma'am. I was wonderin' if you could perhaps find room for another one?'

'But I . . . I thought you'd decided to stay at home?' I gasped.

'I had, but a woman's entitled to change her mind, ain't she? An' if truth be told . . . Well, it ain't the same at home since me old man passed away. But now . . . are you goin' to keep me standin' out here on the step to freeze all day or what?'

I almost dragged her over the doorstep in my delight, and once inside she stood gazing around her before she said, 'Well, it's certainly a lovely gaff you've got here. I'll grant you that.'

'So, are you here for a night? For Christmas?'

'For good if you'll have me,' she mumbled, and I suddenly felt as if all my Christmases had come at once.

'*Wh . . . at?* You mean you're actually going to *stay*? But I thought you said they needed you back home?'

'I thought they did,' she admitted as she took off her hat and placed it on the hat stand. 'But the long an' the short of it is they don't. Our Hilda's married, the lads are doin' just fine on their own, an' at the end o' the day I thought it might not be such a bad thing to give 'em all a little bit o' space. They are grown up after all. Now, stop gawpin' an' tell me where his Nibs is.'

'He's out playing in the snow, but he should be back shortly.'

'Good, then that will give us time to have a cuppa and for you to show me round the place, won't it?'

Taking her hand, I hauled her into the kitchen, where she whistled through her teeth as she stared about her.

'Bugger me, this is as big as the whole of my downstairs put together.' Her eyes were shining as she stared around, and I laughed.

'Wait till you see the rest of it,' I warned her. 'It takes me all my time just to keep the fires going, let alone get any cleaning done. I've already told Tommy I want central heating in before next winter. But sit down and let me take your coat. I want to hear about all that's happening at home.'

She handed me her coat, and I pressed her on to a chair before hurrying across the room to put the kettle on.

'I've brought you some photos of our Hilda's wedding.' She was delving in her bag, and by the time I got back to her she had spread them out on the table. I slowly lifted them one by one, and as I studied them my heart began to hammer in my chest. Hilda looked truly beautiful. She was wearing a cream suit cinched in at the waist and a small hat that was placed at a jaunty angle and to which was attached a veil that covered one side of her face. But it wasn't the clothes that made her look beautiful. It was the glow on her face as she gazed up at her husband. I forced myself to look at him, amazed at how different he looked without his outlandish Mohican haircut. Detective Sergeant James Bainbridge. It seemed a very long time ago now that he had bought me flowers, red roses, but he was seven years younger than me and I had told him, 'I have just adopted one son. I don't want another.'

I pulled myself back to the present with a start. That was all in the past now. I was married to Tommy, and although we were going through what Nardy would have termed 'a sticky patch', he was my husband and somehow I had to try and get our marriage back on the right track. The past was the past and best forgotten.

'She looks beautiful,' I said sincerely, and Janet's face softened as she nodded.

'Yes she does. She really loves him, you know? I just hope it works out for them. He almost broke her heart the last time.'

I chose not to answer as I hurried away to make the tea. Instead, with my back to her, I asked, 'And what about the lads?' Lads; they were grown men really, but I knew that Janet would always think of them as her lads.

'Right as ninepence,' she retorted. 'You have them to blame for me bein' here. Between you an' me I reckon they'll be pleased to have the house to 'emselves. You know what they say – while the cat's away, the mice will play.'

I placed the teapot on the tray and carried it back to the table just as the back door opened and Harold and Sandy spilled into the room bringing an icy blast of air with them.

'*Gag!*' His eyes almost popped out of his head and there was a grin on his face that stretched from ear to ear as he hurtled across the kitchen and flung himself into her outstretched arms.

'What *you* bloody doin' here?' He quickly glanced my way for the reprimand that he would usually hear when he swore, but because it was such a special day I decided to turn a deaf ear.

'I thought I'd better come an' make sure as you were behavin' yourself,' she teased.

He looked momentarily worried but then, seeing the twinkle in her eye, his face relaxed and a barrage of questions started. 'So how long will you be stayin'? What time did you come? Is Uncle Max an' Uncle Bill wi' you? An' did Auntie Hilda get married?'

'Whoa!' Janet held her hand up and stopped him mid-flow. 'Slow down, will you? You're makin' me dizzy. Now, in answer to your first question, I shall be stayin' for as long as you can put up with me. No, your uncles ain't here; I figured it were about time the great idle louts started lookin' out for 'emselves, that's if they don't get our May to wait on 'em hand an' foot. An' yes, your Auntie Hilda did get married, an' from what I can see of it she's very happy. Now will that be enough for you to be goin' on with, sir?'

'Oh Gags, I'm *so* glad you're here. This is goin' to be the *best* Christmas ever.'

And as I looked fondly at the two of them, I had the strangest feeling that he might just be right.

Chapter Nine

A T THE ELEVENTH HOUR, Harold and I decided that we should invite the whole family to spend Christmas with us and so Christmas Eve found Janet and me running about like headless chickens. She had gone into Fellburn that morning and returned with the most enormous turkey that I had ever seen. She had then spent the next two hours plucking it, much to Harold's disgust.

'Why couldn't you just 'ave got one o' them frozen ones, Gag?' he had asked and she had almost choked with indignation.

'*Frozen!* Why, I ain't got time for them. Tasteless they are. You'll see tomorrow when you're tuckin' in.'

Stifling a laugh I hurried out of the kitchen as I heard the phone ringing in the hall. It was Tommy and he sounded very agitated.

'I'm afraid I'm going to be late home, dear,' he told me.

I sighed. 'But Tommy, it's Christmas Eve.'

'I know it is, dear, and I'm sorry but there's nothing I can do about it. That container of metal I ordered from abroad hasn't arrived yet and I shall have to wait for it here till they deliver it.'

'Well I suppose you know what you're doing,' I told him tightly, and after apologising yet again he hung up.

I was feeling annoyed when I went back into the kitchen and it must have shown, for Janet piped up, 'What's wrong wi' your face, then? You look like you've lost a bob an' found a tanner!'

'Tommy just rang to say he was going to be late home,' I muttered.

'Oh, as it happens I saw him earlier on when I was down in Fellburn. Him an' two Irish blokes an' that young chap he has workin' for him who always wears a balaclava were just goin' into the Jolly Sailor. I know they were Irish 'cos I heard 'em talkin' as I passed. Mr Tommy didn't see me though.'

I had just opened my mouth to answer her when Hamilton suddenly galloped straight through the back door snorting furiously and waving his hooves in the air. I gulped deep in my throat. This was the first glimpse I had had of him since moving into my new home and I had been beginning to think that I had left him behind in Nardy's flat.

It's those two same Irish blokes that visited the flat, he told me, but trying to ignore his antics I said, 'I'm just going to go and finish wrapping some presents, Janet. Can you manage here?'

'No trouble at all,' she assured me as I hurried back out into the hallway. Hamilton was leaning against the dining-room door, and as I advanced on him I told him, 'Now don't start. Not today. I have a million things to do and I'm sure Tommy's meeting was purely innocent, something to do with his business.'

He put his head to one side and snorted. I walked past him and closed the door firmly between us, but then there he was standing behind the table. This time Begonia and Dusty were with him and for the first time Dusty seemed agitated too. He was shaking his shaggy mane from side to side and there was a fearful look in his eyes.

'Now don't *you* start,' I told him in exasperation, and at that moment I heard the door opening behind me. I turned just in time to see Harold about to enter the room.

'Off with you,' I told him sternly as I shooed him away. 'I've told you this room is out of bounds until all the presents are wrapped.'

'*Oh!*' He sniffed but obediently closed the door. A grin spread across my face. He was so excited about Christmas that I wondered if he would get any sleep at all tonight.

'Now, what was I saying . . .' I turned back to where Hamilton and his menagerie had stood but found that I was alone again. With a shake of my head I lifted a roll of Sellotape from the table and began to wrap the gifts.

Some time later I remembered that I had left the perfume I had bought for Janet in the room along the hallway. It had been used as a second sitting room when we had first moved into the house, but Tommy and I had decided to turn it into a library and he had also adopted it as his study, so that he would not disturb me in mine while I was working. I had hidden Janet's gift in there as Tommy was very strict about his privacy and would not allow her to clean in there. His desk was always organised chaos but he insisted that he knew where everything was, so Janet and I were happy to leave him to his own devices and rarely ventured in there.

As I entered the room now my eyes were drawn to the window where the snow was coming down thick and fast. I moved to stand in front of it, delighting in the snowy landscape. The branches of the leafless trees were bowed with the weight of the snow that had settled on them and everywhere looked clean and bright. Smiling, I turned to get Janet's perfume from the shelf, and as I did so my eyes settled on a cheque that was lying on Tommy's desk. I meandered over to it curiously and as I noticed the amount written on it they almost bulged out of my head. The cheque was made out to Tommy in the amount of £50,000. But what, I asked myself, could he possibly have done to earn such a sum? I realised instantly I would not be able to ask him. If I did, he would know that I had been into his room and he would not be happy about it.

See . . . I told you there was something fishy afoot, didn't I?

'Oh, stop it, Hamilton,' I snapped as he pranced from behind the desk. 'Tommy told me there was a lot of money to be made in scrap. I'm sure there's some perfectly legitimate reason for the amount.'

Gripping the perfume I left the room and hurried back to the dining room, where I closed the door behind me and leaned heavily against it. Fifty thousand pounds, yet Tommy hadn't told me about it. What was he planning to do with it? As a thought occurred to me, I found myself relaxing and a smile spread across my face. I knew that he was renting the yard for now, but he had said quite openly that once he had earned enough he would buy it outright. No doubt he was hoping to surprise me. Feeling much calmer again, I finished wrapping the gifts.

Our guests began to arrive at ten o'clock the next morning and suddenly the house seemed to be bulging at the seams and laughter was bouncing off the walls. Kitty, Harold and the other children immediately disappeared off up to his bedroom once they had opened their presents, and now that Janet was happy that the dinner was cooking nicely, the adults all retired to the living room to enjoy a pre-dinner glass of sherry.

Janet had spent most of the morning speaking on the phone to her eight children, who seemed to be scattered here there and everywhere, but she was in fine good spirits and didn't seem to be missing them at all, which I was grateful for. I had worried that she would fret being away from them at Christmas, but she and Gran seemed quite content in each other's company. Gran had already shown Janet the delights of the local working men's club in Fellburn and Janet often went off to join her there of an evening.

The lights on the tree were twinkling, the smell of roast turkey and Christmas pudding was filling the house and I felt more content than I had in some long time. Tommy had bought me a beautiful diamond bracelet that sparkled in the lights from the tree, and Janet and Gran had sprayed so much perfume on themselves that the room was heavy with it.

We had all just settled down and turned the television on when someone rang the doorbell. I frowned. Who on earth would be visiting on Christmas morning? I wondered.

'I'll get it,' Janet said obligingly as she started to struggle from the chair, but Tommy pushed her back.

'No, you sit there. I'll go.'

I watched him leave the room, then out of curiosity I moved to the window that overlooked the drive to see him deep in conversation with the young man they called the Sand Dancer on the front doorstep.

Flashing a smile at Janet and Gran, I went into the hall and told Tommy, 'Do invite him in, dear. Where are your manners? It's Christmas morning and I'm sure your colleague would like to join us for a drink.'

I smiled at the young man as I spoke. He was wearing that ridiculous balaclava again, and as I looked into his eyes, which were the only part of his face visible, they seemed to bore right through me and for no reason that I could explain I shuddered.

'It's all right, dear. Just a bit of business to sort out, that's all.

Why don't you go and finish your drink?' Tommy's eyes were unsmiling, so without argument I turned and went back the way I had come.

He rejoined us in the lounge shortly afterwards but for some reason he seemed pensive and preoccupied, so after a while I gave up trying to make conversation with him and turned my attention back to Janet and Gran.

The Christmas dinner was a jolly affair, with much laughter and merriment. It began with home-made vegetable soup and prawn cocktails, which just happened to be one of Harold's favourites, followed by turkey with all the trimmings. Much to Harold's disgust, Kitty found the shining silver sixpence in the Christmas pudding, but when we started to pull crackers and allowed each of the children to have a little sip of wine he forgave her.

'Eeh, I reckon these bairns have got hollow legs, the amount they've tucked away,' Gran declared and we all grinned at each other. Gran was already on her fifth glass of wine and more than a little merry.

After dinner we retired to the living room to listen to the Queen's speech while the children played with their presents, and then we all settled down to watch *The Wizard of Oz*.

'Christmas wouldn't be Christmas without this film an' old Bing Crosby in *White Christmas*,' Janet sighed, and Gran chuckled and was soon snoring her head off.

By the time we waved them all off at the door later that night, I was in a mellow mood.

'It's been a grand day, ain't it?' Harold sighed happily.

'*Hasn't* it!' I corrected him.

He rolled his eyes at his gran. '*Hasn't* it,' he repeated, then, 'I wish the snow would go now so as I could have a ride on me new bike.'

I blinked at him. 'But you *love* the snow! I've had a job to keep you and Sandy out of it!'

'*Did* love the snow,' he said indignantly. 'Till I got me new bike.'

Tommy shook his head and disappeared off into his study, and Janet looked at me and shrugged before hurrying away to start on the pile of dirty pots in the kitchen.

George and Mary had invited us all to spend Boxing Day at their house, and it was with some trepidation that I stepped over their doorstep and allowed George to take my mink coat from me. My heart was hammering so loudly that I feared they would all hear it as I flashed them a faltering smile.

This was the house I had been brought up in by my mother. Except for the few short years when she had been married to George, we had lived here alone and it had not been a happy time. When she died she had left the house to me and I had then foolishly married Howard Stickle, who I had soon discovered had only married me for this very reason. It was in this house that Howard had tried to burn me to death, almost causing the deaths of George and his family too. It was *still* my house, although it had now been renovated, but was it any wonder that I still shuddered each and every time I stepped over the threshold. At one time this house had meant the whole world to me, and it came to me with a little shock that I now owned three properties. I wondered what my mother would have thought of that. Poor plain little Maisie, the owner of three properties! Thankfully, my gloomy thoughts were interrupted when Mary took my hand and dragged me into the small lounge.

'Come on,' she urged, pushing a glass of sherry into my hand. 'You're not allowed to have sad thoughts today. And guess what I've cooked for dinner?'

'*Turkey!*' the children shouted in unison and I felt myself begin to relax a little.

We had all just finished our lunch when Tommy went into the small hallway and came back with his overcoat over his arm. 'Do excuse me,' he addressed George. 'But I shall have to pop down to the yard to feed Zeus.'

Zeus was an enormous German Shepherd that Tommy had recently bought to act as a guard dog at the yard when it was shut.

'Actually, I think I'll come with you.' George made to rise from his seat. 'Happen I could do wi' walkin' a bit o' that turkey off. I've eaten so much over the last couple o' days I feel fit to burst.'

'No, no, I wouldn't do that if I were you,' Tommy told him quickly. 'Zeus isn't the most gentle of creatures, which is why I bought him as a guard dog. He'd have your leg off as soon as look at you, and I'd hate you to end up in the hospital on Boxing Day.'

George looked a little disgruntled but settled back into his chair as with a nod Tommy hurried from the room.

'He's a bit uptight, ain't he?' he commented.

Feeling the need to defend Tommy again I said airily, 'Oh, I think he's just tired, that's all. He so wants to make a go of this business that he's working long hours and I think it's catching up with him.'

I saw Gran and Janet exchange a glance as I quickly turned my attention to the television, and suddenly I just longed to be back in my own home again.

Tommy returned almost two hours later, closely followed by Harold and George's youngest two who had all been out on their sledges. Harold's cheeks were glowing and as I looked into his happy shining eyes I felt blessed. Gran was on her third bottle of Guinness and there was a party atmosphere in the air.

'Come on, hinny,' she said as she waved her glass at me, sending drops of Guinness flying in all directions. 'Have a proper drink an' let your hair down a bit. It would do her good, wouldn't it, our Georgie?'

Georgie winked at me before replying good-naturedly, 'Happen Maisie knows what she wants, Ma.'

By now, Janet was itching to get home so that she could phone her family again, so shortly afterwards we said our good-byes and went back to The Chimneys. It had been a wonderful Christmas all in all and one that I would remember with great affection.

In January a thaw set in and Harold replaced his sledge with his bicycle. He would spend hours pedalling up and down the drive with poor Sandy bounding behind him trying to keep up. He was doing amazingly well at school and was now in the choir, which I was thrilled about. He had also joined the youth club that Father Makin had told us about down in Fellburn and was settling into his new life far better than I had dared to hope he would.

Janet too had settled in well, although I sometimes got the impression that she was beginning to miss her family, particularly Hilda, who was now four months pregnant.

'I just spoke to James,' she informed me one evening when she came off the phone. 'He tells me that Hilda ain't so good. She's breathless all the while by all accounts. I've told him to make her get her arse off to the doctor's and get a check-up.'

A picture of James and Hilda sitting in the beautiful drawing room in the flat with the bright curtains suddenly flashed in front of my eyes and I had to swallow a strong taste of envy.

'It's probably just the extra weight she's having to carry about,' I replied.

Janet shook her head. 'No, she shouldn't have put that much on at four months. I had eight kids but I can't ever remember bein' breathless till near the end. I wonder what it could be?'

'Nothing to worry about I shouldn't think, so stop fretting. Hilda is a healthy young woman,' I assured her. 'Now, why don't you sit yourself down and I'll make us a nice strong cup of tea.'

'Thanks all the same, but I've agreed to meet your gran down in Fellburn. They're havin' a session o' bingo at the club at three o'clock an' I told her I'd go with her. Just to keep her company, o' course.'

'Of course,' I agreed, trying hard to keep a straight face, and then, 'Well, go on and get yourself ready. You don't want to keep her waiting, do you?'

She took the stairs two at a time as I made my way back to my study. I was now almost halfway through my latest book and had spoken to Mr Houseman at my publisher's only that very morning about it, promising to have it finished within the next two months.

For the last week I had seen even less of Tommy than I normally did, for he had been backwards and forwards to London twice already on the train. His scrap business seemed to be doing remarkably well from the little he told me about it, but I was forced to admit to myself that the same couldn't be said for our relationship. He had taken to coming in later and later and often now slept in the room across from Harold's, saying that he didn't wish to disturb me. I knew that the fact should have troubled me but found that strangely it didn't. You can't have everything, I told myself, and after all I did have more than most. Tommy had not been so possessive of me since our move to Fellburn; I had a beautiful home, no money worries and a son that I adored. So why, a little voice niggled, did I still not feel truly happy?

Chapter Ten

IT WAS A GLORIOUS MARCH morning and Janet and I were enjoying a quiet cup of tea in the kitchen after getting Tommy off to work and Harold off to school. Suddenly Janet exclaimed, 'Eeh!'

I found myself smiling, for she seemed to be picking up a lot of Gran Carter's sayings of late. Her head was buried in the daily newspaper but now she raised it to explain, 'The undercover SAS have shot three IRA terrorists in London. It says here they trailed them across the Spanish border because they were thought to be planning to bomb the Changing o' the Guard and shot the buggers dead afore they had the chance. The IRA in Belfast have since admitted that all three of 'em were on "active service duty". It don't bear thinkin' about, does it? I just pray to God that none o' my crew were anywhere near at the time.'

'Oh Janet, don't be silly,' I said softly. 'If anything had happened to any of them you would have heard by now. London is a huge place, I'm sure they're all fine.'

'Huh! Well, we should think ourselves lucky then. Think on it, the day this happened Mr Tommy was in London an' all. He's lucky he didn't get in the line o' fire neither.'

'I'm sure he wasn't even aware of what was going on or he

would have told us about it when he got home, wouldn't he?' I pointed out sensibly.

'There is that in it,' she admitted grudgingly. 'And at least they got the sods this time before they murdered anyone, which is more than could be said for back in November when they bombed the Armistice Parade in Enniskillen.' As I carried our cups to the sink she buried her head in the paper again and a silence settled on the room.

After lunch, I found I had well and truly hit writer's block. The more I stared at the sheet of paper in my typewriter the blanker my mind became. Glancing at the clock I saw that it was just after one o'clock so I decided to go for a walk to try and clear my head.

As I put my coat on I could hear Janet humming away in the kitchen as she prepared the vegetables for the evening meal. I passed the door and shouted, 'I'm going out for a breath of fresh air, Janet. I shouldn't be too long.'

'About time too,' came the reply. 'You don't get out near enough for a young woman. You know what they say: all work an' no play makes Jack a dull boy.'

Grinning, I slipped out of the front door and breathed in deeply. The sun was high in the sky though a cold wind was blowing as I set off down the drive. At the end of it I paused to look down on Fellburn. From up here I had a bird's-eye view of Tommy's scrap yard and I was just in time to see a huge lorry towing a great container in through the gates.

I decided to surprise him with a visit and set off with a spring in my step. By the time I arrived at the gates some while later I was breathless and my cheeks were glowing. I thought how pleased he would be to see me. I shall have to make more of an effort and do things like this more often, I told myself as I slipped through the enormous metal gates. Zeus was chained in a far corner of the yard in front of a large kennel, but the instant he saw me he leaped forward, straining on his chain and barking loudly enough to waken the dead. Almost immediately the Sand Dancer appeared from the building. I could not see his expression, for he was still wearing the ridiculous balaclava. A grey knitted one this time instead of the usual black. Being in a good mood, I found myself smiling as I wondered if he bothered to take it off to go to bed, before asking politely, 'Is Mr Balfour in?'

He had been about to disappear back into the building, but now he paused to stare at me and I felt goose bumps forming on my arms as I looked into his cold grey eyes. They seemed to be burning with malice.

'I said . . . is Mr Balfour here, *please*?' I could not keep the note of annoyance from my voice, and he thumbed towards the office before turning abruptly and walking away.

Bristling with indignation at his rudeness, I stormed towards the small office to the side of the yard, determined to tell Tommy what I thought of his ignorant young employee. However, the moment I set foot through the door, all thoughts of the Sand Dancer fled as I found myself confronted by the two Irishmen who had visited the flat in London.

Seeing my astonishment, Tommy almost sprang from his chair, and grabbing my elbow hauled me unceremoniously out into the yard again before hissing, 'Just what the hell are *you* doing here?' through clenched teeth.

'Since when does a wife have to make an appointment to visit her husband at work?' I shot back as I rubbed at my elbow and glared at him. 'And what are those men doing here, Tommy? I thought they were the ones who trashed our flat in London?'

He ran a hand distractedly through his hair and his manner changed as he implored, '*Please*, Maisie, don't go interfering in something you know nothing about. Go home and I'll explain everything this evening when I get in.'

I stared back at him. This was not the Tommy I knew. The man standing in front of me now looked as frightened as a rabbit trapped in car headlights.

My anger dispersed as quickly as it had come and my shoulders sagged as a cold hand closed around my heart. There was something not right here; I could feel it in every bone in my body.

'Very well,' I said resignedly. 'But I shall be waiting and I shall be expecting an explanation.' With what little dignity I could muster I turned on my heel and walked calmly out of the yard as Zeus went into yet another paroxysm of barking and strained at his chain to get to me.

Once outside, I paused to look up and down the road. A smart black limousine was parked some yards away and I wondered if this belonged to the Irishmen who were visiting my husband. If it did, they were certainly not short of a bob or two.

I walked into the town and visited the toyshop, where I treated Harold to a bell for his new bicycle that he had had his eye on. It was a very loud red affair and I knew he would be thrilled when he got home and saw it. I then briefly thought of cutting through the streets and paying Gran a quick visit, but I wasn't feeling in a happy mood any more, so instead I slowly began the long climb back up Brampton Hill towards home, wishing that I had never bothered to come out in the first place. I was halfway up it when I became aware of Hamilton galloping alongside me. I turned to him and said, 'Don't start; I'm really not in the mood right now.' I was certain that if anyone saw me speaking to myself, no doubt the word would be all round Fellburn before nightfall that Miriam Carter really did speak to imaginary creatures.

Things are not right!

'Do you really think I don't know that? I might be what's termed a little slow, Hamilton, but I'm not *entirely* thick!'

So what are you going to do about it?

'What *can* I do about it?'

At that point, an old gentleman who was cycling down the hill at breakneck speed towards me swerved wildly and almost fell off his bicycle.

I stuck my chin in the air and marched on.

You've got to confront him. Have it out.

When I looked round again, I saw that Dusty had now joined Hamilton and was trotting along at his side. To my surprise he spoke for the first time and I was so shocked that I came to an abrupt halt.

I really do think my friend is right, he said in the most perfect English I had ever heard. You *must* quell any funny business that husband of yours is up to!

He might have been schooled at Oxford University, his grammar was so correct, and the words sounded incongruous coming from the mouth of such a mangy-looking beast.

'I . . . I intend to do that this very evening,' I gabbled in reply and Dusty inclined his head. I moved on in silence for some time then, and when I got to the end of the drive leading to The Chimneys I turned to ask Hamilton, 'Where is Begonia today?' but found myself talking to fresh air. There was no sign of either of the companions who had escorted me up the hill. Sighing heavily, I set off down the drive.

That afternoon Janet was going to the community hall with Gran for what she termed a get-together and a knees-up. I waited until she had left, and when I was quite sure that she was a safe distance down the drive I did something I had never done before. I slipped into Tommy's study and started to root about. First I checked the drawers of his desk, but there seemed to be nothing untoward there; merely his chequebook and orders relating to his business. Next I peeped amongst the books on the shelves ranged along the wall. Again nothing. I felt like a thief in my own home and was just about to leave the room when I noticed that the lid of a large storage box situated beneath the window was slightly open. Tommy usually used it to store old newspapers, and every now and again when he had read them all he would carry them out to the dustbin.

Crossing to it, I lifted the lid. Just as I had thought, there was nothing in there but papers. I was about to close it again when I decided to lay them flat so that the lid would shut properly, and as I did so I felt something hard and unyielding beneath them.

Lifting the papers out of the box, I gasped as my eyes settled on what appeared to be a dismantled rifle. For a moment I was so shocked that I was rooted to the spot. What would Tommy be doing with a rifle? And to leave it here, too, where Harold might find it was unforgivable. Hamilton had been right, I decided. I needed to have strong words with him and at the earliest opportunity.

Carefully placing the papers back as I had found them, I crept out of the room with my heart in my mouth. There was something that felt seriously wrong here and it was time I found out what it was.

Harold was thrilled with the new bell for his bicycle.

'I ain't never see one this colour before,' he declared as he admired it. 'It'll look brilliant wi' the yellow mudguards on me bike.' And with that he flew out of the room, intent on fitting it on to his bicycle straight away.

It was just after Harold and I had eaten our tea together in the kitchen that the phone rang. We liked to eat in there when it was just the two of us, as it was much more informal than the dining room. Much warmer too, for I had soon discovered that being on a hill the wind seemed to find every small crevice. I hurried into the hallway to answer it and smiled when Hilda's voice floated down the line to me.

'Hello, Mrs Nardy. Is me mum there?'

'I'm afraid she isn't, Hilda. She went into Fellburn with Gran this afternoon to some do or other at the community hall and I'm not expecting her back till much later this evening. I could get her to ring you though if it's something important.'

She seemed to hesitate before replying, 'No, no . . . it's all right. It's nothing that won't wait.'

'Very well. And how are you, dear?'

'Oh, you know, so-so,' she replied, and I noticed that her voice was flat and sad-sounding. We chatted for another couple of minutes and then I placed the phone down. Hilda really hadn't sounded quite herself, but then, I told myself sternly, because all was not right here I was probably just looking for trouble. With a shrug of my shoulders I went back into the kitchen to help Harold with his homework.

At ten o'clock that night I went and had a leisurely bath, then wandered into my study to do some work while I waited for Janet and Tommy to come home.

Janet was the first to arrive with a broad smile on her face and overly red cheeks. 'Eeh, me and your gran have had a rare old day,' she told me from the doorway. 'I've laughed that much I gave meself a stitch.'

Her evident good mood was infectious and I found myself

smiling with her. 'That's good. I'll go and make you a cup of cocoa before you go up, shall I?'

'You'll do no such thing,' she told me sternly. 'You carry on wi' what you're doin' and I'll go and make us both one.'

I settled back into my seat and went on with my typing till she reappeared with two steaming mugs in her hands. She had just placed mine on the corner of the desk and plonked down in the chair next to it when I remembered Hilda's phone call.

'Oh, Hilda rang earlier,' I told her before I could forget.

'What did she want?'

'She didn't say, just that it was nothing important, but you're welcome to ring her back if you like.'

She glanced at the clock before replying. 'No, I hadn't better. It's gettin' on an' she'll no doubt be in bed. I don't want to disturb her so I'll leave it till the mornin' now.'

'As you like.' I sipped at my cocoa and for the next half an hour listened to Janet's account of what she and Gran had been up to. They were certainly getting on like a house on fire, which I suspected was one reason why Janet had settled here so well. Both being widowed and mothers, they had a lot in common.

Janet went off to bed at just after eleven and I found that I was no longer in the mood to work, so I let Sandy out into the garden while I started to turn off all the lights and lock up.

I then retired to bed, where I lay waiting for Tommy as I tried to concentrate on the book I was reading. I remember looking at the bedside clock just after midnight but then I must have drifted off to sleep, for the next thing I knew, Janet was drawing back the curtains while she balanced a cup of tea in the other hand.

'Goodness me, what time is it?' I asked as I pulled myself up on to the pillows.

'It's just gone nine, but there's no need to rush. I've got Harold off to school so you can have a lie-in if you like.'

'*After nine!*' A swift glance at the clock confirmed her words. 'Why ever didn't you wake me?'

''Cos you've been lookin' a bit peaky for the last few weeks,' she replied in a matter-of-fact voice, 'an' I thought the rest would do you good.'

'Rubbish,' I declared. 'I'm perfectly all right, Janet. Has Mr Tommy left for work too?'

I saw a faint blush appear in her cheeks as she smoothed a crease in the bedspread and avoided my eyes.

'That I couldn't tell you,' she muttered. 'He must have left before I got up.'

'Oh, I see.' I frowned. He certainly hadn't joined me in our bed, so I could only suppose that because he had come in late again he had slept in the room across the corridor. I waited until Janet had left the room then, climbing out of bed, I slipped my dressing gown on and hurried across the landing. One glance at the bed when I opened the door confirmed that it had not been slept in, and my stomach sank. Tommy had been coming home at all hours for some time now but he had never stayed out all night before. My mind began to work overtime. What if he'd had an accident and was lying in hospital somewhere? Still in my dressing gown, I ran down the stairs and quickly dialled the yard. To my relief he answered straight away.

'Tommy, where have you been? I've been worried sick,' I told him tensely.

'Sorry, love. I got caught up in a business deal and it was so late by the time it was over that I decided it wasn't worth coming home, so I slept in the office.'

'*In the office?*' I repeated incredulously. 'But where did you manage to sleep? There's barely room to swing a cat around in there.'

'Oh, you'd be surprised how comfortable this old chair is when you're tired,' he responded cheerfully. 'But now I really must get on, Maisie. Don't worry, I should be home early this evening.'

I bit back the sarcastic comment that had sprung to my lips. I had been about to say, 'That will make a change,' but I thought better of it, and then I thought of the gun in his study and my stomach was instantly in knots again. Whatever time he decided to roll home, I knew that I would be having strong words with him.

Gran turned up just in time for mid-morning coffee, huffing and puffing as if she had climbed a mountain. 'I ain't sure if Brampton Hill is gettin' steeper or whether it's just me gettin' older,' she complained as she sank down on a chair at the kitchen table. Then, looking at me, she asked, 'An' what's up wi' your face, hinny? It looks like a slapped arse.'

'Oh Gran!'

'Don't oh Gran me, lass. You can't pull the wool over my eyes. I know you too well, you're as soft as clouts as I've told you afore, an' I know summat ain't right, so why don't you tell me what it is?'

I opened my mouth to tell her nothing was wrong but then promptly clamped it shut again as tears trembled on my eye-lashes.

Gran watched me for a moment with a look of deep concern on her face, then, leaning towards me, she said, 'It's Tommy, ain't it? A blind man on a gallopin' hoss can see that things ain't quite right between you, pet.'

Her kindness was my undoing, and now all the weeks of

worrying rose to the surface and the tears I had tried so hard to blink back rolled down my cheeks unchecked.

'I don't know,' she said sadly after a time when I remained tight-lipped. 'I'd hoped wi' Tommy it would be a case of third time lucky, but it ain't turnin' out to be so, is it? What is it wi' you that attracts trouble, I wonder?'

'N . . . Nardy wasn't trouble,' I said between sobs, and now she took my hand and squeezed it gently as she said softly, 'No, I'll grant you that, hinny. There weren't a finer man walkin' than Nardy. He was one o' nature's true gentlemen. It's just a bloody shame as he were taken young. But then they reckon as the good go first. Still, there ain't no point weepin' over that now. What's amiss atween you an' Tommy?'

'I don't quite know,' I told her quietly.

She seemed to be thinking for a time before she eventually asked, 'He ain't into gambling, is he?'

When my head snapped up she held her hand out as if to ward off a blow. 'Now don't get goin' off on your high horse,' she warned. 'I wasn't goin' to tell you this, but the reason I ask is because Georgie was in Newcastle last night an' he happened to see Tommy there. He was goin' into the casino on the waterfront wi' another couple o' blokes an' that weird young chap that works for him who always wears a balaclava.'

I screwed my eyes up tight as my worst fears were confirmed. I had wondered if Tommy was still gambling and now I had every reason to believe that he was. So much for the move here and our fresh start, I thought wryly. The problem now confronting me was, what was I going to do about it?

Chapter Eleven

TOMMY KEPT HIS promise that evening and arrived home just as Janet was about to serve the dinner.

'That's good timing,' she told him cheerily. 'Go through to the dining room an' I'll have this dished up in less than a minute.'

I followed him through and watched as he lifted the whisky decanter and poured himself a glass. It was as I was watching him that it hit me like a blow to the stomach how much weight he had lost; funny, but I hadn't noticed it before, and he was very pale too.

I was longing to confront him with what Gran had told me earlier in the day but decided to wait until Janet and Harold had retired for the night. I owed him that much at least.

Thankfully, Harold chattered nonstop all through the meal, despite the fact that I asked him twice not to speak with his mouth full. I was glad of the fact deep down; it disguised the uncomfortable silence that seemed to have fallen between me and Tommy.

Eventually, when the meal was over, Janet began to clear the table and Harold scampered away to his room to play with his train set, yet another present he had received for Christmas. As Tommy and I were heading for the living room, the phone rang. It was Hilda again, so after calling Janet to take the call I followed him through, softly closing the door behind him.

I watched as he flopped on to the settee and ran a weary hand across his eyes before saying, 'I think it's time you and I had a good talk, don't you, Tommy?'

He looked instantly defensive as he shot back, 'Talk? What about?'

'About everything.' Sitting sedately on the edge of the settee, I folded my hands primly in my lap before continuing. 'Things aren't right between us, Tommy, nor have they been for some time. Is there anything that's worrying you that you'd like to tell me about?'

He looked away as he replied. 'No, of course there isn't. Why would there be?'

I pursed my lips but then said quietly, 'Tommy . . . why is there a gun in your study?'

Now his head whipped round and the colour flooded into his cheeks as he shouted, 'Have you been prying in my study?'

'Of course I haven't.' It was me avoiding his eyes now as guilt stabbed at me sharp as a knife. 'I found it quite by accident while I was tidying up in there.'

'I've told you *I'll* keep that room tidy,' he snapped, but then his voice dropped back to a normal level and his shoulders sagged. 'It's not what you think, Maisie, I assure you. There's nothing sinister in it. I happened to come across the gun amongst a load of old scrap that came into the yard and I thought it might be worth something, so I held on to it instead of letting it be melted down. I don't even know if it works, to be honest.'

'Oh!' I was forced to admit that his explanation sounded plausible, and feeling rather stupid for thinking the worst of him, I quickly moved on to another matter. 'And what about your gambling?'

'What do you mean . . . what about my gambling? We moved here to get away from that, didn't we?'

'Yes, we did, but I have reason to believe that you're still doing it. In fact I know that you went into the casino in Newcastle last night when you told me you were working.'

'I *was* working,' he insisted. 'It just so happens that the client I was seeing wanted to meet there. Was I supposed to tell him that I'm not allowed to step into a casino?'

'And what about those two Irishmen who were in your office when I called at the yard? They were the same two that I met back in London, the ones that you thought had trashed the flat.'

'Yes, they were,' he told me without hesitation. 'And as it happens they put a lot of work my way. In business you have to put aside any differences you had in the past and make your money where you can. I don't like having to work with them, I can assure you, but they give me access to some very valuable clients. They did what they did back in London because I owed them money, but I'm working hard to try and put that behind me now. Can't that be enough for you, Maisie?'

I suddenly felt very foolish for jumping to conclusions and so I now smiled at him tremulously as I told him apologetically, 'I'm so sorry for doubting you, dear. It's just that I'd begun to wonder if you regretted marrying me.'

'Oh Maisie, my dear, *never* think that, please. You are the best thing that ever happened to me. I know I've neglected you lately, but it was only because I'd made such a mess of things in London. I wanted to prove to you that I could make a go of the business and I realise that in the process I've left you alone too much. I'm *so* sorry.' He was kneeling on the floor in front of me now holding both my hands in his, and he looked so repentant that I felt ashamed for thinking badly of him.

'No, it's *me* that should be sorry,' I told him in a small voice. 'I should have trusted you and not been so quick to think the worst.'

'Then in that case let's start again,' he whispered as he drew me to my feet and led me unresisting to our room, where we loved as we had not loved in what seemed like a very long time.

I floated down to breakfast the next morning in a much happier frame of mind. Tommy had gone out of his way to be loving and attentive the night before, and for the first time in weeks I was feeling optimistic that we would be able to get our marriage back on to a good footing. My happy mood dispersed almost immediately when I found Janet sitting at the kitchen table sniffing into a handkerchief.

'Why, Janet, whatever is the matter?' I cried as I hurried across to place my arm about her shoulder.

She sniffed loudly. 'It's our Hilda,' she told me tearfully. 'James took her to the doctor's to get her checked out 'cos of her breathlessness and the doctor referred her to the hospital to have some tests done.' She gulped and dabbed at her eyes before going on. 'It seems that the tests showed she had a heart condition.'

'Oh!' Shock washed over me as I sank down on to the seat at the side of her. 'What sort of heart condition?'

'She said somethin' about a heart murmur an' the valves not workin' right,' Janet said brokenly. 'You wouldn't credit it, would you? I mean, she's twenty-eight an' it's never been picked up on. I could count on one hand how many times she's been to the doctor's in the whole of her life. She's always seemed so healthy.'

117

'Well it's probably the strain of the pregnancy that made it noticeable,' I said lamely.

'So why didn't they find out the last time she was in this condition?'

'Because she wasn't in that condition for long, was she, before she had the . . .' My voice trailed away.

Janet nodded miserably and then, looking decidedly uncomfortable, asked tentatively, 'Would you mind very much if I popped back to London to make sure she's all right? They're on about takin' her into hospital until after the baby's born so that they can keep an eye on her, an' I just feel as if I should be there.'

'Of *course* you must go,' I replied without hesitation. 'Now you just sit there while I make you a nice strong cup of tea and then we'll phone the station and see what time trains run from Newcastle. I'm sure George won't mind taking you to the station if he isn't at work. If he is, I'll order you a taxi to take you into Newcastle. And try not to worry too much. Now that they have detected a problem, I'm sure they'll keep a close eye on it.'

She nodded miserably as I hurried away to put the kettle on, and while I did so I was selfishly thinking, Why is it that every time I start to feel any happiness, something happens to spoil it? I instantly felt ashamed and tried doubly hard to put Janet's mind at rest.

While she was packing a case shortly afterwards I rang George and was relieved to find him at home. He was a lorry driver and was often out on a run, so I was thankful to catch him. 'I'll be there in fifteen minutes, lass,' he told me. 'You ring the train station and I'll make sure she gets there on time.'

'Thank you, George.'

'Think nothin' of it. That's what family is for,' he told me kindly before placing the phone down.

There was a lump swelling in my throat. That's what family is for, he had said, and yet he had no blood ties to me whatsoever. Once, what seemed a lifetime ago, he had married my mother and for the first time in my life I had known kindness. Even when he and my mother had split up, George and Gran had continued to keep an eye on me, and now I wondered what I would have done without them through all those years. But it wasn't the time to be thinking about such things right now. Janet was almost beside herself with worry and I must concentrate on her.

As promised, George was there within fifteen minutes, by which time Janet's case was packed and ready to go at the side of the door. I helped her on with her coat, and as she fastened her hat on to her head I asked tentatively, 'How long do you think you'll be staying for?'

She shrugged. 'I can't rightly say till I see how she is,' she answered truthfully, and then putting her arms about me she said, 'I'm sorry to rush off like this.'

'Don't you dare apologise,' I scolded her. 'Hilda is family. Of course you must go, but . . . there will always be a place here for you, Janet.'

She blinked and then, chewing on her lip, said, 'I ain't even had time to say goodbye to Harold. Will you explain what's happened for me?'

'Of course I will. Now get off with you else you'll miss your train.' I prodded her gently towards the front door, where George was standing with her case in his hand, and after a final hug she followed him down the steps and got into the car. Within seconds they were driving away and I waved until they turned the bend in the drive and were lost to sight. Then I turned back and stared up at the grand façade of The Chimneys. There was no denying it was a beautiful house, a grand house, in fact, and yet strangely it still didn't feel like home. Giving myself a mental shake, I squared my shoulders and walked back inside.

When Harold arrived home from school that afternoon he looked about and asked, 'Where's Gag?' She was usually waiting for him and it was if he had sensed she wasn't there.

'Aunt Hilda isn't too grand, so she's gone back to look after her for a while.'

'How long is a while? She is comin' back, ain't she?'

'We'll have to wait and see, won't we?' I said brightly as I noted his downcast face. 'Now come on, I've got you a snack ready in the kitchen to keep you going till dinner.'

He trailed into the kitchen with Sandy close on his heels and slumped dejectedly on a chair at the table. His relationship with his gran had always been a very volatile one and I was forever having to stop her from clouting him for some misdemeanour or another. But in that instant I realised just how strong the bond between them was and hoped that Janet would return for his sake as well as my own. It was true what they said, blood was thicker than water, not that I didn't regard Harold as my own. Since the day I had signed the adoption papers he had meant everything to me. He was the child I had once lost and every child I would never have. Thankfully, his glum mood dispersed within minutes and he asked, 'Can I go out on me bike for a bit? It ain't rainin'.'

'Yes, of course you can.' I smiled at him. 'But change out of your uniform first and don't be going too far, mind.'

His face bright again, he scampered from the room with Sandy following close behind. I began to clear the table. I too was already missing Janet's presence in the house, but I determined I would keep myself busy so that I wouldn't have too much time to think about it.

Once again that evening, Tommy was home in time for dinner and we all ate it together in the kitchen.

'How are things at the yard?' I asked him conversationally and he shrugged.

'Oh, you know, not bad. I've got a container full of copper due in tomorrow from abroad so I might be a bit late home.'

'Things are going well then?'

He nodded. 'As well as you would expect a new business to do. The chaps I have working for me are a good bunch. Not afraid of hard work, so I shouldn't grumble.'

There had been a question playing on my mind for some time, and now I asked, 'And what about the young man. The one they call the Sand Dancer? He's a bit of a strange character, isn't he? What's his real name?'

'To be honest, I couldn't tell you,' Tommy admitted as he ladled another helping of cabbage on to his plate. 'I pay him a backhander. You know, he doesn't go through the books. I think I heard one of the chaps call him Robbie or something like that once, and I believe he comes from South Shields, but he tends to keep himself very much to himself, which suits me right down to the ground as long as he does his work.'

I nodded slowly, supposing that he was right, but all the same there was something about that young man that I hadn't taken to. It was his eyes; whenever he looked at me they seemed to bore right through me. Still, I consoled myself, it wasn't as if *I* had to work with him, and as Tommy had pointed out, so long as he did his job and didn't cause any trouble I wasn't likely to see him that often.

I was about to start serving up the pudding when someone rang the doorbell. Excusing myself, I hurried into the hallway to answer it. I was delighted to find Dr Kane standing on the doorstep and hauled him through the door, exclaiming, 'Oh Mike, this is a lovely surprise. What brings you up here?'

He shook the black bag in his hand. 'I had a call to do on Brampton Hill straight after surgery and I thought seeing as I was passing I'd pop in. I'm not disturbing you, am I?'

'Disturbing me? Of course you're not,' I gushed with genuine pleasure. 'We were just having dinner, why don't you come and join us?'

'Well if you're sure there's enough, I'd love to.' As he spoke, I was helping him off with his coat. 'As it happens Jane is away staying at her sister's and I was facing a sandwich when I got home.'

'I'm sure we can do better than that. But you'll have to excuse us. I wasn't expecting company, so we're dining in the kitchen.'

'Sounds good to me,' he replied as he followed me down the hallway. He greeted Tommy and Harold while I fetched another plate and started to load food on to it, and the atmosphere was light as he told us funny stories about some of his patients.

'You need to watch it, though, young fellow-me-lad,' he said, wagging his fork at Harold. 'There's an outbreak of chickenpox down in Fellburn.'

'Yuck!' Harold screwed his face up in disgust. 'I could bloody well do without that!'

As I glared at him across the table, Harold bowed his head in shame but Dr Kane threw his head back and laughed aloud, then wiped his hairy chin on his napkin. 'You haven't managed to get him completely house-trained yet, then, Maisie?'

'Most of the time I have,' I told him primly. 'It's just when he gets excited about anything, he tends to revert back to his London lingo.'

'Well don't go changing him too much,' he said with a twinkle in his eye. 'The lad's got spirit an' you don't get too far in this world without it.'

He then turned his attention to Tommy and for the rest of the meal they talked of politics and the state of the country. When everyone had finished, I shooed the men off to the living room for a glass of brandy and Harold off for his bath while I cleared the table.

When I eventually rejoined them, Tommy rose from his seat and said, 'I hope you'll excuse me, Mike. I have a container coming tomorrow and I need to go and get the paperwork ready for it.'

'You get yourself away, man,' Dr Kane told him good-naturedly. 'I'm sure me and Maisie here will find somethin' to talk about.'

Once Tommy had done just that, I replenished the doctor's glass and poured myself a small sherry.

'Well!' he said when I joined him on the settee. 'This is nice, Maisie. It isn't often you and I get to have a good old chinwag. Tell me, how are you settling back in Fellburn? If you don't mind me saying, you're looking a bit peaky. Feeling all right, are you?'

'Which question would you like me to answer first?' I asked with a hint of sarcasm as I raised an eyebrow. 'I'm settling back in OK. It's very strange to be back after being used to living in London, but I suppose I'll get used to it. I know that Howard Stickle is dead and buried, but every time I go out I expect to see him. Secondly, I'm fine, so don't start fussing. It's been a long while since I queued to see you in the surgery every Monday morning. In my head I can still clearly hear that woman who used to say to me every week, "Bye, are you here again, lass?" Water Lily you called her, didn't you, if I remember correctly, because she had something wrong with her waterworks. It never occurred to her that she was there every week too.'

We both laughed, but then Mike's great hairy face became serious as he said, 'And how are things between you and Tommy?'

'That's a very personal question.' I could feel myself flushing but it was no good trying to pull the wool over Mike's eyes. He had always been able to read me like a book.

'We, er . . . we've been going through a rough time,' I muttered. 'But I hope we're coming through it now.'

'Mm . . .' Mike patted his chin, then said in his abrupt way, 'He's changed!'

'What do you mean, changed?' I was indignant now.

'Just what I said; no more, no less. He's changed, and from where I'm sitting, not for the good.'

I was so surprised that for a moment I could think of nothing to say. I had thought that Tommy and I had managed to hide our differences from the world, but if Dr Kane was anything to go by we hadn't done a very good job of it.

'Furthermore,' he went on in a low voice, 'there's whispers in Fellburn that he's got his fingers into all sorts of pies, and not all legal ones.'

'Mike, *really.*' I bounced out of my chair. 'I would have thought you were above listening to idle tittle-tattle.'

'Not when it involves you.' As his eyes bored into me, I felt colour flame into my cheeks.

'Tommy is working really hard to build his business up,' I muttered, feeling like a naughty schoolgirl who had been called in front of the headmaster. 'The trouble with that lot down there,' I thumbed towards the town, 'is that they're jealous.'

'There could be an element of truth in that,' he admitted. 'But all the same . . . be careful, Maisie.'

I was dumbfounded. What was I supposed to be careful of? Keen to get on to a different subject now, I poured myself another drink and settled back into my chair. 'I think Tommy is hoping to take *Spring Fever* out later this month. She hasn't been out over the winter so no doubt he'll be happier then. I know Harold is looking forward to it.'

'I thought he might sell her after what happened to that captain of his.'

Again I was on the defensive as I snapped, 'What happened to the Captain was nothing more than a tragic accident, Mike.'

Placing his glass on a nearby table he shrugged. 'I can see I'm rubbing you up the wrong way tonight, so this might be a good time to take my leave. I ought to be going anyway, else the damned cat will think I've left home. He'll no doubt have clawed a hole through the door by now.'

I fetched his coat and once he had put it on followed him to the door, where he paused to say, 'You know, Maisie, I've come to think a great deal of you over the years. If anything I've said has offended you, then I'm sorry, but you should know me by now. Jane is always telling me my mouth will get me hung.'

I placed my arms around this great bear of a man's neck and hugged him. Over the years, Mike had been my salvation and I could never be angry with him for long.

'Don't worry about me, I'm a big girl now,' I told him softly, and then the old Mike was back as he pushed me playfully away from him and laughed.

'A big girl, you say? Well, from where I'm standing all I see is a woman who's only knee high to a grasshopper. But I won't interfere again. Now go in out of the cold and I'll see you the next time I'm passing.'

I watched him drive away, and as I turned to walk back into the house Harold came hurtling towards me in his pyjamas, smelling of shampoo and talcum powder.

As I hugged him to me, I found I was smiling. While I had Harold I could face anything life cared to throw at me.

Chapter Twelve

JANET RANG ME the next day to say that Hilda had been admitted to hospital and that there was a likelihood she would have to stay there until after the baby was born in June.

'An' the thing is,' she told me warily, 'I don't really like to leave her while she's like this.'

'Then don't,' I replied promptly. 'If you came back you'd only worry. You stay there and keep your eye on her. How is James doing, by the way?'

I heard a loud sigh travel along the phone wire before she said, 'You'd never believe it if you was to see 'em together now. He seems to worship the ground she walks on. He's wanderin' round like a lost soul, so I've moved into the flat to keep me eye on him for her.'

I suddenly had a vision of the drawing room back in London where she was speaking from right now and a wave of home-sickness washed over me. It was funny, whenever I thought of home I still thought of the flat, probably because it was the only place where I had ever been truly happy.

'I'm glad they're both so contented,' I told her truthfully. 'You say hello to Hilda from me when you next go to see her. In actual fact I might have time to visit her myself next week. I have to come to London to see my publisher, so if I've time I'll pop in.'

'Then why don't you stay overnight at the flat?' she invited.

I hadn't considered doing this, but now that Janet had suggested it, I found that it did make sense. Gran had already offered to have Harold and Sandy for the night, so I had nothing to rush back for. Tommy was more than capable of looking after himself for one night.

'I might just take you up on that offer,' I said now. 'I'll get in touch a little nearer the time and let you know what day I'm coming, shall I?'

'You just do that.' Her voice was brighter now. 'Bye for now then.'

'Bye, Janet.'

As I put the phone down I tried to ignore the little worm of excitement that was wriggling its way around my stomach. It's because I'm going to London, I told myself, but then a voice from behind me said, Oh no it's not. It's because you're going to see James.

Whirling about I saw Hamilton leaning against the banisters with his lips stretched back from his teeth in a wide smile.

'Don't be so ridiculous!' I retaliated sharply. 'I hadn't even thought of James!'

Mmm . . . really?

'Yes, *really*.' Snatching my coat from the hall stand, I started to pull it on as I glared at him. 'Now if you'll excuse me, I'm going to put an ad in the local shop window for a temporary cleaner until Janet gets back. Or did you already know that too?'

I stamped out of the house but within seconds Hamilton was trotting along at my side, his long mane whipping in the wind. That was something I had soon discovered about living on Brampton Hill. Even on a clear day it tended to be breezy.

Hamilton accompanied me all the way down the hill till we reached the end of the road that would take me to the corner shop. The journey was made in silence yet I found his company comforting. For many years he had had the knack of appearing when I was troubled about something, and despite the fact that I had been annoyed with him I could never stay angry for long.

I'll be off now then, he informed me as I paused to look at him, and aware that two women were walking towards me I simply inclined my head.

'Hello, Miss Carter,' one of them said as she came abreast of me, and I smiled a greeting as I hurried past.

When I arrived home later that afternoon I prepared the meal ready for the evening then went straight through to my study. If I was to get the book finished and deliver the manuscript to Bernard Houseman at my publisher's next week as I had promised, then I was now working to a very tight deadline. Thankfully, it was one of those days when the words seemed to flow and by the time Harold arrived home from school I had made good progress.

'I've got choir practice tonight at the church,' he informed me as I poured him a glass of milk. One of the things I had soon discovered about Harold when he first came to live with me in London was that although his spoken grammar still left a lot to be desired, despite all my attempts to correct it, when he started to sing he had the voice of an angel. It was a fact I was very proud of, which was why I had been so thrilled when we moved back to Fellburn and he was instantly admitted into the school choir. They practised twice a week at the church and I usually walked him down there with Sandy. I would then visit Gran until it was time to pick him up and we would all walk home together again.

I knew that Tommy was going to be late home tonight, so I told Harold, 'We'll go a little early if you like and you can go on your bike. We'll drop it off at Gran's and then you can walk round to the church.'

His face lit up at the suggestion and I smiled. I was sure he would have taken that bicycle to bed with him if I had let him. He seemed to spend most of his leisure time either riding it or cleaning it.

When we arrived at Gran's house early that evening the heat of the living room took my breath away. Gran always kept a fire burning winter or summer and the room was stifling.

She smiled wryly as I stripped off my coat and cardigan. 'It's all right for young 'uns. You don't feel the cold like us old folks do.'

I grinned as my eyes travelled around the cramped little living room. Nothing had changed in it for as long as I could remember. The chair that was pushed up to the side of the fire was the same one that I had sat in as a child, and the sideboard was still full of photographs in frames of all shapes and sizes. If anything there were even more of them now, for Gran had finally taken to the four children that George had adopted when he married Mary and their photos had been added to the rest.

'Harold gone off to choir practice, has he?' she asked and I nodded as I made for the kitchen to put the kettle on.

'Will you still be all right to have Sandy and Harold one evening next week?' I shouted through the open kitchen doorway.

'Why wouldn't I be? I ain't quite in me dotage yet you know, lass.'

I knew that Gran was missing Janet just as much if not more than I was, for they had formed a strong friendship in the time that Janet had been staying with me and seemed to be always off on some jaunt or another together.

'Heard from Janet, have you?' she shouted, almost as if she had been able to read my mind.

I quickly told her about the latest phone call and she clucked with concern.

'A dicky ticker *an'* pregnant,' she muttered. 'Don't sound like a very good combination to me.'

'Well, all we can do is keep our fingers crossed that everything goes well at the birth,' I said matter-of-factly.

She nodded in agreement, setting her double chin wobbling, but we had no time to say any more on the matter, for at that moment George arrived with Kitty, his youngest.

I went back into the living room to join them as he placed a large box down on the chenille tablecloth. 'There you go, Ma. I reckon you'll find there's everythin' you asked for there.'

When I raised a questioning eyebrow at him he told me, 'It's her arthritis playin' her up. You know what a stubborn old sod she is at the best o' times. She could barely walk this mornin' so I offered to fetch her shoppin' for her.'

Gran flushed deeply before saying, 'There's no need to speak as if I ain't in the room, our Georgie. Me back might be playin' me up but me mind's still as sharp as a razor an' you'd best not forget it.'

'It's a bloody good match for that tongue o' yours then,' he quipped and I found myself smiling from one to the other of them. I sometimes thought these two should have been on the television as a double act. They were certainly entertaining enough when they got going.

'Anyway,' he said now, 'I'd best be off. I've promised to take Gordon, John an' Kitty to the pictures, ain't I, pet?'

Kitty nodded eagerly as she grinned up at him, then, leaning towards Gran, told her, 'Our Betty's got a boyfriend, ain't she, Da?'

At eighteen, Betty was the oldest of George's adopted brood and a lovely girl, so Kitty's statement did not shock me. I was only surprised that she hadn't had one before.

George, however, looked none too happy about the fact and Gran told him sternly, 'It's no use lookin' like that. They all have to grow up an' fly the nest sometime, lad. What's up; ain't you taken with him?'

George looked decidedly uncomfortable. Keeping his eyes averted from me, he told her, 'I don't mind her havin' a boyfriend, Ma. It's who it is that's the problem.'

'Oh aye, an' who would that be then?'

'It's, er . . . that strange lad that works at Tommy's yard.'

'You mean the one they call the Sand Dancer?' I gasped incredulously.

George nodded, 'That's him all right, though Betty says his name is Robbie. He rents that little flat over the shop in South Street.'

'Oh!' I found myself smiling as I said, 'And has she ever managed to catch sight of him without his balaclava on? I never have and all I've ever managed to get out of him is a grunt.'

'Same here,' George agreed. 'When he calls for her he waits at the bottom o' the street, though I've told her she's welcome to bring him in. He seems an unsociable little bugger to me an' I reckon our Betty could do a lot better for herself. She's a canny-lookin' little lass an' could have the pick of any lad she wanted from where I'm standin'. Not that my opinion counts, o' course. Mary's told me to keep me nose out of it. She reckons that if Betty knows I ain't taken wi' the lad it'll just make her all the more determined to see him an' she says she has to learn by her own mistakes.'

'I'll go along wi' that.' Gran's head wagged from side to side. 'You made enough, Lord knows, afore you met Mary, her mam bein' one of 'em.' She thumbed towards me and smiled apologetically now before going on. 'Now *there* were a woman who thought she were a cut above the rest if ever I saw one. The only good thing to come out o' that marriage were this one here.' She again inclined her head towards me as George shrugged.

'I dare say you're right, but I still have a bad feelin' about the lad.'

'That's as maybe. But keep your lip buttoned an' happen it will blow itself out afore you know it. It usually does at that age an' our Betty is a sensible girl so you should have nothin' to worry about.'

By now, Kitty was pulling gently on George's hand, the one he had lost two fingers from on the night of the fire, and as he looked down at her his face softened. I was trying hard not to look at the scars on the poor child's legs. These injuries too had been sustained on the night Howard Stickle had tried to burn me to death in my bed.

Despite the cloying heat of the room I shuddered involuntarily. Thoughts of my first husband could always have this effect on me, even though I knew he was dead and buried.

'Right, lass, we'll be off afore you pull me arm out of its socket.' George planted a kiss on his mother's cheek then did the same to mine, and swinging about said cheerily, 'Come on then. There's no peace for the wicked.'

Kitty waved as he steered her through the door, and turning her attention back to me, Gran asked drily, 'Are we goin' to have that cup o' tea or what? I'm as parched as a bone an' I've no doubt the kettle will have boiled dry be now!'

Smiling widely I walked back into the kitchen, thinking what a kind man George was and how lucky those children were to have him as their dad. I certainly had been, if only for a short time.

By the time Harold arrived back from his choir practice I was having difficulty in breathing and was glad of an excuse to say my goodbyes and get out into the night air again. Harold skipped off to the back yard to collect his bicycle and met me at the end of the entry, and we set off with him riding ahead and me and Sandy trailing behind trying to keep up with him. It was a beautiful evening; the sky overhead was sprinkled with stars and as I walked along watching Harold's sturdy little legs pumping the pedals I felt blessed.

Tommy and I were preparing for bed much later that evening when I started to tell him of the day's events. I first told him of Janet's phone call and her offer of me staying the night in London the following week; though for some reason I chose not to tell him that I would be staying at the flat. I then went on to tell him that Betty was seeing the Sand Dancer.

He paused in the act of buttoning his pyjamas to ask, 'Are you sure about that?'

'Well, George is. He doesn't seem too happy about the fact, between you and me. He reckons the lad is strange.'

Tommy shrugged. 'I have to agree with him there. But at the end of the day it's nothing to do with us, is it? The lad works hard, which is to his credit, and I suppose Betty is free to see whom she pleases. No doubt it will fizzle out anyway.'

'That's what Gran said.' I jumped into bed and pulled the covers up. Minutes later, Tommy joined me but almost instantly he switched off the bedside light and turned on his side and I was left to stare up at the ceiling as I thought of my trip to London the following week.

★

'You *will* come back, won't yer?' Harold was blinking rapidly as I bent to his level and kissed him. I had just dropped him and Sandy off at Gran's and now George was about to run me to the train station in Newcastle with my case.

'Do you *really* need to ask?' I was blinking too now and suddenly felt as if I was leaving home altogether instead of going away for one night.

'Now come on, laddie,' George said encouragingly as he ruffled Harold's hair affectionately. 'I was thinkin' when I got back from droppin' your ma off at the station, you, me, Gordon an' John might take a trip to the swimmin' baths. All lads together. What do you say, eh?'

Harold sniffed. 'I ain't brought me trunks.'

'Well that's easily remedied,' George boomed. 'I dare say our John will have a spare pair you can use. So are you up for it or what?'

There was a tremulous smile on Harold's face now as he nodded, and I sighed with relief as George lifted my case and hustled me towards the door. Harold ran to me and gave me a final hug, then Gran joined him and put her arm about his shoulders.

'An' I was thinkin' for us tea we might go to the chippie. You could have one o' them battered sausages you're so fond of, eh?'

His smile stretched from ear to ear now, which went a long way to relieving the guilt I was feeling.

'Come on,' Gran went on bossily. 'While we're waitin' for George to get back we'll take Sandy for a run, shall we?'

When Harold had scampered away she turned to me and pecked me on the cheek. 'Get off then. We'll be as right as ninepence. After bringin' my Georgie up I'm bloody sure I can handle one bairn for the night. An' give me love to Janet an' tell

135

her to hurry up an' get her arse back here. It ain't the same at bingo without her. Have a good time, lass, but be careful. I can't say as I'm happy about you goin', not wi' all them bloody IRA bombs goin' off all over the place. You just take care now, d'you hear me?'

I climbed into the car beside George, and as he pulled away I looked over my shoulder just in time to see Gran and Harold setting off down the road with Sandy on his lead between them.

'Don't get worryin' about Harold,' George told me. 'Him an' me ma will have a rare old time of it while you're away if I'm any judge. Between you an' me I think she misses havin' a nipper about the place, which is why my lot are so fond of spendin' time round there with her. She spoils 'em.' He took his eyes away from the road just long enough to glance at me appreciatively. 'An' if you don't mind me sayin', lass, you're lookin' grand today. Every inch the famous author.'

I self-consciously smoothed down the pencil skirt I was wearing and patted my hair. I was wearing one of the suits that Nardy had bought me when we lived in London. It had cost a ridiculous amount of money but he had insisted I should have it because he said it made me look sophisticated. This was not a label I would ever have attached to myself but I had to admit that whenever I wore the suit it made me feel good about myself. It was a very light pearl grey with a fitted jacket and slightly padded shoulders. Today I had chosen to wear a deep blue top beneath it, which with the help of a little eye shadow made my eyes look bluer than the nondescript grey they really were. I had also washed and blow-dried my hair and for once it was doing as it was told, so all in all I was feeling pretty good.

Once we were at the station George carried my overnight case to the train for me. When he had taken it on board and lifted it into the luggage rack, he hastily kissed me before saying,

'Right, I'd better get off sharpish then. Otherwise the train will be pulling out and you might find you're stuck wi' me all the way to London.'

I laughed as he hurried away, and then waved at him through the window until the guard blew his whistle and the train pulled out of the huge old station. Then I settled back in my seat for the long journey ahead with the weirdest feeling that I was going home.

Chapter Thirteen

I ARRIVED IN LONDON shortly after one o'clock and took a taxi to Chapman's Yard. As I stepped out on to the cobbles I found myself thinking of the very first time I had come here. I had submitted my first book to the publisher's that were housed here and had been shocked to receive a very nice letter from them saying that they would like me to come and meet them so that we could discuss the possibility of them publishing it. I had met my beloved Nardy for the very first time on that day, but it all seemed a very long time ago now. So much had happened since then and not all of it good, although I still considered that meeting Nardy had been the best thing that had ever happened to me. That, and adopting Harold of course.

I paid the driver and lifting my small case made for the brass sign with the publisher's name on it. Bernard Houseman, or 'God the Father', as Tommy had always referred to him, was waiting for me and he hugged me to his enlarging stomach as he exclaimed, 'Why, Maisie, you don't seem to grow any older. You must tell me your secret.'

Laughing, I returned his hug. 'Flattery will get you everywhere, Bernard. But now, here it is.' So saying, I took from my bag a heavy manuscript and placed it in his hands, and he smiled as he slid it on to his desk.

'Let's hope this is another bestseller, eh? But first things first. Have you eaten?'

'Not yet,' I admitted. 'I'm not too keen on those pre-packed sandwiches they serve up on the train.'

'Good, because it so happens I've booked us in for lunch at the Ritz. I felt like treating you.'

'*The Ritz!*' My eyes stretched. 'You're pushing the boat out a bit, aren't you?'

'Well, we have to look after our authors. And as it happens, I have a bit of good news for you.' There was a twinkle in his eyes as he lifted his jacket and slipped it on before taking my elbow and steering me back towards the door.

'Come on, we'll take a cab,' he told me. 'My stomach thinks my throat's cut. I haven't eaten a thing since breakfast.'

And so we went to the Ritz, and I felt like a queen as I sat beneath the sparkling crystal chandeliers and waiters in smart black coats waited on us as if we were royalty.

The second we sat down, Bernard ordered a bottle of champagne. I had three glasses during the meal and by the time it was finished I felt relaxed and happy.

'So *now* are you going to tell me what this good news is?' I asked. I had been trying to contain my curiosity throughout the meal, but the champagne had loosened my tongue and the question just popped out.

Bernard raised his hand to the waiter, who instantly refilled our glasses, then, leaning towards me, he smiled broadly. 'I've just sold your last two books to the States.'

I blinked rapidly as I tried to take in what he was telling me. My books selling in the States! It was unbelievable, yet I could see by the look on his face that he wasn't lying and all I could say was '*Oh!*'

'Yes, you might well say *Oh!* From now on, my dear, the sky is the limit for you, so many congratulations. Before you know it your name could be famous all over the world.'

I gulped on my champagne and promptly choked, and Bernard rose from his chair laughing and slapped me on the back.

'I . . . I can't quite take it in,' I mumbled as I wiped my mouth on a napkin.

'I've also sold you to three other countries,' he informed me. 'Which means your books will be translated into other languages. What do you think of that?'

What *did* I think of that? It was too much to take in and I must have appeared rather gormless as my head wagged from side to side and my mouth hung slackly open.

Bernard reached out and gently pressed my chin, saying, 'Shut it up, Maisie, else you'll be catching flies.' And when he laughed I now found myself laughing with him. Oh, it was turning out to be a good day, a grand day in fact, there was no doubt about it! How I wished that Nardy could have been there to share it with me. He would have been so proud. I instantly felt guilty for not thinking of Tommy but pushed the thought away. I wouldn't allow myself to think of sad things today.

I watched Bernard pay the bill without a qualm although I know it must have amounted to an awful lot of money. Then he took the elbow of my short arm and led me back through the dazzling foyer. Outside the hotel, a man dressed in a grand uniform hurried down the steps and promptly hailed a cab for us.

'Thank you, sir.' Bernard pressed a handsome tip into the man's hand before helping me into the cab, and before I could blink we were back in the midst of the traffic again, heading back to the office.

It was almost two hours later when Bernard handed me into

yet another cab in the cobbled yard that led to his office. During that time he had briefly glanced through the new manuscript and read the synopsis before assuring me that he felt we had another bestseller on our hands. So was it any wonder that as he waved me away I had the sensation of floating? I was on cloud nine, there was no doubt about it, and the cloud did not disperse till the cab pulled up in front of the flat. It was then that I came back down to earth with a bump as I fumbled in my purse, all fingers and thumbs. I watched the cab pull away from the kerb before turning to look at the façade of my old home. I had spent the happiest years of my life here and it would always hold a special place in my heart, which was why I had been reluctant to sell it. Even though I no longer lived there, it was nice to know that it was still mine in name.

I wondered if James would be home, but then pushing the thought away I hitched my bag higher and entered the building.

When I emerged from the lift on to the outer landing that led to the flat I felt as if I had never been away. I still had a key but now that someone else was living there I chose to ring the doorbell rather than use it.

Within seconds the door was flung open and there was Janet, her whole face beaming as she exclaimed, 'Oh, it's good to see you! Come on in and get your coat off.'

I went into the hallway, where Janet hung my coat up on the hat stand, and then walked into the lounge. I looked around. Everything was just as I had left it. The bright curtains and coverings on the suite still gave the room a sunny feel. The furniture was still in the same position. The only thing that was different was the contents of the display cabinets. I had taken Nardy's treasures with me to The Chimneys and Hilda had replaced them with some very tasteful pieces of Doulton and Royal Albert.

'Why, everywhere looks lovely,' I told Janet, and she smiled before hurrying away to put the kettle on. I meanwhile took my small overnight case to the guest room at the far end of the hallway and slowly unpacked it. I knew that it would feel strange not to sleep in what I still thought of as mine and Nardy's room, but I had to accept that I was merely a visitor here now.

When I went back into the lounge Janet was just placing a tray of tea and biscuits on a small table to the side of the settee. As she started to pour the tea into two china cups I asked, 'So how is Hilda then?'

She sighed before saying, 'Not so good, to be honest. Apparently this heart problem they found is a lot more serious than we first thought, so they're havin' to keep a very close eye on her.'

'Will she be staying in now until after the birth?'

'Yes she will; there's no doubt about that. In fact, they've already said they may have to induce the baby a bit early. I don't mind tellin' you I'm worried sick. An' James ain't much better, bless him.'

'Where is he now?' I asked.

Janet added some sugar lumps to the cups before replying. 'He's at work. On some undercover operation again, all very cloak an' dagger, but then it's his job at the end o' the day, ain't it? Mind you, he's still managin' to get home most nights so as he can go an' see Hilda.'

'I see.' I lifted my cup and sipped at my tea so that I wouldn't have to say anything as I wondered how I would feel when I saw him again. We spent the rest of the afternoon talking about home and Harold and the things that were happening back in Fellburn.

Janet cooked a lovely dinner that evening but I was still full from the meal I had eaten at the Ritz, so while she served up I decided to go and have a little lie-down. It had been a long day and I must have been more tired than I thought, because the next thing I knew Janet was tapping at the door. As I started awake I heard her say, 'We'll be leavin' for the hospital in ten minutes, if that suits you.'

I was shocked to realise I had fallen asleep but I answered quickly. 'That will be fine, Janet. I'll just tidy myself up a bit and then I'll be ready to go.'

Hastily running a comb through my hair, I applied some lipstick and slipped my high heels back on before rushing back out to join them. The first thing I saw when I opened the bedroom door was James straightening his tie in the hall mirror. As he caught sight of me over his shoulder he said, 'Hello, Maisie. How are you? It's nice to see you again.'

I felt colour rush into my cheeks, but my voice was steady as I replied, 'I'm very well, thank you. And you?'

'Oh, you know, I shouldn't grumble.'

He looked so far removed from the Mohican he had once masqueraded as that I barely recognised him. Instead of the outlandish gear and the heavy boots he used to wear he was dressed in a smart pinstriped suit and a white collar and tie. But it was his hair that was the biggest shock, for it had grown now and was cut neatly into a style that framed his handsome face.

'It's, er . . . very good of you to stop off so you could go and see Hilda,' he said, obviously feeling as ill at ease as I did.

'It's my pleasure. Though I wish I was going to see her under happier circumstances.' A silence stretched between us now and it was James who finally broke it when he said, 'So how are you enjoying life back in Fellburn? Janet tells us you have a beautiful house there.'

'Oh, it's a grand house all right.'

'And Tommy . . . is he well? Is his business taking off?'

'In answer to both questions, yes, thank you. He is well and I believe the business is doing splendidly.'

Again the silence settled, this time broken by Janet, who bustled into the hallway and announced, 'Come on then, you pair. Visiting time will be over if we mess about for much longer.'

We followed her out into the lift, and once outside I climbed into the back of James's car, leaving Janet to travel with him in the front.

When we arrived at the hospital my first glimpse of Hilda shocked me. I hadn't been sure quite what to expect, but it certainly wasn't the radiant-looking young woman who was smiling at us from the bed. Her eyes lit up at the sight of her husband and her skin seemed to have a glow about it. There was nothing about her to suggest that everything wasn't exactly as it should be, apart from the machine she was hooked up to that was monitoring her heartbeats and a very faint blue tinge about her lips. She was dressed in a pretty nightgown and her hair was shining. Her stomach was pronounced and rounded now, and as she greeted first James and then Janet and me her hand rested on it protectively.

'Oh, Mrs Nar . . . Balfour. I can't believe you've gone to all this trouble to come and see me,' she said as I bent to kiss her cheek.

'It was my pleasure,' I assured her. 'But tell me, dear. How are you?'

Shrugging her slight shoulders, Hilda grinned ruefully. 'Well I shall certainly be a lot better when they let me out of this place.' Then, turning her attention back to James, she told him, 'The doctors have been round to see me today and they've said that once the birth is out of the way they're going to operate on my heart valves. Now don't look so worried,' she scolded him as she saw his face fall. 'I've got too much to live for to go anywhere but home just yet.'

As Janet took a handkerchief from her bag and noisily blew her nose, Hilda sighed. 'Oh dear, I wouldn't have told you if I'd known you were both going to fly off into a panic. I've got two and a half months to go, that's all, and then I'll have the operation and be as right as rain, you'll see.'

'Of course you will.'

I wasn't sure if James was trying to reassure her or himself, but now I said brightly, 'Is there anything you need, dear? I noticed that the hospital shop is still open, so I could always pop down if there's anything you fancy.'

Laughing, she pointed towards the locker at the side of the bed, which seemed to be groaning beneath the heap of flowers, magazines, fruit and chocolates piled upon it.

'It's very good of you to ask, but as you can see, James seems to think they don't feed me in here. By the time I come home I shall be as big as the back end of a bus.'

We all laughed now, and for the rest of the visiting hour the atmosphere was light as I told them of some of the antics Harold had been getting up to. Ten minutes before we were due to leave, James and Janet rose from their seats and Janet said, 'We're going to give you two a few minutes alone now. Hilda sees us every day and must be sick of the sight of us by now. You two have a good old chinwag and we'll see you down in the hospital café when the bell goes. James here can treat me to a nice cup o' tea.'

They both kissed Hilda soundly and with a final wave trotted off down the ward.

'So,' I said brightly, 'how are you enjoying living in the flat, Hilda?'

'Oh, it's absolutely wonderful. I never knew that I could be so happy.' As she reached out to squeeze my hand I had to blink rapidly to hold back the tears that had sprung to my eyes. She went on, 'I feel as if I'm on holiday every day living there, but I was meaning to ask, would you mind very much if James decorated the guest room as a nursery? It would be very tastefully done, I promise. In fact, I was hoping that you might give him a few tips. You have such an eye for colour. And we *would* put it back as it was if ever you wanted us to leave.'

'I think there's very little likelihood of that,' I assured her. 'And no, I wouldn't mind at all. The problem is I'm catching the train home tomorrow morning. I've left Sandy and Harold with Gran. But perhaps I could pop back over the next few weeks and James and I could go and pick some paper if you give me an idea what you'd like.'

'I'd like it to be done in pink,' she said without hesitation. 'I just know somehow that this is going to be a little girl and I want her to be loved.'

'Well, I rather think that is a foregone conclusion with you and James as her parents.'

Becoming serious now, she took my hand again and her next words caused my other hand to fly to my mouth. 'Look out for her, Mrs Balfour,' she said softly. 'And James, *especially* James. He . . . he has a great fondness for you.'

When I shook my head in denial she smiled. 'I know that he loves me. He shows it every day and the time I have had with him has been the best of my life. I have known more love in the short time we have spent together than most people experience in their whole life, but . . .' She bowed her head, and when she eventually lifted it again I saw tears glistening on her lashes. 'I have this feeling . . . I can't explain it but it's there all the same. A feeling that I might not be around to see my baby grow up.

If that should happen, will you promise me that you will look out for them?'

'Hilda, *really.*' I was so choked that the words came out harshly. 'I don't think that you should be talking like this. Of course you will see your baby grow up. You're a young woman with your whole life ahead of you. You and James will grow old together. Anyone can see that you were made for each other.'

'Even so . . . *promise* me that you'll look out for them.'

'Well of course I would, but I won't have to.'

At that moment the bell heralding the end of visiting time rang and it was with a sense of relief that I rose from my chair to look down on her.

'Now you do as you're told,' I said gently. 'And I'll come back as soon as I can to get that paper for the nursery. In fact, I might even get a later train and go shopping for it tomorrow if you're sure that you're happy to leave the choice to me.'

'I'm more than happy. If you'll just choose the paint and paper, James will get someone in to do it and I will feel better knowing that the baby's room is all ready for it to come home to.'

'Then that's what I shall do,' I told her, forcing a brightness to my voice. Leaning towards her I kissed her on the forehead.

She clung on to my hand for a second and there was a funny look in her eye as she said softly, 'Goodbye, Mrs Balfour.'

'Not goodbye, dear. It's cheerio for now. I promise I shall do my best to come and see you again as soon as I can.'

She nodded as I set off down the ward. At the doors I turned to wave and saw that her eyes were still tight on me, and for no reason that I could explain I felt a cold shiver run up my spine. Hurrying through the doors I headed for the small hospital café, trying to ignore the sense of foreboding that had settled about me like a cloak.

★

Back at the flat I told James and Janet what Hilda had asked me to do as we all sat enjoying a glass of wine together.

'Gran won't mind if I'm a little late collecting Harold and Sandy,' I said. 'I could phone her and explain and then I could go shopping for the wallpaper in the morning.'

'I think that's an excellent idea,' Janet told me. 'It would be no good me tryin' to choose it. It would end up a right mish-mash o' colours an' our Hilda wants everythin' to be just right for this little 'un.'

'Well it just so happens that I don't have to go into work tomorrow,' James piped up. 'So I could take you into London if you liked.'

'There then, that's settled,' Janet said. 'That way at least the baby's dad will be involved in the choice. Our Hilda would like that. Don't ask me to put the paper on the walls, though. I remember I once spent the whole day paperin' the downstairs loo, an' when our Rod got in from work he pointed out it were all on upside down. Him an' our Max had to strip the whole bloody lot off an' start all over again.' At this she held her sides and roared with laughter, and it was so infectious that soon James and I were laughing too.

I was still smiling when I went to phone Tommy some time later, but all I got was the sound of the phone ringing in the empty house at the other end. The smile slipped from my face as I slowly made my way to the guest room. As I opened the door, there was Hamilton sitting on the bed with his front legs crossed, and Dusty, who looked even mangier than I remembered, standing beside him.

Up to his tricks again, is he?

Crossing to the dressing table, I sat down heavily on the stool as I answered. 'I'm sure he's just working late.'

148

He would *have* to be working *very* late if he still isn't in at this time! This came from Dusty, and once again I was shocked at his beautiful use of English. He sounded more like an Oxford professor than an old donkey who looked as if he had been rescued from the knacker's yard.

'But that's what you have to do when you're trying to build a business up,' I said testily, and when there was no reply I glanced back over my shoulder to find that I was alone again.

Sighing, I prepared for bed, and fell asleep with visions of pink nurseries and a beautiful baby girl floating in front of my eyes.

Chapter Fourteen

JANET WOKE ME the next morning with a cup of tea. I took it from her gratefully. It was one of the things I had missed since she had moved back to London.

'James has gone to get a mornin' paper,' she informed me. 'I thought I'd wait breakfast till you were both up and about.'

'Oh, just toast and cereal will do for me,' I told her, but she put her hands on her hips and glared at me.

'No disrespect meant, but it's no wonder you're no further through than a line prop. You need a good breakfast inside you to set you up for the day, so come on, shake a leg. The bacon is on an' I want you to get somethin' substantial inside you.'

Knowing that it would be useless to argue, I finished my tea, and after slipping into my dressing gown I joined her in the kitchen. James had just got back and he smiled at me cheerfully over the top of the newspaper.

'I was just reading about the new law they're hoping to pass in May,' he told me. 'They're planning to allow sixty-five thousand pubs in England and Wales to stay open from eleven in the morning till eleven at night.'

'Huh! I can see that causin' ructions,' Janet declared as she put two fat juicy sausages on his plate. 'As if the drunken buggers can't get enough down their necks in ordinary openin' hours.'

James and I exchanged wry smiles as I resignedly set about tackling the piled plate that Janet put in front of me.

We were in the middle of the shop with samples of nursery paper spread out in front of us when the old maternal instinct reared its ugly head again. It had not shown itself for some time now. In fact, I had been content since I had adopted Harold, but now here it was again; a raw pain eating away at my insides. I found myself wondering what the baby I had lost would have looked like. Would it have been a little boy or a girl? I had hated and feared the man who had impregnated me, for Howard was cruel, and yet I knew deep down that I would have loved the child had it been born. I had had to deal not only with the loss of my first baby, but also with the knowledge that there would never be another because of the rare blood that coursed through my veins.

But now was not the time for feeling sorry for myself. I had promised Hilda that I would choose the paper and so I now looked from one to another. They were all beautiful in their own way, but I felt I knew what Hilda would have wanted, could she have chosen it herself, so I pointed to one in particular.

'This is lovely,' I remarked to James, and he nodded in agreement. The paper had a white background, which made it look bright, and all across it were Beatrix Potter animals. 'You could do the paintwork and the curtains in pale pink,' I told him, 'to pick out the pink in the paper.'

'I must say I do like that one. It isn't as fussy as some of the others and I think Hilda would approve too.'

'Are we decided then?'

'Yes, I rather think we are.' Smiling widely, he went to find the assistant, and shortly afterwards we left the shop, each clutching a bag containing four rolls of paper. He had also bought a large tin of pale pink paint.

'Will you be getting a decorator in to do it?' I asked as he stepped to the kerb to hail a cab.

'That was the idea,' he admitted. 'But to tell you the truth I rather fancy having a go at it myself now. It is for my baby after all, isn't it?'

I smiled wryly, wondering if he realised just how lucky he was. I would have given anything in the world to be choosing the paper for my baby's nursery, but then, my childbearing days would soon be drawing to an end and I did have Harold, a fact I thanked God for every day of my life. As a cab pulled up beside us, James ushered me inside and asked, 'What time does your train leave?'

'Oh, I thought I'd get on the one o'clock one from King's Cross. I should be home for tea then. If I'm not, I shall have Harold on the phone checking up on me.'

'Still a character, is he?'

'Very much so.' I laughed now. 'Between you and me, I don't think anyone will ever tame Harold completely, and if I were to be honest I'm not sure that I'd really want that to happen.'

He smiled as he sat back in the seat. 'I think I know what you mean. He might have a mouth on him but he's also got a big heart. He loves you, Maisie . . . But then we all do.'

I turned my head and stared through the car window so that he wouldn't see the colour that had crept up my neck and into my cheeks. Thankfully within minutes the taxi drew to a halt outside the flat and I left James to pay the driver as I staggered towards the lift loaded down with wallpaper. I shouldn't have come back here, I thought. It was a mistake, but I'll be sure not to make the same one again.

Janet oohed and aahed at our choice of paper, and forcing a smile I left her to it and hurried to the guest room to pack my bag. Suddenly I just wanted to be gone from there. To be back with Harold and Tommy and everything that was familiar. I knew without a doubt now that this part of my life was over and I mustn't look back.

'I'll run you to the station,' James offered when I carried my small case back into the lounge shortly afterwards, but I shook my head.

'No, it's fine, really. I'll hop in a cab. But thanks for the offer.'

He did not argue and for that I was grateful. We said goodbye politely and then Janet came down in the lift with me to the ground floor. Her eyes were misty and I pushed her gently in the shoulder saying, 'Now we'll have none of that. You'll have me at it if you start.'

'I'll come out and wait with you,' she offered, but I turned her about and pushed her back in the direction of the lift.

'Oh no you will *not*. You get back up there and see to some lunch for James.'

'Oh dear . . .' Her hand flew to her mouth. 'What was I thinkin' of! What about *your* lunch? It's a long time till teatime an' you said yourself you don't like the sandwiches on the train.'

'Don't get worrying about that. I shall have time to grab some lunch at the station if I hurry. Goodbye, Janet. Take care and give Hilda my love.'

I stepped out into the street now and almost instantly a cab drew in to the kerb and I climbed inside. I was going home, but I had very mixed feelings about it.

★

I was halfway to Newcastle when the sun slipped behind a cloud. Within minutes it was raining cats and dogs and continued to do so for the rest of the journey. I stepped from the station in Newcastle to find the rain bouncing off the pavements and gratefully clambered into the first taxi I could find. I had intended to phone Tommy to ask him to pick me up, but with the weather as it was I didn't fancy standing about waiting for him. Once the taxi pulled up at Gran's house I paid the driver, then clutching my bag I made a rush for the front door, which thankfully was unlocked.

'Eeh, pet. You look like a drowned rat,' Gran declared. She had never been one for beating about the bush, which, strangely, was one of the many things I loved about her. You always knew exactly where you stood with Gran.

'Mum!' Harold shot across the room like a bullet from a gun, closely followed by Sandy, and suddenly I was being hugged and licked all at the same time.

'Hello, you two. Have you been good for Gran?' I asked as I held Harold at arm's length and smiled down into his face.

'Good as blood . . . good as gold, ain't I, Gran?'

I looked towards her for confirmation, and she nodded as she struggled from the chair.

'He has, I have to admit. In fact he's been a good help like. I ain't had to lift the coal bucket once since you left an' he's made me that many cups o' tea I've lost count of 'em. But how did it go, hinny? With your publisher, I mean. An' how is young Hilda?'

As she put the kettle on to boil I quickly told her the good news that Bernard Houseman had passed on to me, then went on to tell her about my visit to Hilda.

'Poor lass.' She looked sad as she thought of the girl's plight, then asked, 'An' what about Janet? Is she thinkin' o' comin' back here or is she goin' to stay on till after the birth?'

'I think she'll stay there to be near Hilda, and to be honest I think I'd do the same if she was my daughter. She really isn't well, although strangely enough, she looks the picture of health. Apparently this heart condition is a lot more severe than they realised to start with.'

'Then may the Blessed Mother watch over her,' Gran muttered, and without another word she pottered away again to make the tea.

'Have you heard from Tommy?' I asked when we were sitting in front of the fire some time later.

Gran shook her head. 'No I ain't, lass. Not so much as a peep. I thought he might pop in to see Harold on his way home last night, but happen he worked late an' thought better of it. I've no doubt he'll be waitin' for you, though, when you get home.'

I nodded, and as I glanced at Harold I saw him yawn and stretch his arms above his head. 'Come on, sleepy head,' I teased. 'Let's get you home and tucked into bed, eh?'

He instantly rose and began to stuff his things into a bag. 'Are we walkin'?' he asked.

Glancing towards the window I saw that it had stopped raining, so I told him, 'We may as well. Sandy will enjoy it and it won't take us long if we get a move on.'

We both kissed Gran, and in no time at all were on our way. The streets were quiet and soon we were climbing Brampton Hill. I was surprised to find how tired I was, and the bag I was carrying was getting heavier by the minute, but I kept my chatter cheerful as I held Harold's hand and we walked along together side by side. It was dark by the time we turned in to the long drive leading to The Chimneys, and as we came round the bend I was disappointed to see that the house was in darkness.

'Don't look like Mr Tommy's home yet,' Harold commented, and swallowing my annoyance I nodded. I had hoped that he would make an effort to be back from work to greet us tonight, but it was more than obvious that I was in for a disappointment, as the dark windows testified.

We were standing on the front steps and I was fumbling in the darkness for my keys, which had somehow disappeared into the depths of my bag, when Harold suddenly put his hand out and with a touch the door swung open into the dark hallway. At the same time he exclaimed, 'Mum, where's all this water coming from?'

Glancing down, I saw water running over the steps. With my heart in my mouth I told him, 'Stand there and don't come in until I tell you to.'

I walked, or perhaps I should say splashed, into the hall and clicked on the light before crying out in dismay. There was water pouring down the stairs and the Chinese rugs in the hallway were floating. Water was flooding through the ceilings too, but before I could see any more there was a loud flash from the ceiling light and I was plunged into darkness.

'What's happenin'?' Harold's voice floated to me from outside, and trying to stay calm I told him, 'Just stay there. It looks like we've had a flood.'

Groping my way along the walls, I hurried into the kitchen, where I found the taps turned on full with the plug jammed deep in the sink. I found the same in the downstairs closet, and after managing to climb the stairs the same again in the bathrooms. I turned them all off but it was obvious the damage had been done, although I would not be able to see the full extent of it until the next day.

As I slowly paddled back along the landing I tried not to slip on the sodden stair carpet. I leaned heavily on the banister rail and picked my way back downstairs. Some inner voice was telling me that this had been done deliberately. But who would do such a thing? If Howard Stickle had still been alive I would have sworn that it was him, but he was dead and buried. There was no time to think on it for now, though, for I realised that we were not going to be able to stay here, at least not tonight.

Stepping back outside, I tried to keep my voice light as I told Harold, 'I think we're going to have to go back to Gran's, dear; for tonight at least. We'll phone Tommy at work from there and tell him what's happened, then we can come back in the morning when it's light and see what needs doing. Don't look so worried. I'm sure it was an accident. Probably just a burst pipe or something.' I hated lying to him, but what was the alternative? If I told him that I thought someone had done it deliberately, it would unnerve him, and right at that moment I just wanted to get him as far away from there as possible.

His steps were slow now as I led him back down the drive, and guilt flooded through me. Poor little chap, he looked worn out. And my house; my beautiful house. Would it ever be the same again? And who could hate me enough to do such a thing? Fear was making the hairs on the back of my neck stand to attention. What if the person who had turned the taps on was still there, watching me from one of the windows? I suddenly realised that I had left both our bags back on the steps, but never for a second did I consider going back for them. We would have to manage for one night, that was all there was to it. Wild horses wouldn't have dragged me back to that house on my own. A picture of the two Irishmen flashed in front of my eyes, and slowly my fear turned to anger. They had trashed our flat back in London, so could it be them who had flooded The Chimneys? For now, I could have no way of knowing. All I did know was that I needed to get us all as far away from there as possible. Clutching Sandy's lead in one hand and Harold's cold little hand in the other, I hauled them along.

We were halfway down Brampton Hill and fear had lent speed to my tired feet when Harold declared, 'I'm tired. Can't you slow down a bit?'

'I'm sorry, dear. I didn't mean to wear you out. I'm just a little upset about finding the house flooded, I suppose. Come along, we've not got much further to go now and we'll have you tucked up in bed at Gran's before you know it.'

It was then that Hamilton joined us. He was rearing on to his back legs and his nostrils were flaring as he picked up on my distress. I was surprisingly pleased to see him, perhaps because I didn't feel quite so alone and vulnerable with him there.

There's something not right about all this!

I glanced down at Harold to make sure he wasn't looking up at me before nodding in agreement.

When Gran answered the front door on my first knock, her eyes almost popped out of her head with shock.

'Why, pet. Whatever brings you back here? Have you forgotten your key?'

'No, Gran. I haven't forgotten my key, but I was rather hoping you could put us all up for another night.'

My eyes must have warned her that I didn't want to say too much in front of Harold, and now she was ushering us all back over the doorstep as she said, 'O' course an' you're welcome, you know that. But this bairn looks worn out. Why don't you go an' hop into bed, Harold? I'll bring you a nice hot cup o' cocoa up presently.'

'But we left me bag wi' me pyjamas in back at the house,' he protested.

'Eeh, that's nothin' to go frettin' about,' she told him as she helped him off with his coat. 'I dare say it won't be the end o' the world if you kip in your vest an' your underpants for just one night. Now off with you an' take Sandy here with you.'

Harold obediently headed for the stairs door. The second it had closed behind him Gran turned to me and said, 'That Tommy has lifted his hand to you, ain't he? Why, the cowardly bugger, I'll get our Georgie to knock his bloody block—'

'Gran, this is *nothing* to do with Tommy,' I answered wearily. 'In fact I haven't even seen him. The house was in darkness when we got home, and when I went to open the door I realised it had been forced, and then . . .' I had to swallow deeply before I went on as a picture of my ruined home flashed in front of my eyes. 'I . . . I made Harold wait outside with Sandy and when I went in I discovered that someone had turned every tap in the house on and left them running. They'd put the plugs in too. The whole place is flooded, the lights have blown; it looked like the weight of the water had brought some of the ceilings down and . . . and . . .'

The tears that I had held back finally came now, and she was round the table in a flash and hugging me to her as she cried, 'Eeh, ain't I always said that trouble has a way o' following you about, hinny? What a thing to happen – but who would do such a thing? Does Tommy know owt about it?'

'I . . . I don't know. I haven't managed to speak to him yet. He must still be at work. Would you mind if I rang him?'

She pushed me towards the phone, saying, 'You call him, lass. An' then ring the police. Whoever has done this wants a shot up his arse. Meanwhile I'm goin' to make you a nice cup o' hot, sweet tea. You certainly look like you could use one.'

I rang the yard's number with shaking fingers but there was no reply, although I allowed the phone to ring for a long time. Sighing, I eventually placed the phone back in its cradle. Wherever Tommy was, he certainly wasn't at the yard.

'What should I do now?' I asked when Gran came back into the room some minutes later with a steaming mug in her hand.

'Ring the police, lass, an' let them deal with it.'

I slowly shook my head. 'I don't think there's much point in doing that tonight. The lights have blown, so they wouldn't be able to see anything if they went there. Plus, I'd rather talk to Tommy before I ring them. He's bound to come here looking for us when he gets home and finds out what's happened.'

Gran shrugged. 'Have it your own way, pet. But I have to say, if it were my house I'd have 'em out right now.'

We settled on to the imitation leather settee to wait for Tommy to arrive, but by eleven o'clock there was still no sign of him and Gran was yawning widely.

'I'm goin' to have to go up, lass,' she told me apologetic-ally. 'I'm that tired I could do wi' a couple o' matchsticks to keep me eyes open. I suggest you do the same. You look all in. If Tommy should turn up we'd hear him through the bedroom window.'

'Thanks, Gran, but I'll wait up just a while longer if you don't mind. You go on up and I'll see you in the morning . . . and thanks for doing this. Putting us up, I mean.'

'Huh! You've no need to thank me, pet. I've considered you family since the day our Georgie put that ring on your mam's finger. Though I have to be honest an' say I never considered her so. Thought she were a cut above the rest that woman did. But then I shouldn't speak ill o' the dead, should I?'

She paused to stroke my cheek as she passed, saying, 'Good night, hinny. I'll see you the morrow.'

'Good night, Gran.'

I listened to her climb the stairs, then the chain flush in the toilet and the creaking of her old brass bed as she climbed into it, and then there was only silence as I sat there waiting for Tommy.

Chapter Fifteen

'MUM, WAKE UP. Ain't you been to bed? It's mornin'.'
I started awake and gasped as I tried to sit up. I
had fallen asleep on the settee and there was a crick
in my neck from how I had half sat and half lain all night.

Glancing at the clock on the mantelpiece I was shocked to
see that it was after eight. I had no idea what time I had dozed
off but I was stiff and sore and worried now that Tommy hadn't
put in an appearance.

'What am I gonna do about school?' Harold asked. 'Me
uniform is in me bag we left on the steps back home.'

'Then you'll have to have a day off, won't you?'

His face brightened considerably at the prospect, and
heading for the kitchen he suggested, 'I'll make us a cup o' tea
then, shall I? I could take Gran's up to her in bed. She'd like that,
wouldn't she?'

I nodded as he disappeared into Gran's small kitchen. Where
could Tommy have got to? And just when I really needed him
too.

Another hour passed. By then we had all had breakfast,
although I had had to force mine down me, and now I was
longing to get back to the house so that I could see just how
much damage had been done.

'I'll not let you go back there on your own.' Gran was horrified when I suggested it. 'Give the yard another ring an' see if Tommy's turned in to work yet.'

And so I did as she suggested, but my call was answered by one of the men that worked there who informed me that they hadn't seen Tommy since lunchtime the previous day.

'Right, there's nothin' else for it then,' Gran said when I told her. 'I'll give our Georgie a ring an' he can run you up there. An' if the damage is as bad as you fear, it might be there'll be no other choice but to ring the police. If you don't, your insurance might not be too quick to pay out. You can leave Harold here wi' me till you get a gliff o' what's happenin'.' She pottered away to ring George as I stared towards the window with a worried frown on my face. Where the hell could Tommy have got to?

I had sent Harold off to give Sandy his early morning walk and was thankful that he didn't seem too worried about what was happening at least.

George arrived twenty minutes later, his face solemn. 'Come on then, pet,' he said kindly. 'Let's go an' have a look at the damage, eh? I couldn't believe it when Ma told me what had happened. Eeh, there's some wicked buggers about – there's no doubt about it.'

Gran followed us to the door, where she told us, 'Take as long as you like. Harold will be fine here wi' me. I might just take him into the market. He'll like that.'

The journey to The Chimneys was made in silence, and when George drew to a halt in front of the steps he got out of the car and waited for me to join him. The front door was still swinging open and suddenly I panicked. I didn't want to go inside and look at the damage, for I had a feeling that I wasn't going to like what I would see.

George seemed to sense my feelings, and he slid his arm

around my waist and said quietly, 'Come on, pet. There's no sense in puttin' it off. Let's go in an' see the worst, eh? An' keep your chin up. It might not be as bad as you're expectin'.'

I nodded numbly as I followed him up the steps. He pushed the door open and we stepped inside. The first thing we saw was the beautiful chandelier I had so admired on the day I had first come to view the house. It was lying in a million pieces on the hall floor, smashed beyond repair, and above it there was a gaping hole in the ceiling where it had hung. A lot of the water had drained away through the open door but we still found ourselves paddling in an inch of water as we gingerly stepped around the chandelier.

'Oh George.' My distress must have been evident as we stepped into the living room, for now George's face was set in grim lines as he hugged me protectively into his side. The carpet was squelching beneath our feet and all of the furniture was running with water that had come through the ceiling, which again was hanging in places, with great lumps of plaster spread across the floor.

'Oh George,' I said yet again. For it seemed that my vocabulary could not move beyond those two words at this point.

We next went into the dining room and then on into the kitchen, where the devastation was even worse than it had been in the other rooms. But then, I reasoned, it would be: one of the bathrooms was above the kitchen and so had taken the worst of the flood. I looked up at the joists and could see the bath leaning drunkenly in the room above me. Barely a square foot of ceiling was where it should be in this room; the rest was spread across the table and the floor.

'I'm going to call the police. Whoever is responsible for this should be hung, drawn and quartered!' I had not seen George so angry since the night Howard Stickle had tried to burn us to death in our beds. He turned away from me without a word and splashed along the hallway to the phone, which he soon discovered was not working.

'Wait here,' he told me grimly. 'I'm going to go next door and ask them if I can use their phone.'

I nodded numbly. Once I had heard him leave the house, I slowly climbed the stairs. I knew that it was a foolish thing to do. The floors, or what was left of them, were probably unsafe by now, but I had to see what the upstairs was like.

The only two rooms that appeared to be untouched by the floods were Harold's room and the one that Tommy had taken to using when he came in late. I supposed that this was because they were at the end of the landing. Most of the water had escaped down the stairs and into the two bedrooms next to the bathroom, one of which was mine.

I stood with my hand pressed across my mouth as I forced back tears. Thankfully, the house was well insured, but even so I had no idea how long it would be before it was habitable again, and where were we to live in the meantime? We certainly couldn't live here.

When George came back he joined me and led me back downstairs. 'The police are on their way, lass. They'll catch the buggers who did it, never you fear. If they don't I bloody will, an' the way I'm feelin' at the minute I'd tear the sods limb from limb.'

The police did arrive twenty minutes later and then the questions began. Endless questions that I tried to answer as best I could. Did I know of anyone who might have a grudge against me? Had I upset anyone lately? I shook my head to each one, willing it to be over, for I was beginning to feel almost as if it was my fault. But at last they were finished and told me, 'You'd best inform your insurance company, ma'am. They'll need to get someone out to assess the damage. Meantime we'll start our inquiries. If we have any news, where can we reach you?'

It was George who answered. 'She'll be stayin' at me ma's for now.' He gave them Gran's address, and the policeman wrote it down, then closed his notebook and told him, 'Thank you, sir.' When he had left, George and I just stood there surveying the ruins of my once beautiful home.

'Right, there's no point us trying to do anythin' till the insurance people have come out.' George began to lead me towards the stairs again, saying, 'Let's get some clothes for you an' Harold. Hopefully the things in the wardrobe should be all right.'

I packed two small cases with what Harold and I would need for the next few days, then asked, 'What about Tommy's clothes?'

'I reckon he's big enough to come an' pack his own, *when* he deems to put in an appearance.'

Lifting the cases without another word, George carried them back downstairs, and as I followed him, I found myself wondering how long it would be before we could come home again.

'O' course you can stay, hinny. An' for as long as you like,' Gran said without hesitation when George told her how bad it was back at the house. 'Eeh, I'd love to get me hands on the buggers responsible. I'd wring their bloody necks for 'em!'

I had the beginnings of a headache pricking behind my eyes now as she added, 'You go an' put your stuff away, pet, an' have yourself a little lie-down. Harold's gone to play wi' John round at George's for a time, so there's nothin' spoilin'. Go on an' do as you're told.'

I gratefully climbed the stairs, wondering what Tommy would think of all this when he finally showed up. I didn't have too long to wait, for he arrived shortly after lunchtime saying, 'What's been going on? I've just been up to the house and the insurance men are there. They told me you were staying here, so I came straight away.'

'Aye, well happen it's a shame you didn't come straight away home *yesterday*. Happen none o' this would have happened then,' Gran told him sternly. 'Just where the bloody hell have you been hidin' yourself anyway? Maisie sat up half the night waitin' for you, me lad.'

Tommy flushed to the roots of his hair, but keeping his voice even he told us, 'I was caught up with a customer and ended up having to go to London.'

'Mm, an' it were too much trouble to phone us to tell us, were it?'

Ignoring the sarcasm in her tone, he turned to me and said contritely, 'I'm so sorry, Maisie. Gran is quite right, I *should* have phoned, but I hadn't expected to be gone as long as I was. Now . . . tell me what's happened.'

'I rather think you know if you've been up to the house.' My head was throbbing now and like Gran, I was angry with him for just disappearing off. It didn't help matters when Hamilton suddenly bounded across the room and started to kick Tommy from behind. I closed my eyes and bowed my head, but when I looked back up he was still there.

'Well, according to the assessor, it could be months before we can move back in, so where are we going to stay meantime?'

'Here, o' course. Where else would you go?' Gran snapped. 'We're family, an' in times o' trouble families stick together. At least they do in this neck o' the woods. So I reckon the best thing you could do is go an' get some clothes together an' make

167

the most of it. I know this place ain't quite what you're used to, but it's better than kippin' on the streets.'

'Of course . . . and thank you.' Tommy looked none too pleased about the arrangement, but from where I was standing he didn't have much choice. He moved towards the door, and after flashing Gran a weak smile, I closed it firmly between us. Once in the privacy of her small front parlour I asked Tommy in a low voice, 'You don't think those two men you've been associating with could have had anything to do with this, do you? I mean . . . they *did* trash our flat in London, didn't they?'

He took my hands in his and looking down at me assured me, 'I'm sure it was absolutely nothing to do with them, dear. It was probably a gang of vandals from Bog's End who saw the house was empty and decided to cause some havoc. I have to get back to work now, but as soon as I've done I'll collect some clothes and join you here as Gran suggested. And try not to worry too much. I'm sure it won't be for too long.'

I watched him climb into his car and drive away, and all the while my mind was working overtime. If I was to stay here for any length of time I would need to collect my typewriter. Gran would probably allow me to work in the parlour where it was quiet. And there were things that Harold would want too; his beloved bicycle being top of the list.

George had promised to call back later in the afternoon, and I wondered if it would be too much of an imposition to ask him if he would mind running me back to The Chimneys again, but what he told me when he first arrived pushed all thoughts of the things I was going to need from my mind for a while.

It was almost three o'clock when he appeared through the kitchen door, and this time Mary was with him and neither of them looked to be in the best of moods.

'Whoever did that to your house must have done it after

eight o'clock last night,' he immediately informed me, and when I raised a quizzical eyebrow he hurried on, 'That lad our Betty is seein', the one they call the Sand Dancer, it seems he needed to pass an urgent phone message on to Tommy, so he an' our Betty walked up there some time after seven. All was well then from all accounts, so it must have happened between then an' when you an' Harold arrived home.'

'But I was home for eight thirty or near as damn it,' I replied. 'Surely that amount of water couldn't have built up and done all that damage in such a short time? Is Betty *quite* sure that everything was all right when they got there?'

'She reckons so, though to be honest she did say that this Robbie, as she calls him, got her to stay at the end o' the drive to save her the walk. She says when he got back to her some minutes later he just said as there was no one in an' then the two of 'em came away. But I reckon he'd have noticed if the door had been forced, don't you?'

Alarm bells were clanging in my mind but I couldn't quite put my finger on why. In the end I assumed it was because I hadn't taken to the young man. It was something about his eyes; they reminded me of a snake's and seemed to bore into you . . . And surely he would have known that Tommy was in London, so why would he go to the house to pass on a message?

My thoughts were distracted when I heard someone say, 'Feelin' any better about our Betty seein' him now, are you?'

This was from Gran and now it was Mary who answered. 'No, I can't say as I am, to be honest. I've asked her to bring him home to tea but he won't come. Betty says he's shy an' likes to keep himself to himself but I'm not so sure. He sounds a bit of a weird character. I mean, what do we know about him apart from the fact that he comes from South Shields? He could be anybody, an' our Betty is such a trustin' girl. I'm sorry if I sound like an overprotective mother, but our Betty is so besotted she won't hear a wrong word said about him.'

I could see that Mary was concerned and my heart went out to her. If I had been blessed with a daughter I too would have been worried about her seeing such a strange young man.

The subject now changed, however, when George asked, 'Is there anythin' else you need from the house, Maisie? If there is, I could run you up there now. We dropped Gordon off at the pictures wi' our Kitty an' John so he'll be happy enough for a couple of hours.'

'There is as a matter of fact,' I admitted. 'But I feel like I'm putting you to an awful lot of trouble, George. If you have anything planned, Tommy could always fetch them for me tonight.'

'Rubbish!' His big square face broke into a smile. 'Come on, there's no time like the present. Mary can keep Gran company while we nip back up there.'

In no time at all we were in the car again and heading back towards Brampton Hill. The assessors were still there when we arrived, and also a locksmith who was replacing the lock on the front door so that we could secure it until such a time as we were able to move back in.

Whilst George was loading my typewriter into his car and Harold's bicycle into the boot, I approached one of the men and asked, 'How long do you think the taps would have been running to cause all this damage?'

His lips set into a straight line as he stared about him thoughtfully, and then he said, 'Well obviously there's no sure way of knowing, ma'am. But I would think it would have had to be at least a couple of hours to bring the ceilings down as it did and such. Why do you ask?'

'Oh,' I shrugged, 'I suppose I was just curious, that's all.'

170

He nodded as he went about his business and I stared off into space. If the taps had been running for some time, then the Sand Dancer should have seen some sign of it when he'd visited the house before Harold and I arrived home. But then, I told myself, perhaps he had seen the dark windows from the drive and not bothered going all the way up to the front door. Yes, that was probably it, I tried to convince myself, but I would mention it to Tommy anyway. Then I set about helping George get the rest of our things into the car.

As promised, Tommy arrived at Gran's in time for dinner that evening. Harold had been delighted to have his bicycle back and since getting home from the pictures had spent most of his time riding up and down the street on it. I had a secret inkling that he was quite happy to be staying at Gran's. For one thing, there were more children here for him to play with than there were up on Brampton Hill, and secondly, Gran spoiled him shamelessly. This at least was something to be happy about. I had enough worries at present without having to add Harold to the list.

The meal passed uneventfully, and when it was over I sent Harold off for a bath while I washed the pots up for Gran. Luckily, she was off to the community centre that evening, which would give Tommy and me a little time alone once Harold was in bed.

'Be seein' you later, help yourself to whatever you want,' she told us as she set off with a spring in her step some time later. I had the feeling that Gran was quite enjoying having people in the house again.

We were now finally alone, and as we settled down in front of the fire, Tommy took my hand and said quietly, 'We don't seem to be having much luck lately, do we, Maisie?'

'It all depends on how you look at it,' I answered quietly. I was over the worst of the shock now. 'We still have each other, and at the end of the day, The Chimneys is only bricks and mortar. The damage can be repaired. As long as I have you and Harold I can face anything. There is one thing that's worrying me, though. George called round earlier and told me that Robbie, the young man you call the Sand Dancer, went up to the house last night with a message for you before Harold and I set off for home. It's funny that he didn't notice anything amiss, isn't it? And why would he go knowing you were in London?'

'Well, it would have been dark, and he probably intended to leave the message with you. But I'll have a word with him tomorrow if it will make you feel any better,' he promised.

I nodded as I stared into the fire and for now the subject was dropped, though the niggling little feeling inside me that something wasn't quite right persisted.

Chapter Sixteen

IT WAS THE FIRST week in May when I received a phone call at Gran's from Janet to tell us that the doctors at the hospital in London had decided to induce Hilda's baby the following day.

'But isn't it a little early?' I queried.

I could hear the concern in Janet's voice when she answered. 'Yes, almost a month by her dates, but they reckon they daren't leave her to go any longer. The baby is puttin' too much pressure on her heart so they've decided to get it over with.'

'I see.' There seemed so little I could say to ease her concern, but then an idea occurred to me and I asked, 'Would you like me to come, Janet? I could be with you by this evening if it would make you feel any better. We haven't moved back into our house yet after the flood and I'm sure Gran wouldn't mind looking after Harold for me.'

'I, er . . . I couldn't ask you to do that.'

'Why not? As I said, Harold and Tommy will be perfectly fine here with Gran for a few days, and you sound as if you could do with a bit of support.'

In truth, as much as I loved Gran, I was now missing my own home and my own space and the thought of a few days away was a welcome one.

'Well . . . if you're sure it wouldn't be puttin' you to any bother, it would be nice to have someone here to talk to. Them great louts o' mine don't understand how I'm feelin', see, good as they are. It ain't like havin' another woman to talk to, is it?'

'Of course it isn't. Now you just sit tight. I'll phone the train station and throw a few things in my bag, and hopefully I'll be there for teatime, so put the kettle on.'

'I'll do that,' she said, sounding considerably more cheerful now, and I put the phone down and hurried away to tell Gran what I proposed to do. As I had thought, she had no objections at all.

'You get yourself away, pet,' she said instantly. 'An' stay as long as they need you. Harold an' Tommy will be perfectly all right here wi' me.'

I first phoned the train station and then a taxi, and by the time it arrived I was waiting by the door with my bag packed. 'Tell Harold I'll ring him tonight,' I told Gran as the taxi driver placed my small case in his boot. 'I'll stop by the yard on my way to the station and tell Tommy myself, if he's there, that is.'

Gran kissed me and pushed me towards the taxi, saying, 'Go on then, you don't want to be missin' your train. But be sure to phone me once the baby's been born, won't you? An' give Janet my love an' tell her I'll be thinkin' of 'em all.'

I waved as the taxi pulled away from the kerb, but then the smile slid from my face as I stared out of the window. The hospital must have cause for concern if they're going to bring the baby early, I thought.

As luck would have it, Tommy was just striding across the yard towards his office when the cab pulled up outside the enormous gates.

'Would you wait for me, please?' I asked the driver, and then I went haring off after Tommy. 'Oh Tommy, I'm so glad I've caught you,' I babbled breathlessly, and went hastily on to explain what had happened.

'I see,' he said with a deep frown on his face. 'And just how long do you intend to be gone?'

I put my head to one side and I stared at him before answering. 'I don't know yet. That will all depend on how Hilda is after the birth. Why? Do you have a problem with me going?'

'Not with you *going* exactly, but I *do* have a problem,' he muttered, dropping his eyes and fiddling with a pen on his desk.

'And what would that be?'

'I, er . . . Well, I was going to ask you tonight as it happens. You see, I find myself a bit strapped for cash and I was wondering . . . Could you possibly lend me a bit, just till I get some of the money in that's owing from my customers?'

'Oh, is that all.' I felt relief flood through me as I fumbled in my handbag for my chequebook. 'How much do you need?'

I was waiting with my pen poised, and once again Tommy looked away as he mumbled, 'Twenty thousand pounds.'

'*Twenty thousand pounds!*' I stared at him incredulously, and suddenly I was remembering the cheque I had found in his office back at The Chimneys to the tune of fifty thousand pounds. What had he done with that? And if the business was doing as well as he kept telling me, why did he still need help?

'Look, I know it's a large amount, but I should be able to pay you back within the month. As I said, I have a lot of money owing, and once it comes in we'll be laughing again.'

Lowering my eyes, I slowly wrote the cheque out and silently handed it to him. He took it without a word as I turned and made towards the door.

It was there that I paused as he said, 'Have a good time, Maisie. And be sure to ring me, won't you?'

I nodded and went on my way without replying. What was there to say?

King's Cross station was teeming with people going home from work when I arrived in London that evening. I carried my small case outside and was soon settled in the back of a London cab heading towards the flat. Janet must have been waiting for me, for the second the lift doors opened on the landing she exploded out of the door and hugged me to her as if I was a returning hero back from the wars.

'Oh, it's good to see you.' Grabbing my arm, she propelled me into the flat and proceeded to almost drag my coat from my arms. 'Come on into the kitchen, I've got a pot o' coffee on. Or would you prefer tea?'

'Coffee will be fine, thanks,' I assured her as I settled on to a chair, then glancing around I asked, 'Is James not in?'

'No.' Her head wagged from side to side. 'He's at the hospital with Hilda. Been there for most of the day, he has.'

'And how is she?'

'Not good and I'd be a liar to say otherwise.' Janet sighed as she stared from the kitchen window to the fenced garden across the road. 'I've seen a big change in her this last couple of weeks. She seems to get breathless just sittin' up in bed, which is why they've decided to bring the baby early. I just pray that everythin' goes well. She's so longin' for this child. But hark at me rabbitin' on. How are things at your end?'

'Oh, not too bad. They reckon we might be able to move back into the house sometime next month. The work that's had to be done is unbelievable, though. Most of the downstairs ceilings had to be replaced for a start, and every room except for two of the bedrooms has had to be redecorated. I seem to have spent most of the last month rushing around choosing paint and wallpaper. Still, not much longer now and hopefully we'll be able to return to some sort of normality.'

Janet smiled as she said, 'I reckon that's something we're hoping for at both ends, eh?' And we then sat down together to catch up on all the gossip.

It was almost nine o'clock when James returned from the hospital, and the first thing I noticed was how tired he looked.

He nodded towards me as Janet asked, 'So how is she tonight, then?'

'Bright as a button,' he said with a shake of his shoulders. 'All I could get out of her was, "This time tomorrow it will be all over." It seems that she can hardly wait. The only thing she's upset about is the fact that they've warned her that the baby will probably have to go into intensive care for a few days for observation. It's routine when babies are brought early, apparently.'

'We can cope wi' that. Just so long as everything goes to plan,' Janet told him, and now a smile spread across his face as he said, 'Just think – this time tomorrow, God willing, I shall be a father.'

Janet chuckled. 'That you will, an' let's just hope you're still lookin' as pleased about it when you're up to your knees in bottles an' nappies an' the little soul is keepin' you up half the night.'

We all laughed now as James disappeared off into the drawing room and returned with a bottle of brandy. 'I think we should all wet the baby's head,' he told us as he went to get some glasses from the kitchen cupboard.

'Ain't you supposed to do that *after* the baby's born?'

'I'm not sure, but if I feel like doing it now there's no law against it, is there?'

'I suppose not,' Janet admitted as he passed her a generous tumblerful. She sipped at it, and shuddered before asking, 'So what time are they plannin' to start her off, then?'

'I've got to be at the hospital for nine in the morning. That's when they're going to inject her, though they've warned me that first babies have a habit of taking their time, so it could be hours before she gives birth.'

'Don't I know it,' Janet said ruefully. 'Over twenty-four hours I were wi' me first. I'd begun to think the little sod were never goin' to put in an appearance, and then when he did I wished he hadn't bothered. I don't mind tellin' you, he had a face like a slapped arse. Can't say as it's improved much wi' time either!'

She was laughing now; no doubt the brandy was helping there, and the rest of the evening passed pleasantly. I rang Harold at eight o'clock to say good night, and during our conversation he informed me that Tommy wasn't home yet. I wasn't really surprised. Tommy had made no secret of the fact that he longed to be back in our own house, and I had a sneaky suspicion that he was using the situation we found ourselves in as an excuse to work longer hours.

We were all up bright and early the next morning, although none of us could face breakfast. The air was charged with tension and James looked like a condemned man, as Janet tactlessly pointed out.

'I shall be fine when it's all over and I know they're both all right,' he told her, and in that moment I realised that he did truly love Hilda and the knowledge made a little worm of envy wriggle its way around my stomach.

'*Promise* to phone us throughout the day an' keep us updated,' Janet implored him as he walked into the lift.

'Of course I will,' he promised, and then the lift doors closed and all we could do was wait.

It was probably one of the longest days I had ever been forced to endure as we hovered by the phone waiting for news. As promised, James rang us at regular intervals, but by teatime it seemed that Hilda was no nearer to giving birth than she had been in the morning.

'They've decided to do a Caesarean,' he told us finally, and Janet's face paled to the colour of lint.

'But *why*?' she snapped uncharacteristically down the phone.

'Because Hilda is exhausted and the baby appears to be distressed. They're getting her ready for theatre right now.'

'That's it then,' Janet said with quiet determination. 'I'll be damned if I'm goin' to sit here chewin' me nails for a second longer. I'll be there in a jiffy, I don't care if I have to sit in the waitin' room all night.' And with that she slammed the phone down and hurried away to get her bag and her coat.

'I'll come with you, shall I?'

'Yes please, love. I'd be grateful o' the company to tell you the truth.'

We arrived at the hospital shortly afterwards to find James pacing up and down the waiting room like a caged animal.

'They've taken her into theatre,' he informed us. 'All we can do now is wait. According to the doctor it shouldn't take long.'

Janet sat down heavily on the nearest chair, nursing her bag to her, until the door suddenly swung open and a doctor still wearing his gown and mask appeared.

'Congratulations, Mr Bainbridge,' he told James as he lowered his mask. 'You have a beautiful baby girl. We've taken her into the intensive care unit so that we can keep our eye on her for a couple of days, but she appears to be healthy. She was a good weight too, almost seven pounds, which is excellent for a premature baby.' He shook James' hand soundly as the proud

179

new father's mouth fell into a gape and he declared, 'Well, fancy that, I have a baby!'

'Well what were you expectin'?' Janet quipped as she dabbed at her eyes with a handkerchief. Turning to the doctor, she asked, 'An' Hilda, is she all right?'

The doctor's face became solemn as he said, 'I have to be honest and say that the birth has taken it out of her, but never fear; we are keeping a very close eye on her. She'll probably be asleep for some hours, so it might be best if you all went home, after you've had a peep at the baby of course.'

James was obviously in shock and it was Janet who now said, 'Oh yes, we'd love a peep at the baby, please.'

'Very well, if you'll just wait here for a while, I'll get someone to come and take you down to intensive care when the little one has been all cleaned up. And congratulations again, she really is a lovely baby.'

James was pumping the doctor's hand up and down now, and there was a broad smile on his face as he told him, 'Thank you, Doctor. Thank you.'

The doctor smiled back as he took his leave, and now James seemed to be glowing as he said, 'Would you believe it, eh? I'm a dad.'

Shortly afterwards a young nurse popped her head round the door to ask, 'Are you waiting to see the Bainbridge baby?'

We all nodded in unison as James almost leapt towards the door, and then we were following her through a labyrinth of corridors that smelled faintly of stale disinfectant and some other odour that I couldn't quite put a name to.

At last she paused in front of some double doors. 'This is the ITU unit. Don't be alarmed to see the baby in an incubator. All the babies in here are in them. Are you ready?'

Without waiting for a reply, she swung the doors open and

we found ourselves in a small ward with incubators stretching along either side of it. There were brightly painted Disney characters splattered in gay profusion across the walls, and even the curtains that hung at the windows were bright and cheerful, nothing at all like the dull ones in the adult wards.

She paused at the end of one incubator and told us with a smile, 'This is your baby. She's quite a looker, isn't she?'

James gazed down on his tiny daughter and his expression would be engraved in my memory for ever, for his whole face lit up in sheer wonder.

Janet was crying and dabbing ineffectively at her face as she too gazed at this tiny girl. She really was the most exquisite little creature I had ever seen, and I too felt tears blinding me as I looked down on the sheer perfection of her. She had a covering of soft blonde hair and her eyelashes were curled on her cheeks.

'Why, she's . . .' James seemed to be lost for words as he sought for a way to describe her, but finally he said softly, 'She's perfect!'

'I'll second that,' Janet said thickly, and turning to the young nurse she asked, 'How long will it be before we're allowed to hold her?'

'Oh, all being well, tomorrow. We just want her to rest for a while because a Caesarean birth is a shock to a baby. If she's still doing well by morning we'll be taking her up to the maternity ward to meet her mum.' Pointing to a little hole in the side of the incubator she told James, 'If you'd like to sit on that chair you can put your hand through there and touch her if you like.'

James needed no second telling, and as he slid his hand into the opening and stroked his daughter's tiny hand her little fingers curled around one of his and I saw that he was on the verge of tears. There was inside me a great mixture of emotions, for while I was thrilled for James and Hilda I was also thinking of the child I had lost. Would my baby have been as perfect as this one? I wondered. I had no time to ponder, for now Janet took my arm and thumbed towards the door as she whispered, 'Come on. Let's leave the new dad to have a few minutes alone wi' his daughter, eh? Happen we'll have time to spoil her tomorrow.' I nodded, and with a final glance at the picture of father and child clear in my mind I followed her out into the corridor.

Before we left the hospital, James was allowed to slip into Hilda's room for a few minutes. When he came out he shook his head and told us, 'She's out for the count. I don't think she'll know much till morning now, but they've told me I can come back early so I can see her meet the baby for the first time.'

Janet's smile seemed to stretch from ear to ear as she nodded her approval. Then leaning towards us she told us, 'Come on, there's nothin' more to be done here for tonight. It just so happens I have a bottle o' champagne chillin' in the fridge an' I've some phone calls I'd like to make.'

We must have looked a merry crowd as we left the hospital, for now we couldn't stop smiling nor did we until we all finally dropped into bed in the early hours of the morning.

James had already left for the hospital when Janet and I finally surfaced. The champagne I had drunk the night before had given me a dull headache and I noticed Janet was looking rather the worse for wear too.

'Oh Lord, me mouth feels like the bottom of a birdcage,' she complained as she gulped at a glassful of water. I chuckled and then headed for the door as I heard the sound of the lift doors swish open in the entrance hall.

It was a young man holding the most enormous bunch of flowers I had ever seen, and as I glanced at the card that was attached to them I saw that they were addressed to Janet. I smiled my thanks before carrying them through to her, and after reading the card she smiled too and blinked back tears as she told me, 'They're from your gran, God bless her soul.'

Despite the fact that we were both suffering from self-inflicted hangovers, we spent the whole morning in the centre of London shopping for baby clothes. By the time we arrived at the hospital in the middle of the afternoon we were loaded down with shopping bags and my arms felt as if they might drop off.

We paused to peep through the glass in the door of Hilda's small private room, and the sight we saw brought a huge choking lump to my throat. Hilda was propped up on pillows with the baby cuddled close to her breast and James was looking on adoringly. Hilda appeared tired and weak and the blue tinge about her lips seemed more pronounced than I remembered it, but she also looked utterly contented.

'Ah, they make a lovely family, don't they?' Janet said proudly, and I could only nod in agreement.

Once inside, we were both allowed a little cuddle with the baby while James and Hilda looked fondly on. I could quite happily have held her all day, but shortly afterwards a stern-faced sister came to tell us, 'I think you ought to leave now. Mrs Bainbridge is still very weak and we don't want to overtire her, now do we?'

Janet looked none too pleased, but all the same she passed the baby back to her mother and asked, 'So, have you decided on a name for her yet?'

'We were thinking of calling her Jessica Rose after me grandma,' Hilda told her. Janet beamed with approval and after planting a kiss on both of their faces headed towards the door. I was about to follow her when Hilda suddenly caught my hand

and said, 'You won't forget the promise you made to me the last time you came, will you?'

I snatched my hand away as a cold finger traced its way up my spine. 'I don't think there's any need for you to worry about that, dear,' I said softly. 'The worst is over now; all you have to do is concentrate on getting better.'

She lay back against the pillows, and leaning towards her I too kissed her before following Janet from the room.

James could speak of nothing else but his amazing wife and his beautiful daughter when he finally got home from the hospital that evening, and the meal Janet had prepared for him eventually grew cold as he chattered on. She smiled at him indulgently, and suddenly feeling in the way I went into the hall to phone Harold and Gran.

It was Harold who answered the phone, and when I heard his voice I missed him so much that I felt like jumping on a train and going home there and then.

'When will you be back?' he asked once I had told him all about the new baby.

'Oh, I should think within a couple of days,' I told him. 'Once we know Hilda is really on the mend I don't think Janet will need me any more. I was only ever here to give her moral support.'

'Good, 'cos I need your mortal support too,' Harold told me indignantly. I stifled a giggle, told him to be good and then went for a welcome bath, where I relaxed as the events of the last few days finally caught up with me. It had been a worrying time, but then, I told myself, all's well that ends well, and I settled back into the hot soapy bubbles with a sigh of contentment.

After my bath I went into the drawing room to say good night, only to find that yet another bottle of champagne had appeared out of the fridge as if by magic.

'Aw, come an' join us,' Janet pleaded. 'We have to drink a toast to Jessica Rose.'

'I thought we did that last night,' I remarked drily.

Janet shook her head. 'Naw, that didn't count 'cos she didn't have a name then.'

'In that case, I'd be delighted to join you.' I grinned as James filled a crystal champagne flute and we duly raised our glasses.

'To Jessica Rose and my beautiful wife,' James said solemnly. We had just taken a sip from our drinks when the phone started to ring in the hall and, cursing softly, James went to answer it.

When he came back into the room we saw at a glance that he was as pale as a ghost.

'What's wrong?' Janet placed her glass down on the small table to the side of her and made to rise from her seat, but James' next words made her fall heavily back into it.

'It was the hospital. Hilda has taken bad. I have to get back there straight away.'

'Oh, dear God. What's wrong with her?'

'They wouldn't say. Just that I needed to get there as soon as I could.' He was pulling his shoes on and struggling with the laces, for his hands, I noticed, were shaking.

I ran into the hall and snatched up his coat, and held it as he slid his long arms into it. Then he was running towards the lift and Janet shouted, 'Keep us informed, won't you?'

Her only answer was the sound of the lift doors as they closed behind him. We looked at each other, then silently sat down to wait for news.

It was just gone four o'clock in the morning when James reappeared. I had been struggling to stay awake but now my eyes stretched wide open.

Janet's fingers were plucking at the hem of her skirt and it was she who finally asked, 'Well . . . don't just stand there like a moron. What's happened?'

James was staring ahead and his eyes had a slightly glazed look as he replied. 'She had a heart attack. The strain of the birth was too much for her.'

'Oh, dear God, *no!*' Janet's hand had flown to her mouth and her eyes appeared to be on stalks as she asked him fearfully, 'She will be all right, won't she?'

He looked her full in the face and in a remarkably calm voice told her, 'I'm sorry, Janet, but Hilda died just over an hour ago.'

Then he turned on his heel and walked away to the room he had shared with his wife for such a short time and closed the door softly behind him. Janet meantime fell in a dead faint on the thick rose-coloured carpet at my feet.

Chapter Seventeen

'ASHES TO ASHES, dust to dust . . .' The vicar's voice droned on as the silent mourners stood at the side of Hilda's grave. Once more I was back in the churchyard behind the small chapel where my beloved Nardy had been cremated, and I felt as if I was caught in the grip of a nightmare. Hilda had been just a young woman with her whole life stretching away in front of her, but now here she was being laid to rest. It just didn't bear thinking about.

Gran had travelled from Fellburn to attend the funeral, and it was she who was supporting Janet as the bereft mother stared down on her daughter's coffin. Harold had gone to stay with Mary and George, and as I thought of him now I suddenly felt the need to feel his small body held tight in my arms. The last week had passed in a blur of tears and sorrow, and Janet seemed to have aged. Gone was the bright smile and ready wit that had made her the person she was, and in her place stood a woman who suddenly looked old and tired. My eyes moved on and came to rest on James, who was standing with his head bowed and his hands joined. He was grim-faced and unapproachable, as he had been since the night of Hilda's death. I had hoped Tommy would come to help me through this terrible day, but he had phoned the flat the night before to tell me that he was unable to leave the yard as they were expecting a container from abroad. Now I felt unbelievably lonely even though I was surrounded by people, and it was a scary feeling; the sort of feeling I had felt as a child when I had only my mother to rely on. A feeling that I had prayed I would never experience again.

I became aware that people were moving away from the grave, and now Gran was beside me taking the elbow of my withered arm as she said, 'Come on, hinny. It's done. Let's get back to the flat, eh?'

I followed her numbly and soon we were back in the bright drawing room, and the caterers that James had fetched in for the occasion were handing round cups of tea. There was a light buffet laid out in the dining room but no one seemed to be very hungry, which I supposed, was hardly surprising. Gran and I joined Janet and James, who were standing by the window, and it was Gran who broke the heavy silence when she asked, 'How's the bairn doin'?'

Just for an instant, Janet's face brightened. 'Oh, she at least is comin' along in leaps an' bounds, bless her. They reckon we could have her home for the weekend if she carries on as she is.'

Gran looked slightly uncomfortable, but never being one to keep her thoughts to herself she now asked, 'An' how are you goin' to cope when she is home? I mean, no doubt James will still have to work, so who will take care of her? Will you fetch someone in?'

The question had been directed at James, who had still not uttered so much as a single word, but it was Janet who answered. 'There'll be no one comin' in apart from me. I shall stay on here an' see to the baby. If that's all right wi' you, James?'

'What . . . ?' James seemed to pull himself together with an enormous effort. 'Oh yes, I'd be grateful of that, Janet.' He then fell silent again as Janet looked at me apologetically.

'I'm afraid this means I won't be comin' back to The Chimneys. I hope you understand.'

'Of course I understand,' I assured her. 'What sort of a grandma would you be if you didn't offer to help out? The baby needs someone close to her to care for her. And speaking of the baby: isn't it time someone was going to see her at the hospital?'

Janet glanced at the clock and frowned. 'Goodness, I hadn't realised what the time was. I suppose I should . . .'

'Look, why don't I go today?' I offered. 'You and James are obviously not up to it.'

'Would you?' Her eyes were brimming with tears again as I gently squeezed her hand.

'It's no trouble at all,' I told her, but my motives were not purely unselfish. I would be glad to escape from the sad atmosphere for a time.

Picking my way through the people who had come back to the flat, I made my way to the door, only stopping to collect my bag on the way. And then I was in the lift and heading for the street, where I took a great gulp of air as I tried to compose myself. I hailed a cab and soon after found myself outside the doors of the ITU unit at the hospital, where the same young nurse who had first led us there on the night the baby was born met me.

'You've come to see the Bainbridge baby, have you?'

When I nodded, she smiled and ushered me inside, and within seconds I was staring down at Jessica, who was awake and looking about with wide blue eyes that were the colour of bluebells. The lid was off the incubator now, and as the nurse leaned into it to lift her out she commented, 'I wasn't sure if anyone would come today with it being the day of the funeral. It's terrible, isn't it, what happened to her mum?'

I nodded as I swallowed the lump that had formed in my throat again and then settled myself into a chair as the nurse placed Jessica in my arms.

'She's actually due for a feed any time now,' she informed me. 'Would you like to give her a bottle?'

I nodded eagerly, and while the nurse hurried away to fetch it I stared down at the beautiful child in my arms. She was so perfect that it was painful to look at her, for she was remarkably like her mother, and I knew then that Hilda would always remain with us through this lovely child she had been forced to leave behind.

The nurse was back within minutes, and after assuring her that I didn't need any help, she left us alone and I offered the teat to the baby. She instantly latched on to it and began to suck greedily as I looked on in wonder. And it was then that a strange feeling swept through me and I had to fight the urge that came on me to cry. She felt so right in my arms, and I asked God, 'Why did you never allow me a child of my very own?'

A movement from the corner of my eye made me look up, and there was Hamilton standing at the side of the incubator with a sad look in his eyes. Begonia was with him too, but it wasn't them I found myself focusing on but the beautiful foal that stood between them. She was a tiny replica of her mother with soft brown eyes and a chocolate and cream coat. And then there was Dusty too, and in that wonderfully correct voice of his he said, In the midst of life we are in death. That is the way of the world unfortunately. But God is good. Things will come right in the end.

'How *can* they come right?' I answered in a low voice. 'When this little innocent is without a mother?'

She will never want for love, he said wisely, and now I found myself looking back at the foal again and my voice was gentle as I told Hamilton and Begonia, 'She is truly beautiful.'

Hamilton nodded, and I saw that both he and Begonia were staring down at the baby in my arms with a look of deep sadness on their faces. All things happen for a reason, he told me. I found that hard to believe at this moment in time, and I too lowered my head to stare down at Jessica. When I raised it again they were all gone, and so for the rest of my visit I concentrated my efforts on the child that was nestling against me, for all the world as if she belonged there.

I visited the hospital again the next day, and the day after that, and on the third day the nurse met me with a broad grin on her face to inform me, 'The doctors have done their rounds this morning and they've said she can go home tomorrow. That's wonderful news, isn't it?'

'Yes, yes, it is.' There was this great hole opening up inside me, for I knew that once Jessica was home it would be Janet who would take over the care of her. For just these few short days I had grown close to her and realised now that I had come to look on her as my own. But then I pulled myself together as I thought of Harold. Now that Jessica was going home, I could return to him with a clear conscience. And Sandy of course. Oh, how I had missed them both. With a little jolt I realised that I hadn't included Tommy, but I put that down to the fact that since moving back to Fellburn we had seen little of each other. Still, I told myself optimistically, the house will be ready to move back into soon and then hopefully we will all be able to get back to some sort of normality. I returned my attention to the baby, revelling in the smell of her and locking each of her tiny features away in my memory. No doubt I would notice a huge change in her the next time I saw her. Babies had a habit of changing overnight.

Both Janet and James, when he got back from work that evening, were delighted when I told them about Jessica being allowed to come home. Janet had felt that James had returned to work too soon, but I had pointed out that this was probably his way to dealing with the tragedy.

'I'd better just go and check everything's ready in the nursery,' she told me, starting to panic.

I followed her to the room that had now been decorated with the paper James and I had chosen and was saddened to think that Hilda had never even got the chance to see it. Perhaps that was why she had asked me to pick it, because she had known that she wouldn't be able to? This room had always been bright and sunny, but now with the soft colours and the new white cot standing ready and waiting for its brand-new little occupant, it looked stunning.

'I suppose you'll be thinkin' o' headin' back home now?' Janet looked at me questioningly as she folded a small pile of matinee coats she had knitted over the previous months, and I nodded in confirmation.

'Well yes, I thought perhaps the day after tomorrow. I feel very guilty about leaving Harold for so long. But are you quite sure that you'll manage? I'm told that new babies can be hard work.'

Janet chuckled ruefully as she said, 'That's an understatement if ever I heard one. But don't you get worryin' about me. I'm an old hand when it comes to babies after havin' eight o' me own, an' it ain't as if I'll be carin' for her by meself, is it? Once James gets home from work of an evenin' he'll be takin' over, so we'll get by. Between you, me an' the gatepost, I can't wait to have her home; she's all I've got o' my Hilda now, ain't she? That alone will make her special.'

I nodded as I blinked rapidly to stop the tears that had started to my eyes from falling. An idea had been forming in my head all day and I had been about to offer to take Jessica home with me. But now I saw that Janet was intent on keeping the child within the family, and deep inside I knew that this was just as it should be. The days ahead would not be easy for them, but I had a feeling that Jessica would lack for nothing, least of all love, in their care.

James fetched her home from the hospital the following afternoon, and for the first time since Hilda's death there was laughter and smiles in the flat as we watched in fascination as Jessica's expressions changed.

James was every inch the devoted father and couldn't seem to get enough of her. He had taken yet another day off work especially for the occasion, and when he returned home from the hospital with Jessica in a Moses basket he was beaming with pride.

'The doctors are really pleased with her,' he told us as he lifted her from her basket. 'They said she's doing remarkably well for a premature baby. And she's very good, you know. I think the nurses were sad to see her go.'

I saw the love in his eyes as he gazed down on his little daughter and once again a pain of envy stabbed through my heart. But then I brightened as I thought of Harold. I had spoken to him on the phone the night before and he had been so excited when I told him that I was coming home that I had almost burst with pride.

Janet and James were now billing and cooing over the new addition to the family, so I took the opportunity to slip away to my room and pack my case. Perhaps it was a good thing that I was going home after all. The longer I stayed near Jessica the closer I was getting to her, and the harder the parting would be. In a positive frame of mind now I went to run myself a bath. I intended to catch an early train the next morning so that I could be at Gran's to greet Harold home from school.

Much later that evening I made James and myself a cup of cocoa and we settled down in the drawing room to drink it. Janet had gone to bed, exhausted by the happenings of the last two weeks, and Jessica was settled contentedly in her brand-new nursery.

'I don't think I've thanked you yet for all you've done for us over the last couple of weeks,' James told me as I tucked my feet beneath me. 'But I am grateful, Maisie, more than you'll ever know. It's helped having you here.'

'Nonsense, I haven't done that much,' I protested as a flush rose to my cheeks.

'Oh but you have, and I won't forget it.'

'I just hope you'll manage all right when I'm gone, what with the strange hours you have to work. How is work going, by the way? I haven't had time to ask you before what with . . . well, one thing and another.'

'Same as ever,' he said with a wry grin. 'Being an under-cover cop you never know what you'll be doing next, but I can tell you I'm working on something very big at the minute.'

'How big?' I asked as my curiosity got the better of me. For a moment I thought he was going to clam up as he usually did when his work was mentioned, but to my surprise he leaned towards me and said in a low voice, 'If I was to say the IRA, would that be big enough for you?'

'*The IRA!*' My voice must have betrayed my fear, because he smiled now and after taking a sip of his drink went on.

'Obviously I can't say too much. But we had a tip-off some time ago. It was after that loyalist gunman fired on an IRA funeral in Belfast back in March. He killed three people and managed to wound fifty others. Three days after that, members of an IRA funeral cortege lynched two British soldiers. It was then we had word about a possible bombing on the underground, and we've been following leads undercover ever since. You'd be surprised to know that for every attack that's successful we've managed to foil another, but of course, the ones that *are* successful always get into the papers.'

'But . . . but surely what you're doing is dangerous?'

He shrugged. 'That's all part of working undercover. The safety of the public has a price, as do all things in this life, including that little one there.' As his eyes settled on the baby, he suddenly stood up, and realising that he wasn't going to say any more on the subject, I rose too.

'Well, I suppose I'd better get myself off to bed. I've an early start in the morning. Good night, James.'

'Good night, Maisie.'

I walked across the room, aware of his eyes boring into my back, and at the door I paused to look back and say softly, 'James . . . please be careful.'

For long moments he sat as if he had been cast in stone. Our eyes were locked, but then he nodded and I went on my way. Once in the privacy of my room I sank on to the end of the bed, and now the tears that I had held back rolled unchecked down my cheeks, and yet I had no idea why I was crying. Eventually I gave myself a mental shake, and after climbing into bed I eventually fell asleep with a picture of Harold bowling down Brampton Hill on his bicycle and Hamilton's beautiful foal floating in front of my eyes.

After a tearful goodbye to Janet and the baby the following morning I set off for the station bright and early. James had already left for work and I was strangely relieved that I had missed him. Before going on to the platform I rang Gran from a phone booth to tell her what time to expect me. I then went to treat myself to some magazines and buy my ticket before boarding the train. I felt frivolous today and went first class, which ensured I had a comfortable seat and that I could get a decent lunch from the dining car. The journey passed pleasantly, and when the train finally chugged through Durham I began to feel excited. Very soon now I would see Harold and Sandy again, and I found that I could hardly wait.

My good mood was heightened when I heaved my case down the steps of the train to see a familiar figure striding up and down the platform peering into the carriages.

'Mike . . . what are *you* doing here?'

His hairy face broke into a grin as he hurried along and hugged me to his great chest.

'I happened to see your gran this morning. She told me you were due back and that George couldn't fetch you 'cos he's off on a run, so I thought I'd do the honours. I can't be too long, though, I've got afternoon surgery, so come along; get a shufty on, eh?'

'Oh Mike, that's so kind of you. It's good to be back.' My face was stretched in a smile as I stared up at this dear doctor who probably knew more about me than any other person on earth. But now that the niceties were over, Mike grabbed my elbow with one hand and my case with the other as he started to haul me along.

'I dare say you won't feel quite so pleased when you catch sight of young Harold.' He was chuckling now.

'Why?' My voice must have betrayed my fear because he instantly told me, 'Oh, nothing too serious apart from a very severe case of chickenpox. You can't put a pin on the poor little chap where there isn't a spot. Mary's crew have got it too, all apart from young Betty. I reckon Gordon's the worst of the lot.'

'Oh no!' I groaned. We were outside the station now and he was leading me towards the car. 'Is he very ill?' I asked.

'Bright as a button now that the spots have come out,' he assured me.

'But why didn't Gran tell me? I've phoned her every day since I've been away and she never said a word.'

'I suppose she thought you had enough on your plate back there in London.' He shook his head and his face was solemn as he said, 'That was a bad do. Poor Hilda, eh?'

I nodded as I settled into the passenger seat. Twenty minutes later, when he drew the car to a stop outside Gran's house, I completely forgot my manners as I jumped out of the passenger door and flew into the house.

Harold was sitting at the kitchen table doing a jigsaw, but the second he saw me he leaped across the room and flung his arms about my waist. Sandy too made his presence known and leapt into my arms, and there I was trying to cuddle both of them at the same time as we all laughed with delight at being together again.

Eventually I managed to place Sandy on the floor, and holding Harold at arm's length I tried not to laugh. He was daubed in calamine lotion from head to foot and looked a sorry sight indeed. Even his ears were covered in spots.

But then my mood became solemn when the smile slid from

his face and looking up at me he said, 'You ain't going to go away for a long time again, are yer, Mum?'

'If I have my way we'll never be parted again,' I told him sincerely, and then, ignoring the lotion that was rubbing off all over my expensive jacket, I hugged him to me and thought how very lucky I was.

Chapter Eighteen

I T WAS THE DAY we were due to move back into our own house, but instead of feeling excited about it I was feeling apprehensive.

'It'll be quiet here without you all,' Gran commented as she loaded yet more of Harold's toys into a large cardboard box. Harold was now fully recovered from his chickenpox and was back at school, so we had the rest of the day to move our things back to The Chimneys.

'I really don't know what we'd have done without you over the last couple of months,' I admitted.

Gran smiled. 'What's mine is yours, pet, includin' me home,' she answered, and then sitting back on her heels she exclaimed, 'Eeh, I'm right lookin' forward to seein' Janet an' the bairn.'

She was travelling to London the next day to spend a few days at the flat with Janet, who had informed us that Jessica was coming along in leaps and bounds.

'You won't recognise her the next time you see her,' she had told me only the night before when I had spoken to her on the phone, and I could well believe her.

'I suppose I should have held me horses an' seen you settled back into your own place first afore I went gallivantin' off though,' Gran now said.

I paused in the act of loading some more of Harold's clothes into a case to scowl at her. 'You should have done no such thing! We're quite capable of seeing to ourselves, thank you very much.'

Tommy appeared just then and lifted yet another box with a resigned sigh before taking it out to the van he had loaned for the day. 'I can't believe how much of our stuff is here,' he grumbled.

Gran rolled her eyes as he disappeared back out of the door. 'Men, eh? Never happy they ain't lessin' they have somethin' to moan about.'

An hour later the van was loaded to the roof and now all that was left to do was say our goodbyes. For now at least. I fixed Sandy's lead on as Gran followed me out to Tommy, who was impatiently strumming his fingers on the steering wheel and glancing constantly at his watch. He had taken the morning off work to move our possessions back to The Chimneys, but now it was obvious that he wanted to be away.

'Thanks again, Gran. And give my love to them all in London, won't you? Oh, and be sure to ring me when you're coming back and I'll make sure someone is there to meet you at the station, but take your time and enjoy the break. There's nothing to hurry back for, so make the most of it.'

'Will you just get in an' stop frettin'?' Gran gently pushed me towards the van, and realising that I was rambling on I climbed up into the high seat beside Tommy.

I waved as he pulled away until we turned a bend in the road and Gran was lost to sight, then I sat back in my seat praying that we wouldn't be met by any reporters when we arrived back at our house. They had somehow got hold of the news about the flood and had had a field day with the story for weeks, with headlines such as *Vandals Target Author's Home*, and *Vendetta*

Against Local Author. I was heartily sick of the whole thing now and just wanted us to get back to some sort of normality.

The decorators were just loading the last of their equipment into their van when we pulled up at the bottom of the steps, and Mr Breen, their boss, strode over to greet us with an oily smile on his face.

To hear the man anyone would have thought he had done the whole of the redecorating single-handed, but I happened to know that this wasn't so. On the rare occasions I had ventured up to the house to see how the work was progressing, he had been strutting about shouting out orders to the harassed-looking men who worked for him. That had done little to endear him to me, though I was forced to admit his workers had done a first-class job.

'Ah, Miss Carter.' Waltzing towards the van, he extended his hand.

'It's Mrs Balfour,' I told him coldly as I shook it reluctantly.

'What . . . ? Oh yes, yes, of course it is. Do forgive me, dear lady. It's just that it isn't every day I get to do a job for a celebrity.'

As an author, I spent most of my days locked away from the world in my study with imaginary characters, which I hardly thought amounted to being classed as a celebrity, but even so I simply smiled as I climbed the steps and looked about the hallway. I had chosen a simple cream paper for in here that made it look bright and airy, and I was pleased to see that the new chandelier I had chosen looked equally as nice as the original one that had been smashed beyond repair. While the house was being redecorated we had also taken the opportunity of having central heating fitted throughout, which I knew would save me hours of making up fires and emptying ash cans in the winter, although I had to admit it would take me some time to get used to the modern-looking radiators that were now attached to the walls in each room. I could hear Tommy talking to Mr Breen on the drive so I now made my way into the living room, where again I was pleasantly surprised. The colour scheme for this room was red and gold and it looked warm and inviting. The original curtains still hung at the windows, and I was pleased to see that after being dry-cleaned they looked as good as new, but the carpets that had been there when I had bought the house had shrunk and so new ones had been fitted throughout. I slowly worked my way through the house, pleased with the results in each room, and yet I felt no sense of homecoming, which I considered to be quite strange. It's probably because I haven't settled back in, I tried to convince myself, yet deep down I wondered if I would ever be truly happy here again. I somehow felt that my home had been violated and could only hope that the feeling would pass. The only two rooms that were unchanged were the last two rooms on either end of the upstairs landing, and it was in one of these that Tommy finally found me after he had given Mr Breen and his men a generous tip and sent them on their way.

'So is everything to madam's satisfaction then?' he asked as he breezed into the room that he had taken to sleeping in.

I nodded. 'Yes, in fairness I have to say you would never have known it had been flooded, but . . .'

'But *what*?'

'I suppose I just feel a bit strange here at the minute, that's all. I'm not sure that I'll ever feel safe here again on my own after what's happened.'

There was a twinkle in his eye now as he told me, 'Then in that case I'm glad I've done what I've done.'

'Oh yes, and what would that be?'

'Well, seeing as Janet won't be coming back for the

foreseeable future, I took the liberty of interviewing a few of the village women to come in and do some cleaning for you.'

When I raised my eyebrow he laughed and held up his hand as if to ward off a blow. 'Now don't look like that till you've given the woman I chose a chance. She's a bit of a character I have to admit, but her references were excellent and she came highly recommended. Her name is Mrs Pringle and she'll be coming up to meet you later this afternoon to sort out what hours you'd like her to work.'

'Oh!' I was surprised, but as I let it sink in I had to admit it made sense. The Chimneys was a large house to keep clean, and if there was someone to help me it would free up more time for me to write. I certainly hadn't had much time lately, and the next deadline for my new book was creeping ominously closer.

'Well, I don't suppose it will hurt for me to meet her,' I admitted grudgingly. 'But I'm not making any promises. If I don't think she's going to be suitable I shall send her on her way.'

'Fair enough.' He turned and went back down the stairs to continue unloading the van, and after a few moments I followed him.

The moment I met Mrs Pringle later that afternoon, I saw what Tommy had meant when he told me she was 'a bit of a character'. To say that she was larger than life in every way would have been an understatement, for she was an Amazon of a woman with a booming voice to match.

'Mrs Balfour?' She held her great ham of a hand out to me when I opened the door to her with a wide smile on her face, and then without waiting to be asked she stepped past me into the hall saying, 'Eeh, that hill is a killer, especially in this heat. I shall be as thin as a rake by the time I've puffed up an' down that a few times, an' that wouldn't be a bad thing, would it?'

Not quite knowing what to say, I simply inclined my head as she took a hold of my hand and pumped it up and down. She stood head and shoulders above me and was dressed in the most outlandish, garish outfit I had ever seen, which consisted of a shocking pink blouse that strained across her ample bosom and a gypsy-style skirt that fell in tiers resembling Joseph's coat of many colours. Her hair was bright ginger and back-combed until it almost stood on end, and her make-up looked as if it might have been applied with a trowel, yet strangely I found myself warming to her. She was what Gran would have termed as blousy or common as muck, but her smile was warm and sincere, and her green eyes were striking.

'So,' she said after staring at the pile of boxes Tommy had left by the door. 'Your hubby were sayin' as you could do wi' someone to give you a hand wi' the housework, washin' and ironin'. I'm a dab hand at cookin' an' all, so if you just tell me the hours you'd like me to work I can fall in wi' whatever you want. My bairns are all grown up now an' able to fend for themselves, apart from our Francis, that is. He's ten an' a right little tearaway I don't mind tellin' you.'

I placed my hand across my mouth at this point to cover the smile that had spread across my lips. Francis seemed like an awfully grand name for someone who originated from Bog's End, but before I could comment on it she went on, 'Me bloke had an accident down on the docks some months back so I suppose you could say that only leaves me to be the bread-winner now. The lads don't chip in much, the selfish buggers. Hurt his back the poor bugger did, but that's another story.'

I was trying to assess how old she was, and guessed that she must be about the same age as me even though she was dressed more like a teenager. But then as Gran was fond of saying, you should never judge a book by its cover, and Mrs Pringle did seem keen.

'Look, come through to the living room,' I now said. 'And perhaps we could discuss hours and pay and such.'

'Suits me, pet.' She followed me across the hallway, and once we were seated she looked around with a broad smile on her face before shaking her head and saying, 'How the other half live, eh? No disrespect intended like. I live down in Bog's End an' it's a far cry from this, I don't mind tellin' you. Still, I pride meself on the fact that it's as neat as a new pin. Me husband is always tellin' me you could eat your dinner off my floor.'

'Right.' Feeling slightly out of my depth I asked her tentatively, 'Do you think you could work every day? Apart from Sunday, that is. Perhaps three or four hours a day?'

'No problem at all, pet,' she assured me. 'When would you like me to start?'

'When could you start?'

'Well, judgin' by all them boxes piled high in the hall there's no time like the present. What say I roll me sleeves up an' get stuck in right now?'

'Oh!' Again she had taken me by surprise, but after a moment I nodded. 'Yes, if you're sure it wouldn't be putting you out. Most of the boxes are full of my son's toys. He's at school at present but it would be nice if we could have them all put away for him by the time he gets home. We've been staying down at my gran's. The house was flooded, you see, and . . .'

'I know all about that,' she told me. 'It were plastered all across the papers for days.' Her head wagged from side to side and then leaning slightly towards me she asked, 'Did they catch the rotten sods that did it yet?'

'No, I'm afraid they haven't. It was probably just some

opportunist vandals from down in Bog's . . .' My voice trailed away as I looked at her apologetically but she waved her hand in the air dismissively.

'Don't worry about sayin' that in front o' me. I know better than anyone that some o' the scum o' the earth live down there. But we ain't all tarred wi' the same brush, I assure you.'

'Oh no, no, I'm sure you're not.' I could feel my cheeks glowing with embarrassment now and with a little shock I found myself thinking, Why! I'm turning into a snob. Me, Maisie Rochester, who was brought up not a stone's throw away from Bog's End myself. I tried to make amends when I asked her, 'Would you like a cup of tea before you start?'

'Now *that's* what I like to hear!' Her large face lit up in a smile revealing a set of beautiful straight white teeth. She followed me into the kitchen, and while I was filling the kettle at the sink she began to peep in all the cupboards.

'Just gettin' me bearin's,' she explained when she saw me watching her. 'Everythin' has its place an' I want to put everythin' back where it should go.'

It was then that I did something I had not done in what seemed like a very long time, for my head went back and I bellowed with laughter. 'Oh Mrs Pringle,' I gasped. 'I have the feeling you and I are going to get along just fine.'

She put her head to one side, setting her double chin wobbling, and said abruptly, 'It's right glad I am to hear it. But why don't you call me Polly? Everyone else does. Mrs Pringle is a bit formal, ain't it?'

Polly Pringle, Polly Pringle! The name was rolling round and round in my head and now I was laughing so much that I feared I might choke. Oblivious to the joke, Polly came to join me at the sink and elbowed me aside, ordering, 'Oh go an' sit down, you daft ha'porth. You're good to neither man nor beast in this state. I heard that authors could be a bit eccentric an' now I know they weren't kiddin'. Still, I'd rather you be as you are than some stuck-up trollop wi' her nose in the air.'

So I dutifully sat down and left her to it, and we then enjoyed the first of many tea breaks we would share together, and as I looked at her over the rim of my cup I was thinking, Why, she's like a breath of fresh air!

Over dinner that evening I told Tommy of my meeting with Polly Pringle, and he smiled as he said, 'Sounds to me like you've taken to her.'

'Oh, I have. It would be hard not to take to her, she's got such a sunny nature. But she also seems like she's going to be good at her job too. She was only here for two hours this afternoon and during that time she emptied every box in the hall and even cleaned the kitchen.'

'Good, good.'

I got the distinct impression that Tommy was only listening to me with half an ear, but then I had got used to that just lately. Harold meanwhile had ploughed through his meal as if he hadn't eaten for a month and he now swiped his hand across his mouth before asking with his mouth full, 'Please can I leave the table?'

'What's the rush?'

He gulped and swallowed his food before telling me, 'I've got choir practice down at the church tonight but I want to get out an' have half an hour on me bike first. Is that OK?'

'I suppose so,' I told him indulgently. 'But don't get going beyond the end of the drive or you'll be late.'

'In actual fact I have an appointment too,' Tommy said as he rose from the table. 'Will you excuse me, dear?'

'But where are you going?' I was trying hard to keep the

disappointment out of my voice and failing miserably. 'Being as it's our first night back at home, I was hoping that we'd spend it together.'

'Sorry.' He shrugged his shoulders. 'Duty calls, I'm afraid. But there'll be other nights.'

'Of course.' I began to collect the dirty dishes together as I wondered what I would do with myself this evening. Usually I visited Gran after dropping Harold off for choir practice, but as she was now in London visiting Janet I felt at a bit of a loose end. I briefly played with the idea of visiting George and Mary instead but then decided against it when I realised it was Mary's night for bingo. I'll take Sandy for a nice walk along the waterfront, I decided instead as I was washing the pots up, and resigned to having nothing better to do, I set to work with a vengeance.

I had dropped Harold off, and now with Sandy firmly attached to his lead I was strolling along the quay. I had once made the mistake of allowing him off his lead, which had turned into a total disaster as Sandy had a very bad habit of chasing after anything on four legs. It was a beautiful evening with a cool breeze blowing in off the sea, and as I strolled along I decided that this hadn't been such a bad idea after all. It was nice to have some quiet time to myself and it provided a good opportunity to do some people-watching. Tommy used to tease me about that, but as I had told him, it's the stuff that books are made of. I might see someone who would catch my eye for any number of reasons. It could be a particular way they walked or talked, or even some mannerism that they probably weren't aware that they had, and then before I knew it I would find them becoming a character in one of my books.

Tonight looked set to be no different, for in front of me I

saw an old sea captain standing with a pipe in his mouth as he puffed away and stared out to sea with a faraway expression in his eyes. I wonder what he's thinking about, I thought and instantly my mind was working overtime. I was so absorbed in the man that it was a while before I became aware of a young couple who appeared to be in the middle of a fierce argument. When I transferred my attention from the captain to them I realised with a little shock that the young woman was Betty, George's stepdaughter. But this was Betty as I had never seen her before. Normally she was a placid, sweet-natured girl, but this evening her face was flushed and I could see from the way she was gesticulating that she was shouting, although I was too far away to hear what she was saying. The young man she was with had his back to me and I realised with a start that this must be the Sand Dancer. I cursed softly. For the first time he did not have his balaclava on, but I was unable to see his face because of the way he was standing with his back to me. I briefly thought of meandering towards them but then thought better of it. Betty might take it that I was sticking my nose in where it wasn't wanted, so instead I stayed where I was and watched from a distance. Eventually I saw Betty bow her head, then she began to fumble in her handbag and I saw her pass something to him. He nodded and walked away from her, and after a moment Betty turned and began to walk towards me. I quickly started walking again too, and when she came abreast of me I said as if in surprise, 'Why, hello, Betty. Out for a stroll too, are you?'

'Oh hello . . . er, yes, I was just having a stroll and a bit o' fresh air.'

'Then why don't you join us? Sandy and I are doing exactly the same thing. I thought it would pass the time while Harold was at his choir practice. I really should do it more often, to be honest. All those hours of sitting at a typewriter can cause havoc with one's figure.'

She hesitated and nodded absently before falling into step with us, and although I kept up a constant stream of cheerful chatter I knew that she wasn't really listening to a word I was saying. Eventually we came to a bench overlooking the sea, and pressing her on to it I sat beside her and asked, 'Is something wrong, Betty? You seem awfully quiet.'

'What . . . ? Oh, sorry. I was miles away. And no, there isn't anything wrong exactly . . . it's just . . .'

I held my tongue as I waited for her to go on, and suddenly turning to me she looked me full in the face before saying, 'Men are funny creatures, aren't they?'

'What makes you say that, dear?'

'Well it's Robbie, my boyfriend. I've been trying to persuade him to come home with me to meet Mum and Dad but he won't have a bar of it, and yet he . . .' She flushed now before saying quietly, 'He . . . he keeps trying to get me to go to his flat, but I don't feel ready for that yet. The trouble is I'm afraid that if I don't go soon he'll get tired of me and look around for someone else.'

'Then as much as I hate to say this, dear, you should let him. You shouldn't have to do anything you don't want to do until you're good and ready. You just stand your ground, and if he really cares for you he'll wait. If he doesn't, you haven't really lost much anyway, have you?'

When she shook her head miserably I had the urge to take her in my arms and hug her. I could remember only too well how vulnerable I had been to Howard Stickle when I was much the same age as she was now, and I would hate to see her fall into the same trap. The difference between us being that I had been plain, fearful that no one else would ever want me, whereas

Betty was bonny. Oh yes, she was bonny all right. So bonny, in fact, that she could have had her pick of boyfriends if she had chosen to.

She rose from the bench now and her next words made me blink rapidly, for what she said was, 'I can understand why me dad an' me gran love you so much, Maisie. You're a kind person.' And with that she walked away as I sat and watched her go.

See, here you are feeling sorry for yourself when there are people who love you!

I turned my head to see Hamilton sitting on the bench right next to me. He had his front legs resting either side of him and his back legs crossed.

I forced a smile. 'I suppose you're right. I have been a bit down in the dumps lately, haven't I?' I replied as I bent to stroke Sandy's silky ears. 'I suppose I'm just a bit worried about Tommy, that's all. He always seems to be working just lately and . . .'

Hamilton now leapt on to all fours and began to gallop wildly up and down the quay, his tail and his mane flying behind him. I watched in astonishment before saying, 'He *is* working I tell you . . . Of course he is.'

An old man who was walking by gave me a funny look before quickening his steps and hurrying past, and I felt myself blushing.

'*Now* look what you've made me do,' I scolded. But when I looked back, Hamilton had disappeared and I suddenly felt lonely again as I tugged on Sandy's lead and led him back the way we had come to fetch Harold.

Chapter Nineteen

A T NINE O'CLOCK on the dot the next morning Polly Pringle arrived, and from that moment on the day became brighter. She had the living room gleaming in record time and I was shocked at her energy, which seemed to be limitless. And all the time she was working she was singing, which had Sandy following her about adoringly, although it could also have been something to do with the fact that she arrived carrying a large marrow bone for him that she had collected from the butcher's on the way.

At eleven o'clock she brought a cup of coffee into my study for me. Crossing her arms she stared around and declared, 'Eeh, I ain't never been in an author's office afore. So this is where it all happens, is it? I read your last two books, you know, an' I never stopped laughin', you've certainly got a way wi' words.'

'That's perhaps as well seeing as it's how I earn my living,' I replied wryly.

Perching on the edge of the desk she asked, 'So what would you like me to prepare fer your lunch?'

'Oh, don't worry about that, Polly,' I told her hastily. 'I usually just have a sandwich or something seeing as there's only me here. We have our main meal in the evening all together.'

'Fair enough.' Hitching up her enormous breasts she went on, 'I'll see as it's all prepared then, shall I?'

'Well that would be nice,' I admitted. 'I'm trying to get this book finished so any help is much appreciated.'

'Fine, I'll see to it when I've finished the cleanin'.' She was now moving towards the door again, but she paused and, looking a little worried now, said hesitantly, 'There was just one thing as I was meanin' to ask you.'

'And what would that be? Go on, I assure you I don't bite.'

'Well the thing is, I were wonderin' if you'd have any objections to me bringin' my Francis along on a Saturday mornin' seein' as he ain't at school. His dad ain't really up to keepin' an eye on him see, wi' him bein' confined to bed like.'

'I can't see that being a problem,' I assured her. 'In fact, seeing as he's almost the same age as Harold I've no doubt Harold will be delighted. They can keep each other company.'

A look of relief washed over her face. 'Thanks, Mrs . . . what am I supposed to call you anyway?'

'Try Maisie, it's my name.'

'Right then, Maisie it is.' I contained my laughter until the door had closed behind her and then picked up my coffee. Things will never be the same round here again! I thought.

When Tommy arrived home that evening he sniffed at the air appreciatively before saying, 'Something smells good.'

'It's a roast beef dinner with all the trimmings,' I told him. 'But don't thank me for it. Polly prepared everything before she left. All I had to do was turn it on and let it cook.'

'I gather her first day went well then.' He was pouring himself a whisky from the decanter in the living room and I smiled widely.

'You could say that. She went through the housework like a whirlwind and the dinner looks delicious.'

'There you are then,' he said smugly. 'It just goes to show that I can come up with good ideas every now and again, doesn't it?'

Instead of immediately answering him I eyed him with growing concern. His suit seemed to be hanging off him and I realised with a little jolt just how much weight he had lost.

'I think I might give you a double portion,' I commented. 'At the rate you're shedding weight we might lose you down a gap in the pavement. You're not feeling ill are you, Tommy?'

'I'm as fit as a butcher's dog,' he assured me. 'It's just that I've been working hard and I sometimes forget to eat. But hark at you, madam, talk about the pot calling the kettle black. You haven't got an ounce of fat on you yourself.'

'Yes well, that's normal for me but not for you. You really will have to begin to take more care of yourself. All work and no play is no good for anyone. Why don't you take the boat out this weekend? You haven't been out in her for ages and the fresh air would do you good. I'm sure Harold would be happy to keep you company.'

'We'll see,' he said vaguely as he drained his glass, and as I watched him walk from the room I frowned. I had an idea that *Spring Fever* didn't hold quite the same appeal for him since the Captain's death, but then I supposed that this was understandable. Still, I told myself optimistically, no doubt once he had taken her out, he would put the unpleasant memories to one side and begin to enjoy sailing again. But it certainly didn't look like it was going to be any time in the near future, if his reaction to my suggestion was anything to go by. I shrugged before heading off to the kitchen to dish the meal up.

★

Early one morning in July when we were all seated at breakfast in the kitchen, Tommy surprised both Harold and myself when he informed us that he had treated us to tickets to go and see Michael Jackson at Wembley. Harold was a huge fan of this particular pop star and whooped with delight.

'Will we *all* be goin'?' he asked, and I smiled as I looked into his animated face.

'No, I'm afraid I can't spare the time,' Tommy apologised. 'But I'm sure you two will enjoy it. The tour is a sell-out so I was lucky to get tickets.'

'Will we be stayin' overnight in London?' Harold asked.

I supposed that it would make sense. Harold was on his summer holidays from school and we had nothing to rush back for, although I was shocked that Tommy was happy for us to go without him. It was a far cry from when we had lived in London and he could hardly bear me to leave the flat without him. Still, Polly now had the house running like clockwork, and seeing as I saw so little of Tommy, I doubted he would have any objections. His jealousy seemed to have completely disappeared now and I was free to go where I pleased again.

'I suppose I could always ring Janet and ask her if she'd mind us staying at the flat,' I answered hesitantly.

Harold's face lit up. 'Great, that means I'll get to see Gag *and* the baby.'

I busied myself with folding some table napkins so as to hide the flush that had risen in my cheeks. My reasons for suggesting a stay at the flat were not entirely unselfish. It would mean that I got to see Jessica again too . . . and James. My head snapped up and now I saw Hamilton. He was standing behind Tommy with his head to one side and his gums drawn back from his teeth in a wide grin.

Flustered, I told Harold, 'Yes, you will see the baby, dear. That will be nice, won't it?'

Tommy stood up and glanced at the clock. 'Right, I'd better be off then. We have a delivery from abroad due this morning and I'd like to be there when it comes.'

He pecked my cheek in passing and ruffled Harold's hair, and as he passed through the hall I heard Polly arriving. She had, as Gran was fond of saying, a gob like a foghorn, and wouldn't have known what the word quiet meant if it was to jump up and hit her in the face. But for all that I had taken to her and liked having her about the place. During the last week she had been bringing Francis, or Franky as he was known, with her, and he and Harold were getting on famously. While Polly was working they would play in the garden or the woods or spend hours taking it in turns to ride Harold's bicycle.

'I wish *I* had a bike,' I had heard Franky say enviously only the day before, and already I was planning on buying him one of his own for his birthday. His hair, like his mother's, was a fiery ginger, and although he was almost the same age as Harold he barely reached his shoulder. All in all, he was a scrawny little chap, but his saving grace was his startling green eyes. They were the colour of emeralds, heavily fringed with surprisingly thick dark lashes that were so long they curled on his cheeks when he closed his eyes.

He now raced into the kitchen ahead of Polly and instantly asked Harold, 'Are you all set then? Let's get usselves off into the woods, eh? I thought we could have a splodge in the edge o' the lake.'

'I'll bloody splodge you, me laddo, if you come back wi' yer shoes an' socks wet through again,' Polly warned.

Grinning, Harold slid off his seat to go and join him. Shaking her head, Polly declared, 'I don't know – them pair are like

216

partners in crime. What are we goin' to do wi' 'em, eh?'

'Leave them to it I should think,' I answered. 'There's not much they can get up to in the woods or around the lake.'

She smiled ruefully. 'I shouldn't be too sure o' that. Them pair could find mischief to get up to in a padded cell.'

I found myself smiling as she proceeded to tie a large apron around her ample waist. Today she was wearing a long red flowing skirt and a shocking pink blouse that did nothing for her bright ginger hair at all.

'I shall be going away in a couple of weeks,' I informed her. 'Probably only for a night or two, though. Tommy has bought Harold and me tickets to see Michael Jackson at Wembley Stadium, so I'll probably stay at my flat in London. Will you be happy to carry on here on your own?'

'O' course I will.' Her green eyes twinkled as she leaned towards me, and lowering her voice she said, 'An' don't get worryin'. I ain't about to take off wi' the family silver.'

'Oh Polly, such a thought never entered my head,' I retorted indignantly. 'I wouldn't give you a key if I didn't trust you, would I?'

Winking, she took the wax polish and a duster from beneath the sink and headed for the door. 'Only kiddin',' she laughed before disappearing into the lounge.

Throughout this exchange Hamilton had kept a silent presence behind one of the kitchen chairs, but now I looked towards him and, lowering my voice, I asked, 'And what are *you* grinning at?'

Just the fact that you seem very excited about this trip if you're only looking forward to seeing Jessica Rose.

'Why shouldn't I look forward to seeing her? She's a dear little thing.'

Suddenly the smile slid from his face and his great dark eyes were sad when he replied, Yes, she is, but you must always remember that she isn't *your* dear little thing.

I tossed my head with indignation and stared towards the window. 'I assure you I'm quite aware of that fact and I certainly don't need *you* to remind me, thank you very much!'

I turned back to him but he was gone and suddenly I felt dreadful. Every time I saw Hamilton lately I seemed to snap his head off. Still, I consoled myself, there's nothing I can do about it now, and after clearing the table I went to my study to work on my book.

'*What the . . . ?*'

The sound of Polly's raised voice two hours later brought me from my typewriter into the hall, where I saw her standing hands on hips with her mouth gaping as she stared at Harold and Franky in horror.

I stifled a giggle as I followed her eyes. They were standing just inside the front door looking very sorry for themselves indeed. Water was dripping off them to form puddles on the tiles and their hair was plastered to their heads. It was hard to tell what colour their clothes might have been earlier in the day, for now they were mud-coloured from head to foot.

'We made usselves a raft out o' some branches layin' about the lake,' Franky told her solemnly. 'But we hadn't bin on it more than two minutes when it all come apart an' dumped us in the water.'

Unable to conceal my amusement for a moment longer, I burst into laughter as Polly glared at me. 'Didn't I tell you these two would find some mischief to get into?' she demanded indignantly.

'Oh Polly, it's not the end of the world.' I was trying hard to look serious and failing dismally. 'They can go up and have a bath and Franky can borrow an outfit from Harold for the rest of the day. It will probably be a bit big on him but no one's going to mind, are they?'

'I suppose not.' She sniffed her disapproval, then wagged a finger towards her son and told him sternly, 'Go on then. You heard what the missus said. Get yourself away to the bathroom, an' think yerself lucky as I ain't skelped yer arse for you.'

'Yes, Mam.' Franky set off for the staircase, leaving a trail of water behind him as Polly shook her head in exasperation.

'That lad'll be the death o' me,' she mumbled as she went back to her polishing.

Now it was my turn. 'Go on you,' I told Harold. 'You can go and have a bath too, and sort Franky some clothes out, would you?'

He nodded before shooting off to join his accomplice just as Gran came gasping through the open front door. 'What's gone on 'ere then?' she asked as she looked at the puddles on the tiles. 'You ain't had another flood, have you?'

'No, of course I haven't.' I grinned as I took her elbow and steered her towards the kitchen. 'Come on, let's get you a cold drink and you can tell me about your visit to London. How are they all there?'

Instantly forgetting the water she followed me into the kitchen. Once seated she said, 'You know, I'm a bit worried about Janet copin' wi' that bairn. She's a bonny little thing, but no disrespect intended, Janet's gettin' a bit long in the tooth now to be takin' on the care of a babby. It ain't so bad of an' evenin'. Once James gets home he takes over, an' o' course he has to work. But how long will Janet be able to keep it up? I suggested that James should think about takin' on one o' them nannies to come in an' help, but Janet wouldn't hear of it.'

'Well I can understand that,' I said solemnly. 'It's always best if children can be cared for by their own families. But you know, she let me adopt Harold and that hasn't turned out so badly, has it? I've no doubt in a few months' time James will have to consider bringing in some help. Try not to worry about it, though. I'm sure things will work out. They usually do. And it's nice to have you back, Gran. We've missed you.'

'Thanks.' Her wrinkled face creased into a smile. 'If truth be told I'm glad to be back. I enjoyed seein' Janet an' the bairn, but between you an' me I'm never really relaxed while I'm in London, not wi' all them bombs goin' off right, left an' centre. It makes you wonder what the world's comin' to. An' happen you're right, lass, I've no doubt things will sort themselves out regardin' the bairn.' She took a long swallow of the lemonade I'd placed in front of her, then, her face bright again, she asked, 'An' what's been goin' on here? I've no doubt that water in the hall had somethin' to do with his Lordship.'

When I told her about Harold and Franky's escapade on the raft, she threw her head back and laughed aloud. 'That's lads for you. My Georgie were no better when he were little. He were always gettin' himself into some scrape or another, but then that's what lads do, ain't it? You know what I say, while they're mucky, they're healthy.'

I nodded in agreement and the rest of the afternoon was spent pleasantly as she filled me in on all the gossip.

Chapter Twenty

I T WAS HOT WHEN Harold and I arrived in London. He had chatted nonstop all the way there on the train and was now in a state of high excitement. We were due to go to the concert that evening, but first we were going to the flat to drop off our bags and see Janet and the baby.

I wondered where Harold was getting his energy from. The heat was making me feel tired, yet he was still as fresh as he had been when we'd set off from Newcastle earlier in the morning.

'Are we gonna get a taxi?' he chirped.

'No, we're *going* to get a taxi,' I corrected him as I followed him to the exit of the station. The London streets were bustling with sightseers and the traffic was as bad as ever, yet even so, I found that I was looking forward to seeing the flat again. I had missed the feeling of still being close to Nardy that I only found there. Twenty minutes later, I hustled a very excited Harold out of the cab on to the pavement while I paid the driver, then herded him inside and towards the lift. Janet was waiting for us with a wide smile on her face when the doors opened on the landing, and Harold launched himself at her with delight written all across his face.

'*Gag!*' He wrapped his arms about her waist and I realised

then that the bond between them was as strong as ever as she hugged him back.

'My!' She eventually held him at arm's length. 'Whatever are they feedin' you on, lad? You're growin' like a weed, so you are.' Her eyes then found mine and she smiled again as she said, 'I've been waitin' for you all mornin' an' right lookin' forward to you arrivin', I don't mind tellin' you. Come away in, the both of you. The kettles boiled an' I've no doubt you'll both be as dry as a bone.'

We followed her into the flat and then Harold went scampering off into the lounge where Jessica was fast asleep in her Moses basket. I found him staring down at her with a look of awe on his small face. As I approached he exclaimed, 'Cor, she's really lovely, ain't she, Mum?'

'Isn't she,' I again corrected him, then smiling I added, 'Yes, Harold, she is lovely, and like you she's growing. I can hardly believe how's she's changed in the short time since I last saw her.'

'Ah well, babies have a habit o' doin' that.' Janet had come to stand beside us and her face was soft as she smiled down on her granddaughter. 'You blink your eye an' turn around an' you find they've grown up afore you know it.'

I felt sad as I thought on her words and realised that she was right. Harold was already twice the size he had been when I first met him and soon he would be a young man. As we were standing there, Jessica stirred and suddenly looked up at us from bright blue eyes.

Harold whooped with delight as he leaned into her cot and tickled her gently under her chin. She immediately smiled at him and from that moment on he was besotted with her.

'Can I hold her, Gag?' he asked excitedly, and laughing, Janet lifted her from the cot and deposited her gently into his arms.

'There you go then, but don't go droppin' her mind.'

Harold was cradling her as if she was made of fine china and I thought the likelihood of him dropping her was very remote, but all the same I added my warning to hers, saying, 'Why don't you sit down with her? I'd feel safer that way.' At that very moment I became aware of Hamilton standing behind the settee with Begonia, their foal between them and Dusty standing to one side. Their faces were soft as they too stared down at the child, and my eyes were drawn to the foal. She really was a beautiful little thing and I could hardly take my eyes off her. Hamilton seemed to become aware of the fact and his voice was gentle as he said, She's truly lovely too, isn't she?

I wasn't sure whether he was talking about Begonia or his foal but I nodded anyway.

'Come on.' Janet was eager for news of what was happening in Fellburn and started to usher me towards the kitchen. 'Those two will be all right on their own for a while. Come an' tell me what's happenin' back in your neck o' the woods.'

And so I followed her into the kitchen and we had a pleasant chat, and all the while we could hear Harold billing and cooing at Jessica through the open doorway. Some time later I went to unpack our clothes while Harold helped Janet to feed and change the baby. We then had a delicious roast dinner and it was time for Harold and me to leave for the concert.

'Have a good time,' Janet called after us as the lift doors closed. I nodded. Harold was so excited that I had no doubt we would; he had talked of little else for days and I was relieved now that it was finally time for it to happen. He had been bombing about the house warbling Michael Jackson songs at the top of his voice and I wondered if he would quieten down when the concert was over. We had just reached the ground floor when James walked through the door.

'Why, hello, you two. You got here then?'

'I didn't have much choice,' I told him ruefully. 'This concert is all he's talked about for days.'

Harold was now tugging impatiently on my hand and laughing, James told us, 'Off you go then and enjoy it. I don't want to make you late. We'll catch up later, eh?'

I nodded as I was dragged towards the door, and the last I saw of James he was standing there laughing at Harold.

The concert was a huge success. I was concerned that Harold couldn't see most of it as there were so many people there. Had I been strong enough I would have lifted him to see above the heads of the people in front of us, but my withered arm prevented me from doing so. Thankfully, it didn't seem to spoil Harold's enjoyment, which was hardly surprising as the atmosphere was electric, and he sang along with Michael Jackson word perfect throughout his perform- ance. When it was finally over I clung on to his hand for dear life as we were jostled towards the exit by the surging crowd.

'That were one o' the best nights o' my whole life,' Harold declared when we were finally out on the pavement and it was safe to loose his hand again. He was positively beaming, and although I was secretly thinking that we would have seen more of the performance on television, I was glad I had brought him. On the way back to the flat we stopped at a café and he downed two enormous milkshakes and a beefburger. Normally I liked him to eat healthy food but tonight was a treat, so I was willing to make an exception.

Eventually I bundled a very tired but happy little boy back into a taxi and by the time we arrived back at the flat he was fast asleep.

'Come on, dear,' I urged as I shook his arm. 'Let's get you inside and tucked into bed, eh?'

He yawned and stretched as I helped him out of the car on to the pavement. Rubbing the sleep from his eyes he complained, 'But I wanna tell Gag all about it.'

'You *want to*, and you can do that in the morning,' I answered firmly, and without waiting for him to argue I marched him into the foyer.

Janet grinned when she caught sight of him. There was a dry moustache of milkshake on his top lip, red sauce all around his mouth and his eyes were heavy.

'Right, young man, it's off to bed for you,' she ordered, and taking his hand she steered him, protesting loudly, towards the bathroom.

'But *Gag* . . .' I heard no more as the bathroom door closed behind them. Smiling, I went into the kitchen.

James was sitting at the table reading a newspaper. 'How did it go?' he asked.

'Oh, I think we can safely say it was a resounding success,' I replied as I filled the kettle. 'In fact, I'm amazed he hasn't lost his voice. He hasn't stopped singing all night.'

'Good, good, I'm glad he enjoyed it.'

I joined him at the table, noting how tired he looked. 'And how are things with you?'

He shrugged. 'Oh you know, jogging along.'

'It must be hard for you, going to work all day and then coming home to look after a baby.'

'I manage,' he said shortly. 'And Jessica is coming on really well.'

'I've already seen that, and my remark wasn't meant as a criticism.'

'Sorry.' He held his hands out. 'I think I must be a bit touchy at the moment. It's all the night feeds I expect. Plus, I'm really busy at work, and having to stay stationed in London for Jessica is very limiting in my job.'

'Yes, I imagine it would be.'

I went to pour the boiling water into the teapot and busied myself setting the cups out. A silence had fallen between us but it was finally broken when James asked, 'And what about you? How are things back home?'

'All right.'

'Just all right?'

'Well, like you, I'm kept busy, caring for Harold and with my writing.'

'And where does Tommy come into the equation?'

'I don't get to see that much of him any more,' I admitted. 'Since he opened the yard he seems to work all the hours God sent, but then I shouldn't blame him for that, should I?' I deliberately didn't mention the fact that Tommy had no alternative. Since losing his properties and his inheritance to gambling, the yard was now his only source of income.

'Mm . . .'

I could feel my colour rising, and eager to change the subject I poured the tea and pushed a cup towards him before saying, 'I thought I might stay for a couple of days if that's all right with you. It will give Harold a chance to spend a little time with his gran.'

'You can stay for as long as you like,' he assured me. 'It is still your flat after all.'

Janet bustled back in to join us just then and I was relieved. I never felt truly comfortable on my own with James, though I had no idea why.

'He went out like a light,' she chuckled. 'Moanin' an' groanin' he were that he weren't tired, then the second his head hit the pillow he were gone.'

Jessica chose that moment to cry and James instantly stood up and went to tend to her.

'Good as gold he is with that baby,' Janet said sadly. 'Our Hilda would have been proud of him if she could have seen him with her.' Her eyes now welled with tears, and reaching across I gently squeezed her hand. The last few months could not have been easy for her, but I was powerless to help her. We spent a few more minutes talking of this and that and then I retired to bed, tired out, but content that the trip had been worth it just to see the look in Harold's eyes when his idol had strolled on to the stage at Wembley.

Hamilton was waiting for me when I snapped the bedroom light on. He was sitting on the end of the bed and his eyes looked sad.

James looks tired, he commented.

'Yes, I know. But what can I do about it?'

He held his head to the side as he slowly shook it to and fro. You could be there for him.

'I think you're forgetting I am a happily married woman, Hamilton,' I told him tartly.

Happily?

'Yes, *happily!* Now why don't you get back to Begonia and your baby? I'm sure she'll be wondering where you are.'

In a flash he was gone, and as I sank down on to the edge of the bed and stared vacantly off into space I tried to put my thoughts into some sort of order. It was true that James could still evoke strong feelings in me, and I found myself wondering again what might have been. I mentally shook myself as I started to get undressed, deeply ashamed of myself. I had chosen the path I was going to take years ago, and now, to use one of Gran's sayings, I had made my bed and would have to lie on it.

★

The following morning when James had left for work, Janet got Harold and Jessica ready and asked, 'You don't mind if I pinch him for a few hours, do you? I thought this would be a good opportunity for me to take him to see his uncles.'

'Of course I don't mind,' I assured her. 'Be as long as you like. I might get myself off into the centre to do a bit of shopping. It's been ages since I've treated myself.'

'Right you are.' She settled Jessica into the lovely coach-built Marmet pram that Hilda had chosen and trundled her through the hallway with Harold close behind her.

'Be good,' I warned Harold. With a cheeky grin he followed his gran into the lift and I listened to it descending to the ground floor before making my way back into the flat. I had a leisurely bath and had just got changed when I heard the lift doors open again and James appeared.

'You're looking very smart,' he commented as he eyed my blue suit appreciatively. 'Off somewhere nice, are you?'

'Actually, Janet has taken Jessica and Harold out for a few hours so I thought I might do a bit of shopping to pass the time. But what are you doing home? I thought you'd gone to work.'

'I had.' He smiled and his whole face was transformed. 'But as it happens I was owed a day off and I decided this might be a good time to take it. The sun is shining and it's far too nice to be cooped up in the shops, so how about we do a bit of sightseeing instead? They opened a new wing at the Tate Gallery in Albert Dock back in May. Have you been there yet?'

'Well . . . no, I haven't actually,' I heard myself say hesitantly. I could feel my face flaming, but then I thought, What harm could it do? It *was* a beautiful day and he was only offering to take me sightseeing after all, wasn't he?

'Are you quite sure I wouldn't be putting you out?' I asked, and now he threw his head back and laughed before saying, 'Do you know something, Maisie? You can be very annoying at times. If it were putting me out I wouldn't have offered to take you in the first place, would I? It just so happens that I've found myself with a bit of free time on my hands and I fancy a break from routine.'

'Then in that case I think it's a splendid idea,' I told him with an answering smile, and before I had time to change my mind he was walking me towards the door and we were on our way.

We spent a wonderful morning at the Tate Gallery and then James took me to a small French restaurant for lunch, where I had two glasses of wine and finally began to relax over a sumptuous meal.

'Right then.' We were out on the pavement again and he was looking up and down. 'What would you like to do now? Janet won't be home till teatime at least if I know her, so we may as well make the most of it. How about a cruise on the Thames in a riverboat? The weather is perfect for it, isn't it?'

'I suppose it is,' I giggled. After two glasses of wine I was up for anything. We walked along until we came to the banks of the Thames and then he led me down some steep steps to one of the pleasure cruisers that were moored there.

The river was calm and we sat on the top deck admiring the places of interest that we passed. When we reached the Tower of London we got off the boat and spent another pleasant hour wandering about taking in the sights. We were strolling along when an enormous man in shorts and a flowered shirt approached us. 'Would you mind taking a picture of me an' the wife together, honey?' he asked in a broad American accent.

As he pressed the camera into my hand I stuttered, 'Oh, I'd be pleased to but I'm afraid I'm not very good with these things. All my photographs tend to turn out without heads.'

'Then in that case, little lady, I'll get your husband here to do it, eh?' And he pressed the camera towards James as I felt myself blushing furiously.

James grinned from ear to ear and took the camera without a word, snapping the photograph of the plump American and his equally plump wife.

'Thank yer kindly.' The American slapped James on the back when he handed the camera back and shouted, 'You have a good day now, do'ya hear me, son? An' that little wife o' yours!'

Struggling to contain his laughter, James quickly took my arm and propelled me in the opposite direction.

'Well then, *Mrs Bainbridge*,' he teased. 'It appears we look like a couple.'

'Don't be ridiculous,' I snapped, more harshly than I had meant to. 'It was an easy mistake to make seeing that we're together.'

And it was then that he did something that totally took me by surprise, for as our eyes locked he lowered his head and gently kissed me on the lips, and I was so shocked that I allowed him to. When we finally drew apart my heart was hammering in my chest and I stared up at him open-mouthed.

His face too became serious for a time as he stared at me intently, and then he took my arm again and we went on our way, but strangely I suddenly felt sober now and just longed to get back to the flat.

Janet was there when we arrived and Harold ran to meet us with the most enormous water pistol I had ever seen. 'Look what me Uncle Rod bought me,' he gabbled excitedly. 'It can squirt for twenty feet.'

'That's wonderful, just so long as you don't go squirting it in here,' I told him.

The smile slid from his face as he asked, 'What's up, Mum?'

'Don't you mean what's *wrong*? And the answer to that is: nothing, young man. I'm just tired, that's all. Now haven't you got anything to do?'

Harold's face fell a foot and I instantly felt guilty as I flung my handbag on to a chair. Janet was watching me curiously, but she said not a word. Instead she just lifted Jessica from her crib and quietly left the room.

I decided that evening to go home the following day even though I had not intended to. The atmosphere seemed strangely tense between James and me now, and I longed to be back in my own house. I rang The Chimneys late, hoping to speak to Tommy, but although I let the phone ring a dozen times there was no answer. It was as I was going into my bedroom that Hamilton fell into step beside me.

I wonder where he is, then? he said sarcastically.

'Probably in bed by now I should think,' I flung over my shoulder at him as I brushed my hair before climbing into bed.

Mm . . . I wonder?

I found that I was chewing on my lip as I thought about his words. If Tommy wasn't in bed at this time, then where was he? As my hand traced my lips I remembered how it had felt when James kissed me, and I felt so guilty that I almost burst into tears.

You enjoyed it, didn't you? Hamilton's voice came from the darkness and I turned over so that my back was to him. I was just too tired tonight to listen to his ramblings.

'Of course I didn't. It was just the wine I drank at dinnertime that made it happen.'

Are you quite sure of that?

'Yes, of course I am. Now let me go to sleep, won't you? Can't you see that I'm tired?'

When there was no answer I turned my head and squinted

into the darkness, but I saw instantly that I was alone again. I screwed my eyes tight shut, but try as I might sleep eluded me, and it was the early hours of the morning before I finally drifted off with a vision of James and me sailing along the Thames floating in front of my eyes.

Chapter Twenty-One

'AW, DO WE *have* to go home today? Couldn't we stay for just *one* more night?' Harold pleaded at breakfast the next morning.

'Sorry, dear, but I'm afraid we do,' I told him firmly as I dabbed at my mouth with a napkin. 'Just think how Franky will be missing you. I bet he's been miserable stuck up at The Chimneys without you. And didn't you say that there was a fair coming down on the common this week?'

Harold looked slightly placated. 'I did,' he admitted grudgingly, but he looked much happier with the idea of going home all of a sudden. When he had finished his meal I sent him to his room to pack his small case while I stole a final cuddle with Jessica. Janet had bathed her and she smelled of soap and talcum powder. She really was a beautiful baby and once again I found myself envying James and wondering if he realised just how lucky he was to have her. Thankfully he had left for work before Harold and I got up and I felt curiously relieved that I had not had to say goodbye to him.

In no time at all we were packed and ready to go and a very tearful Janet accompanied us down to the foyer with Jessica in her arms.

'You give my love to your gran now,' she told me as she

sniffed loudly. 'I have to admit I miss the old bugg . . . the old dear.'

'Of course I will. Now you take care and I hope we'll see you again very soon. And take care of this little one for me, won't you?' As I spoke I was stroking Jessica's cheek and my heart was breaking at the thought of having to leave her again.

Janet gave me a resounding kiss on the cheek and then she was hugging Harold and there were tears in her voice as she told him, 'You just be a good boy now, d'yer hear me?'

'Yes, Gag.' He endured her kiss then sprinted away to the waiting taxi, leaving me to load our bags into the boot. And then we were waving madly through the back window until Janet and Jessica were lost to sight.

It was late afternoon when we stepped from the train in Newcastle. It had been an uneventful journey and now Harold was eager to be home.

'D'yer reckon Franky will still be there?' he asked as I steered him along the platform.

'There's a possibility, but if he's gone you'll see him tomorrow anyway.'

'Mm, I bet Sandy will be glad to see us.'

'Yes, dear, I'm sure he will.'

'I might go out on me bike for a bit when we get back.'

'Yes, dear.' Harold had chattered all the way back from London and now the sound was like white noise.

Twenty minutes later the taxi drew up at the steps leading to the front door of The Chimneys and Harold's face lit up when he saw Franky pedalling across the lawn towards us on his bike. He was out of the taxi and racing towards his friend before I could blink.

Smiling, I stepped out on to the drive and waited while the

taxi driver took our cases from the boot. I was surprised to see that Tommy's car was parked outside the garage, which meant that he must have finished work early for a change. Polly was obviously still here too, so after paying the driver I entered by the front door. The first thing I saw was Polly standing waiting for me with red-rimmed eyes.

'Oh Maisie, I'm so glad you're back. I've been beside meself all afternoon, which is why I phoned the mister to come home,' she greeted me.

As I dropped the cases on to the hall floor, Tommy appeared out of his study, and I saw at a glance that he seemed troubled too.

'What is it? What's wrong?' Every instinct I had was borne out when Tommy approached me and said, 'Now don't go getting yourself all into a lather. I'm sure it's nothing to worry about, but . . .'

'But *what*?'

'Well, it appears that Franky took Sandy out to play in the woods earlier this afternoon and he's run off.'

'What do you mean, he's run off? Sandy *never* offers to stray, and well you know it.' I could hear the fear in my voice as I suddenly remembered back to the time when Howard Stickle had kidnapped and tortured the poor creature when Nardy was alive. But of course he couldn't have anything to do with Sandy's disappearance this time. Howard Stickle was dead and buried, thank God!

'Look, I've just got home and I'm going out to look for him right now,' Tommy told me.

I shook my head as I tried to take it in. This certainly wasn't the homecoming I had expected.

'How long has he been missing?' I asked, addressing the question to Polly.

Wringing her hands together she stuttered, 'It . . . it must be goin' on for two hours now, lass.'

At that moment Franky and Harold ran into the hall and I saw at a glance that Franky must have told my son the news, because his face was anxious.

'Sandy's gone missin', Mum,' he said tearfully.

I forced a smile to my face. 'Yes, I know, dear. But he can't have gone far. Tommy is going out to look for him right now. Why don't you and Franky go with him? Three pairs of eyes are better than one and I've no doubt you'll find him playing in the woods somewhere.'

The two boys obediently followed Tommy outside, and turning to Polly I asked, 'You haven't noticed anyone hanging about, have you? Anyone that you didn't recognise?'

She chewed on her lip for a moment and stared off into space before saying, 'Now you come to mention it, I did think I saw someone yesterday teatime as I was gettin' ready to leave. I thought I glimpsed someone on the edge o' the lawn next to the woods through the hall window, but then when I got outside I thought I must have imagined it, 'cos there were no one in sight. I can't say as I've spotted anythin' out o' the ordinary today, though.'

As I wearily hung up my jacket, Polly grabbed my hand. Tears started to roll down her face and she sobbed, 'Eeh, I can't tell you how bad I feel about this. The first time you go off an' leave me on trust an' I go an' lose your bloody dog for you.'

'Don't cry, Polly. It isn't your fault,' I said, although I was feeling very close to tears myself. 'Sandy has been playing in those woods ever since we moved here and he's never gone off before. I'm sure Tommy will find him. Now how about a cup of tea while we're waiting? I'm gasping for one.'

She moved woodenly towards the kitchen, and I crossed to

the hall window just in time to see Tommy and the two boys disappear into the woods. It was then that I saw Hamilton come galloping up the drive. His tail was swishing and he looked agitated as he stopped at the bottom of the steps and began to paw at the ground. A cold finger snaked its way up my spine. I had been lucky to get Sandy back the last time he had gone missing, but would I be so lucky this time? I suddenly had a vision of Nardy on the day he had presented him to me and the way Sandy had leapt into my arms, licked my face and stolen my heart. And then when I had lost Nardy, Sandy had been there to share my loneliness and lick away my tears. Now I felt a great hole opening up inside me as I thought of what would happen if I didn't get him back. But no, I scolded myself as I stared out at Hamilton. He *will* come back . . . he has to. I lowered my head and swiped away the scalding tears that were burning my eyes, and when I again looked from the hall window I saw that Dusty was there with Hamilton too now, and he was looking at me, no, through me, and his eyes were great pools of sadness.

I turned and made for the kitchen, unable to look at them any longer, and then the long wait began.

It was dusk when Tommy and the boys returned and I saw instantly by their downcast faces that their search had been unsuccessful.

'We must have searched every inch of that blasted wood,' Tommy told me. 'But there isn't a sign of him. I can only think that he's skirted the trees and somehow got out on to the road. But don't worry, he can't have gone far, and there can't be that many pure white poodles about, can there? I've no doubt someone will be knocking on the door with him any time now.'

'But what if they don't?'

He gazed into my eyes for a moment before answering. 'They will. You have to believe that. Now come along, Polly, get yourself off home else your husband and sons will be sending a search party out for you too.'

She slowly walked into the hall, where, taking Franky's hand, she looked towards me to ask, 'Will you still want me here tomorrow?'

'Of course I will,' I assured her. 'This isn't your fault, Polly, so stop blaming yourself.'

She nodded and left without another word, and I found myself feeling sorry for her as I thought of how I would have felt had I been in her position. Harold meanwhile had collected Sandy's lead from the kitchen and was heading towards the door again.

'Harold, where are you going?' I asked, and as he turned to look at me I could see the misery in his eyes.

'I'm goin' to look for Sandy, o' course. We can't just leave him out there in the dark all night, can we?'

I took the lead gently from his hand and gave him a little push in the direction of the kitchen. 'You just go and get the dinner out of the oven that Polly has cooked for you and we'll see about looking for Sandy in the morning. We're not going to find him in the dark, are we?'

'Why not? He's white, ain't he? He'll show up in the dark,' he snapped with the logic of a child.

'Kitchen, young man, *now*!'

His shoulders sagged and he dragged himself off as if he had the weight of the world on his shoulders. Tommy took my elbow and propelled me towards the study.

'Maisie, I, er . . .'

'*What?*' I knew I must sound impatient, but I was so concerned about Sandy that I was finding it difficult to think of anything else.

'Well, I know this isn't perfect timing and I hate to ask you, but . . . Well, the thing is, I'm a little strapped for cash again and I wondered if you might see your way clear to giving me another loan?'

My mouth gaped open and my voice came out as a squeak. 'A . . . *another* one? How much do you need *this* time?'

Tommy looked terribly embarrassed as he lowered his eyes and muttered, 'Another ten thousand.'

'*Another ten thousand?*' I knew I must be sounding like a parrot but found I couldn't help myself.

'Just until—'

'Just until you get the yard up and running? Yes, I know, Tommy, that's what you told me the last time.'

His face now darkened as he said, 'Who else have I got to turn to if not my own wife? Surely you know I'll pay it back.'

'It isn't a matter of you paying it back.' I was weary now and too tired to get into an argument. 'The thing is, Tommy, I haven't got another ten thousand spare to give you.' I sighed before going on. 'I have money in the flat in London, but as you know that's tied. I also own this house. If you recall, I bought it outright. I then lent some money to you, and in case you hadn't noticed I'm the one who has been paying all the bills since we moved in here, so I'm afraid I just don't have that amount of money to give you until I sign my next contract, and that is still some months away. I suppose I could manage two, or even three thousand at a push if that would be any help?'

He lowered his head and with his hands thrust deep into his jacket pockets began to pace up and down, up and down until I began to feel dizzy and implored him, 'Oh for goodness' sake stand still, can't you?'

He stopped his pacing, and when he looked towards me the look he gave me caused me to grip my withered arm tight into my waist, for his eyes had a fearful, haunted look shining in them. Then he turned on his heel and left the room without so much as another word as a strange feeling of foreboding settled around me like a cloak.

It was now the early hours of the morning. I had retired to bed some while ago only to lie at Tommy's side tossing and turning. Every sound I heard I imagined was Sandy scratching at the outer door to get in, so eventually I had got up and now I was pacing from one downstairs room to another with a glass of whisky in my hand. I had never been a great one for spirits, but tonight I felt the need of something to help me through the dark hours till daylight came and I could resume the search for Sandy. All manner of terrible visions had flashed through my mind. Sandy lying at the side of the road, injured. Sandy floating in the water of the docks after falling in in the darkness. I knew I was torturing myself unnecessarily yet seemed unable to stop it. And so when the first light of dawn finally streaked the sky I sighed with relief and hurried upstairs to get into my clothes. I pulled on the nearest outfit that came to hand and then silently slipped out of the house with Sandy's lead gripped tight in my hand. Tommy and Harold were still fast asleep and no doubt would stay that way for some time to come, so I intended to search the woods by myself. It had been dusk the night before when Tommy and the boys had gone searching for him, and I hoped that I would find some sign of him that they had missed.

'Sandy . . . Sandy . . . come on, boy. Where are you?' My voice echoed eerily amongst the trees but all that answered me was the sound of the birds perched high in the branches as they welcomed the new day with their dawn chorus. The grass underfoot was heavy with dew and high overhead the sky was streaked with flashes of red as if the great hand of some unseen artist had painted them there. Yet another saying of Gran

Carter's suddenly sounded in my ears: Red sky at night, shepherds' delight, red sky in the morning, shepherds' warning. I was not really surprised. The heat had been unbearable for the last few days and I had a feeling we were in for a thunderstorm. Even now, so early in the morning, the atmosphere was humid and oppressive.

It took me an hour to scour the woods from one end to the other, but there was no sign of Sandy and eventually I gave up looking and turned back towards the house. I decided that as soon as it was a respectable hour I would phone the dogs' home to see if by any chance Sandy had been handed in there, and then once Polly arrived to keep her eye on Harold I would widen my search.

Tommy was up when I got home and entered the kitchen, but he barely looked in my direction. He had scarcely spoken since our conversation in the study the night before and appeared to be sulking. Let him, I thought sullenly. Finding Sandy was my main priority at that moment in time, and I was shocked to discover how empty the house felt without him. Normally I would only have to walk out of the front door and back in again and he would greet me as if I had been gone for a month. Now it felt as if a great big hole had opened up and I had lost one of my best friends.

'Er . . . about what we talked about last night,' Tommy now said as he paused at the door. 'Are you quite sure you couldn't manage more than three thousand?'

'I shall be stretching it at that,' I retorted, and he must have sensed that I was prickly because his tone softened when he said, 'Do you think you might be able to find time to get to the bank to draw it out for me today?'

'Wouldn't a cheque do?'

'Cash would be better.'

'Very well. I'm going into town this morning to enquire after Sandy. I'll have it for you by lunchtime.'

He looked at me long and hard for a second, as if there was something he wanted to say, but then he seemed to think better of it and swinging about he muttered, 'Good luck in your search.'

'Thank you.'

He had no sooner set foot out of the door when Hamilton appeared over by the sink with Begonia at his side. Begonia's eyes were sad as she stared at me, and I choked back the tears that had suddenly sprung to my eyes again. Begonia could always have that effect on me, for she had first appeared as Hamilton's bride when I married Nardy. But it was no good making myself even more depressed by thinking of that now. I had Sandy to worry about, so I smiled at her then slipped quietly up to my room to get changed into clothes more suitable for going into town in.

By the time Polly arrived I was ready to go. Harold was having his breakfast in the kitchen, and the second she set foot through the door she asked, 'Has there been any sign of him?'

When I sadly shook my head I saw her eyes well with tears and I realised then that beneath her brazen exterior beat a gentle heart. Franky shot past her to join his friend in the kitchen, and as I made for the front door I asked, 'You won't mind keeping your eye on Harold, will you? He's very subdued so he shouldn't give you any trouble. I want to check that no dogs have been taken in at the vet's and put some missing posters up in the shop windows. I have to go to the bank too but I'll be home for lunchtime at the latest.'

'You be as long as you like, ma'am.'

She was quiet today, nothing like the loud individual I had

grown accustomed to. And suddenly I was ma'am, whereas before she had always called me by my Christian name.

'Look . . .' I found myself feeling sorry for her. 'Don't whip yourself over Sandy going missing, Polly. He's always gone out with the boys and never run off before. It's just one of those things. I'm sure he'll turn up.'

Even as the words were uttered, I wasn't quite sure if I was trying to reassure her or myself. But what I was sure of was that the alternative just didn't bear thinking about.

Chapter Twenty-Two

W HEN I REACHED the town I went into every shop I
passed and asked them if they would put the cards
I had typed out the night before in their windows.
The shop owners were all very obliging, and with that job done
I then made my way to the vet's. I had attended this particular
practice a number of times since moving back to Fellburn, and
when I entered, the receptionist, who looked as if she was a
hundred if she was a day, smiled widely, saying, 'Why, hello, Mrs
Balfour.' She now glanced down at the floor to my side. 'And
where's our bonny lad today then?' Mrs Trip had taken a great
fancy to Sandy the very first day I had taken him there and
always made a great fuss of him.

'I'm afraid he isn't with me.' I took a great gulp of air and
forced myself to go on as I noticed the other animals waiting
with their owners to go in to see the vet. 'Sandy went missing
late yesterday afternoon and I called in the hope that you might
have heard of someone who may have found him.'

Her face solemn now, she slowly shook her head. 'I'm so
sorry, my dear, I'm afraid I haven't, though most of the dogs that
go missing hereabouts usually end up here. Or the police
station, that is . . . Have you tried there?'

'No . . . no, I haven't, but thank you. I'll go there next.'

'Goodbye then, my dear . . . and good luck.'

All the way down the street I was cursing myself. The police station – why hadn't I tried there first? Of course, Mrs Trip was quite right, anyone finding a dog would take it there until the dog warden came to collect it and take it to the dog pound. I hurried down Gower Street and along Avenue Road until I came to the police station. Once at the desk, I breathlessly asked a young constable, 'Have you had any stray dogs brought in since yesterday afternoon? A poodle about so high.' I held my hand to Sandy's height whilst gabbling on. 'He's pure white, very recognisable and very friendly.'

'Would you wait there, ma'am?' He left the desk and disappeared through a door behind him, and as I waited for him to return I impatiently strummed my fingers on the counter.

Within minutes he was back and I swallowed my disappointment as he told me, 'I'm sorry, ma'am, but no. There have been no dogs brought in since last Tuesday. But if you'd care to leave your name and address I'll be sure to get in touch if he does turn up.'

I wearily gave him what he asked for and after thanking him I slowly walked outside into the sunshine. It was unbearably hot and humid although I noticed that great black clouds were rolling in. I looked first one way then another, completely at a loss now as to where to try next. And then I decided that as I was so close I may as well go to the bank to get the money for Tommy before looking anywhere else. My journey took me past the docks, and as I was passing I saw a crowd assembled. They were all shouting as they stood on the edge of the quay, gesticulating at something in the water, though I couldn't hear what they were saying as I was some distance away. I was about to move on when suddenly Hamilton sprang up in front of me almost directly in my path. He was clearly distressed about something and waving his front hoof in the direction of the crowd as he reared on his hind legs.

I frowned as I asked him, 'What's wrong, Hamilton?' And then suddenly it hit me and I knew the answer to my question. 'It's Sandy, isn't it?'

He dropped down back on to all four legs as a solitary tear slid from his eye to run in a perfectly straight line down the length of his magnificent nose. And then I was running, and as I approached the crowd I heard someone shouting, '*What is it, what is it?*' and I realised with a little shock that it was me. I elbowed my way through the onlookers until I came to the edge of the quay, and as I looked down into the swirling waters I saw that a man with a long boat hook was fishing for something in the water. For a while it was impossible to see what it was, for the water was filthy and covered in floating debris, but then he managed to pull his catch to the side and two men immediately dropped on to their bellies and reaching down clutched at something just below the surface and hauled it up on to the cobblestones. My breath was coming in great gasping sighs as I shook my head from side to side in shocked disbelief. It was my Sandy, but not as I had known him. Instead of being pure white, this poor creature was a dirty mud colour and his beautiful intelligent eyes were dull and glazed. Almost before I knew it I had dropped to my knees and was cradling his poor broken body to me as the men bowed their heads in dismay. And then I heard a long wail that echoed across the water and sounded above the noise of the seagulls: '*Noooooooooo . . . !*' And again I realised that the sound had issued from me. Now one of the men had come forward and wringing his cap in his hands said, 'Eeh, come away, hinny. There's nothin' you can be doin' for that poor soul now.'

I remember staring up at him and then nothing more, for a

comforting darkness was creeping towards me and I welcomed it.

'That's it; I think she's coming round.' The voice was a long way away and I didn't want to hear it. It was safe and without pain here in the darkness, but the light was getting brighter despite my efforts to ignore it, and now as I blinked my eyes open I found myself looking up into Mike's hairy face.

'Feelin' better, lass?'

I slowly came to realise that I was lying on the settee in my living room. Gran was there behind Mike's shoulder, her eyes red-rimmed from crying, and Polly was there too, cuddling Harold into the side of her.

'*Wh . . . at?*'

'Ssh now, just lie still. You've had a nasty shock but it will all come back to you in a minute, more's the pity.' This was from Mike again, and just as he had said it suddenly everything did come flooding back and I jerked as I tried to rise. His great hand pressed me back on to the pillows as he barked at Gran, 'Fetch her some brandy, would you? And make it a big one.'

'Aye, lad, straight away.' She almost ran to the decanter to do as she was told, and I saw that her hand was shaking as I muttered brokenly, '*Sandy . . .*'

Mike pursed his lips and his great bushy eyebrows drew together in a frown. 'It was a tragic accident, Maisie, nothing more. Sandy must have got lost and fallen into the water in the dark.'

My head shook from side to side in denial of what he had said. 'Sandy wasn't fond of water. He would have kept his distance. Someone must have thrown him in.'

'Now, now, we'll have none of that talk. Ask yourself, pet, who would do such a thing?'

He pressed the glass to my lips and as I felt the liquid burning its way down my throat I began to cough and feebly tried to push it away. Mike held my head firmly, not releasing his grip until I had drained the glass, and then he said, 'There now, that's better, isn't it? Better than a needle at any rate. Do you think you could sit up now?'

I nodded slowly as he helped me up on to the pillows and gazed around at the people standing about me. They were all crying, with the exception of Mike.

'H . . . how did I get home?' I managed to ask, and again it was Mike who spoke. 'Luckily one of the dock workers knows Georgie, and he recognised you, so he sent round for him and Georgie fetched you home. He's out in the garden now digging a hole for . . .'

I gulped deep in my throat before asking, 'Where is Sandy now?'

'He's out the back, lass. But I wouldn't go out there if I were you. George will do what needs to be done.'

'I want to see him.' Something about the set of my face must have told him that I meant to, for his shoulders sagged as he said wearily, 'As you will, Maisie. Do you want me to come with you?'

'No . . . I think I'd like to be alone with him if you don't mind.'

Mike helped me to my feet and I walked unsteadily towards the door and on towards the back garden. Once in the kitchen doorway I saw George at a distance digging beneath a large oak tree. And then my eyes fell to a blanket that was laid neatly on the steps leading up to the door and I knew that this contained the body of my beloved friend.

Tentatively I bent and drew the blanket back and there he was, still so very precious and dear to me. In my mind's eye I saw him again on the day that Nardy had presented him to me and I felt my heart break all over again, for it was as if I was losing yet another part of Nardy as well as a much-loved pet. It was then that the first clap of thunder sounded overhead, and within seconds the heavens had opened. I sat there drenched to the skin as I held Sandy's lifeless body to me. Eventually George laid down the spade and crossed the lawn, lifting the dog from my arms as if he weighed no more than a feather.

'Let me do the rest, hinny.' His voice was soft and threaded with sadness. 'You get yourself away in now out o' the weather, eh, an' get Ma to make you a nice strong brew.' As he strode away, I lowered my head and sobbed as I had not sobbed since the day I had lost Nardy.

Tommy breezed in at lunchtime. Mike and Gran and her crew had left by then and I was sitting in my study staring off into space. Through the open window I could see Harold and Franky mooching about the garden with dejected looks on their faces. Even Harold's prized bicycle held no charms for the boys today. I could hear Polly working about the house, but there was no singing. The whole household seemed to be feeling Sandy's loss. I had been trying unsuccessfully for the last hour to lose myself in my writing, but today there were no words there to spill out of me and the sheet of paper I had inserted into my typewriter was still blank.

'So.' Tommy paused in the doorway. 'Why has everyone got such long faces? I saw Harold and Franky on my way in and they looked like a wet weekend.'

'Sandy is dead,' I told him bluntly. 'Some dock workers pulled him out of the water earlier this morning. George has been up here and buried him for me.'

'Oh . . . I see.' Tommy sighed deeply. 'I'm sorry to hear that. What a tragic accident to happen.'

'It *wasn't* an accident, I'd stake my life on it!' I shouted and swivelled around in my chair. 'You know as well as I do that Sandy hated the water. He even hated getting his feet wet when I took him down on to the beach. He would *never* have gone near the quay.'

'Now Maisie, try to be reasonable. I realise that you're upset, but think about it. He went missing yesterday. He probably wandered too close to the edge and went over accidentally.'

'*No!*' I shook my head vehemently. 'There's something not right here, I tell you. First the flood and now *this* . . . I think someone has got a vendetta against us.'

'Ah, now I detect an author's imagination at work, dear!'

My eyes were flashing as I stood to face him. 'Think what you like,' I retorted. 'But I'm going to report this to the police. Sandy would never have gone off on his own in the first place. Someone must have taken him and thrown him over the edge of the quay when it was dark.'

'Nonsense! I think you're getting this all out of perspective. What do you think the police would say if you tried to talk to them about it? They'd think you'd lost your marbles, and if you don't calm yourself you might do just that.'

My shoulders suddenly sagged as the anger seeped out of me to be replaced by utter despair. Deep down I knew that he was right, but I was hurting so much that I needed something or someone to lash out at. As the tears squeezed from the corners of my eyes and ran down my cheeks in rivers, Tommy crossed to me and gently pressed me back into my chair. His voice was gentle as he said, 'That's it; let it all out. You'll feel better after you've had a good cry. I'll go and get Polly to make you a nice hot cup of sweet tea.'

'You sound just like Gran,' I sniffed. 'She thinks a cup of tea is the cure for all ills too, but I swear if I drink another drop of the damned stuff I shall drown in it.'

Tommy hovered uncertainly for a time and then tentatively said, 'Look, I know this isn't the best time to ask, but did you manage to get to the bank for the money this morning?'

It had completely gone out of my head and I chewed on my lip now as I looked up at him apologetically. 'I'm so sorry; I was actually on my way there when I saw the commotion going on at the docks. That's when I found . . .' My voice trailed away as Tommy frowned crossly.

'Well, how about you come back into town with me now in the car? You could pop into the bank and get it for me while I wait outside?'

My head wagged from side to side. 'I can hardly go anywhere looking like this, can I? Couldn't it wait until tomorrow?' I had always envied the film stars on television who managed to still look attractive and vulnerable when they cried, never more so than now when I caught sight of myself in the mirror. I looked an absolute mess. My eyes were red-rimmed and swollen and my hair was all over the place after being caught in the downpour earlier on. Gran Carter had once told me that I was as plain as a pikestaff. Well she had never been more right than at this very moment.

Tommy's face had darkened and I saw that he was deeply annoyed. Normally it would have concerned me, but right now it was the least of my worries and I was determined to stand my ground.

'I'll go and get the money out for you tomorrow,' I said quietly. I turned back to my desk, and seconds later I heard the study door slam none too gently behind him. It was then that I realised he had shown no sorrow whatsoever about Sandy's untimely death. He had been more concerned about his damn money! I shook myself mentally. There I went again, cursing, and yet I would jump down Harold's throat when he did the same. It was then that my eyes settled on the basket to the side of my desk. There was a warm blanket inside it and Sandy had loved to lie there, keeping me company when I was working. It struck me afresh that he would never do that again. He would never leap into my arms and cover my face with his warm, wet tongue. Never again would I come out of the bathroom to find my loyal friend waiting for me on the landing with his tail flicking from side to side, or waken in the morning to find he had snuck into my bed during the night and cuddled his warm body into mine. Lowering my head on to my withered arm, I sobbed afresh just as I had done so many years ago when I had lost Bill, my lovely old bull-terrier.

It was late in the afternoon when a tap came on the study door and Polly poked her head into the room. 'Sorry to disturb you, but I'm about ready for the off. Is there anythin' I can get you afore I go?'

'No, no there isn't, Polly, but thanks.'

Still she hovered as if there was something more she wanted to say, and when I raised an eyebrow she stepped into the room and said nervously, 'I were wonderin' . . . You were goin' to take the lads down to the fair on the common tonight if you remember . . . O' course I realise you won't be feelin' up to it now, so I were wonderin' if you'd mind me takin' young Harold home wi' me? I could take 'em round to the fair for an hour after dinner tonight an' then he could stay the night at my place wi' Franky an' I could bring him home in the mornin'. I just thought it might help take his mind off . . . you know?'

'Oh!' I blinked. I had completely forgotten about the

proposed plans for the evening. But then as I thought of Polly's offer I saw that it made sense. Harold was upset enough without having to miss his treat.

'I'd take good care o' him,' she assured me hastily as she saw me considering her idea.

I forced a smile. 'That would be really kind of you, Polly. And of course I trust you implicitly. But let me get you some money. These fairs can be costly places. No doubt the boys will want to go on every ride they come to and I don't want you to be out of pocket.' After rummaging about in my handbag I pressed a five-pound note into her hand and told her, 'Do let me treat Franky too, please.'

'But . . . this is too much!'

'Rubbish! Just make sure they enjoy themselves. Do you want me to come and get an overnight bag ready for him?'

She shook her head, 'Heavens, no. We're quite capable o' doin' that ourselves. Now are you quite sure there's nothing else you want afore I go?'

'Nothing,' I assured her.

Ten minutes later I went out into the hall to say goodbye to Harold, who was looking very tearful.

'Now you have a good time,' I told him as I cuddled his sturdy little body to mine. 'And when you come home in the morning you can tell me all about it, can't you?'

He nodded miserably as I kissed him soundly and pressed him towards the front door. There he suddenly paused and running back to me wrapped his warm arms about my neck and muttered, 'I love you, Mum.'

Deeply touched, I hugged him back and whispered, 'I love you too, dear. More than you can know.' I then released him, and taking Polly's hand he walked away.

I decided that once I had pulled myself together a little I

would use the time to collect all Sandy's things from about the house. It was just too painful to see them everywhere I looked. I watched Harold haring off down the drive on his bicycle with Franky running behind and Polly trying to keep up with them, and as I closed the door behind them I thought, Things are just about as bad as they can be.

Chapter Twenty-Three

GRAN CALLED LATER that evening and I was glad to see her. Once again Tommy was late home from work and the house felt empty.

'How you feelin' now, hinny?' she asked sympathetically.

I shrugged. It had seemed a rather silly question for her to ask under the circumstances.

She followed me into the lounge, and once she was seated with a large glass of sherry in her hand she told me, 'What's happened to Sandy is awful, but don't go thinkin' you're the only one wi' troubles. Our Georgie an' Mary have got their share too. It's young Betty. That weird lad she's been seein', the one they call the Sand Dancer, has dumped her, just like that.' She snapped her fingers and shook her head. 'But not afore he'd drained her post office savin's an' her bank book dry. An' that ain't the worst of it: he's left her wi' her belly full an' all. I reckon if our Georgie could get his hands on him he'd tear him limb from limb, but he's done a runner. The little sod. Probably scarpered back to South Shields where he comes from, an' all I can say is good riddance to bad rubbish, though our Betty ain't sayin' that. The poor lass is heartbroken. Eeh, I just wonder how she's goin' to manage?'

'Are you quite sure he's disappeared?' I asked after I had got

255

over the initial shock of what she'd told me. 'Only he works for Tommy down at the yard and Tommy hasn't mentioned that he's gone missing.'

'He only left yesterday by all accounts, so happen Tommy wouldn't have missed him till today an' then he'd probably have thought the lad were just pinchin' a day off. I would have told you earlier on but your thoughts were . . .' As Gran took a long swallow of her drink and looked away, I frowned. Poor Betty. How she must be hurting. And yet I found myself envying her. At least when she had her child she would have something of the man she had loved to remember him by. If only I could have been so lucky with Nardy . . . I forced my thoughts away from the path they were taking. What was I thinking of? Betty was little more than a child and from now on she would need all the support she could get. Luckily people nowadays were far more accepting of girls who gave birth to children out of wedlock and I supposed that was something to be thankful for at least. She also had the bonus of a loving family behind her, which was another blessing. She would survive, I had no doubt.

'So.' Gran changed the subject. 'Where's Tommy, then?'

'He's not in from work yet,' I told her dully. It was such a regular occurrence that it no longer bothered me.

'An' where's his Lordship?'

'He's gone to stay with Polly for the night. I'd promised to take him and Franky down to the fair but I wasn't feeling up to it, so when Polly offered to take them I thought it was a better option than disappointing him.'

'I see.' Gran sniffed disapprovingly. 'Do you think that was wise? I mean, you hardly know the woman, do you? An' she's not exactly out o' the top drawer, is she?'

'Oh Gran!' I said in exasperation. She could be such a snob

at times. 'In case you'd forgotten, I was born within a stone's throw of Bog's End myself. And Polly has a heart as big as a bucket despite her brash exterior.'

'That's as maybe.' She took another swallow of her drink. 'But it's a bit of a contradiction, ain't it? I mean, sendin' him off to a private school that costs an arm an' a leg each term an' then lettin' him mix wi' the rougher element o' the town.'

Again I said, 'Oh Gran,' and then we lapsed into silence for a while as I stared out of the window to Sandy's burial place. I was just too weary and heartsore to argue with her tonight.

She stayed for another hour, during which time she got through half a bottle of sherry. When she finally rose to leave she seemed slightly unsteady on her feet. 'Shall I give Georgie a ring?' I offered. 'I'm sure he'd come and fetch you and save you the walk home.'

'No, lass. Thanks all the same, but he's got enough on his plate at the minute with our Betty wi'out havin' to worry about me. 'Sides, the fresh air will do me good, providin' I don't go arse over tit.'

Despite how I was feeling, I had to stifle a smile as I followed her to the door. For as far back as I could remember Gran had been there for me and I could not envisage a time when I would ever be without her. But then I had thought that of Sandy too, and now he was gone . . .

She kissed me on the cheek as I opened the front door for her and I watched in amusement as she tottered down the steps clutching her voluminous handbag in front of her.

'Bye, lass.'

'Bye, Gran.'

I waited until she had gone some way down the drive before closing the door. As I turned back into the house, the loneliness hit me like a smack in the face and I experienced feelings I had not felt since losing Nardy. Determined not to give in to them, I set to and began to collect all Sandy's things together. It took me an hour, for there seemed to be something of his in every room, a toy here, a cushion there, a basket here. At last it was done, and I carried them all outside and deposited them at the back of the garage. I would take them all to the stray dogs' home eventually . . . but not yet. The pain was still too raw to part with them for now.

Some time later I had a leisurely bath. I had given up trying to work earlier in the day. For now my inspiration seemed to have fled. Then I warmed myself a glass of milk and retired to bed. If Tommy wanted something to eat he could get it himself when he finally decided to come home. I certainly wasn't in the mood to pander to him after his thoughtless performance earlier in the day.

After a time I must have dropped into a troubled doze, where I found myself trapped in a nightmare. It was a beautiful day and I was walking Sandy through the woods. Harold was there too and so was Dusty, who seemed greatly agitated for some reason. And then I was on the docks, staring down into the dirty swirling water as the men tried to hook my beloved pet out of the water with a boathook. But it wasn't Sandy they were pulling out; it was Harold. He was limp and lifeless and Dusty was leaping about, more energetic than I had ever before seen him. Then I became aware of a sound coming from a long way away and I was struggling through a deep fog to come back to wakefulness. I started as my eyes snapped open, still caught in the grip of the terrible nightmare. My cheeks were wet with tears and I was shocked to discover that my nightdress was clinging to me with cold sweat. I lay there trying to determine where the sound was coming from and suddenly it dawned on me what it was. The phone was ringing down in the hall. A quick glance to the side of me showed that Tommy was still not home, unless he had chosen to sleep in the spare room again, that was. I slung my shaking legs out of the bed and hurried towards the door. Dusty was standing in the shadows, crying, but I was too intent on answering the phone to bother with him now. I sped past him, and all the while my heart was hammering. Who would be ringing at this time of night? Unless it was someone to tell me that something was wrong.

When I reached the hall, I fumbled for the light switch before snatching up the phone. Instantly I heard Polly babbling almost incoherently on the other end.

'Oh, ma'am . . . I'm *so* sorry. I *swear* it weren't my fault . . .'

'Polly, is that you? What isn't your fault? Calm down and tell me what's happened.'

I heard her take a great gulp of air before saying, 'It's Harold . . . I've lost him.'

'What do you mean, you've *lost* him? You can't *lose* a child.' I could feel hysteria creeping up on me and had to force myself not to give in to it.

'We were at the fair an' the lads were havin' a grand old time of it,' she gabbled on. 'An' then Harold went into the Haunted House an' he didn't come out!'

'What do you mean, he didn't come out? Where did he go?'

'I don't know.' She was crying now, I could hear it in her voice.

'Where are you now?' I asked abruptly.

'I'm back at my house. Me lads are all out lookin' for him even as we speak.'

'Right, tell me your address. I shall be there in no time.'

She gave me her address and I slammed the phone down on her, then tore back up the stairs to get dressed. I grabbed the nearest clothes that came to hand, heedless of how I looked, and then I was running down the stairs and out of the house, leaving the front door swinging open behind me.

I vaguely remember noticing that I was wearing odd shoes as I pounded down Brampton Hill, and the strange looks I was attracting. I didn't care. All I knew was that I must find Harold at all costs. He was my main reason for living. And all the while Dusty was galloping along beside me, and I could see that he was just as distressed as I was.

I found Polly's house easily. It was in a row of back-to-backs in Bog's End. Each house looked the same, with only the curtains at the windows to distinguish one from another, and I realised with a little start how privileged I was to be living where I was. The smell of the docks hung heavy on the air here; a curious, cloying odour of oil and rotting fish. The pavements that the front doors opened directly on to were dirty and unswept, and rubbish was blowing along the gutters. I pounded on the door with my fists and within seconds it was opened by Polly, who was wearing a vivid orange two-piece suit that clashed horrendously with her bright ginger hair. The shoulder pads on it were so large that they gave her the appearance of an all-in wrestler, but then as I had discovered very early on in our relationship, Polly was never going to win any prizes for dressing. It was her face that struck me the most, though. It had the customary layer of make-up that always looked as if it had been applied with a trowel, but tonight her mascara was streaked down her cheeks and her eye shadow was smudged up into her eyebrows. Even so, it did nothing to disguise how pale she was. Before I could say a word, she had grabbed my elbow and yanked me into the front room, which I noticed was surprisingly neat and tidy.

'Right . . .' I struggled to get my breath back. My lungs felt as if they were on fire but I was heedless to my own discomfort. 'Now tell me exactly what's happened.'

Polly wrung her hands distractedly as fresh tears spurted from her eyes. 'Well, we was at the fair, as you know, an' the lads were havin' a whale of a time. They'd been on just about every ride there when Harold tells us he wants to go into the Haunted House. I told him he wouldn't like it an' it would likely give him nightmares, but you know what a determined little bugg . . . chap he can be when he gets his mind fixed on sommat, so I told him all right, but you goes in on your own 'cos I ain't settin' foot in there. Our Franky didn't fancy it neither, see? Anyway, in he goes an' me an' Franky waited outside for him, an' waited . . . an' waited. After about twenty minutes or so I approached the chap on the door an' asks him how long does it usually take for people to walk round it? When he told me ten minutes or so I started to get worried an' asked him if he'd go in' an' have a look round for Harold. So off he goes an' after a while he comes back an' says he can't see hide nor hair of him. It were then I started to get worried an' I kicked up such a rumpus that in the end he puts all the lights on inside an' him an' another bloke go back in to have another look. But when they come back out again they both said he definitely weren't in there.'

'Are you sure that there was only the one entrance?'

'I asked that straight off, an' it appears that you could get into it from the other side, so off me an' Frankie goes thinkin' that Harold were probably waitin' for us round the other side. But . . . he weren't,' she finished lamely.

'So where is he then?' I could hear the panic in my voice and

Polly must have heard it too, because now she started to cry once more.

'Me lads are all out right now,' she told me again. 'They've been gone for over an hour so they should be back soon. He couldn't have gone far, could he?'

'Have you phoned the police?'

Her head wagged from side to side. 'Not yet. I thought I'd better phone you first an' see if the lads could find him. The fair will be all shut down now an' everyone will have gone home, so it should make it easier to spot him if he's just got lost.'

'He wouldn't have got lost,' I told her with an edge to my voice. 'Harold walks past the common every day on his way to school. Even if he couldn't have found you he would have known his way back home.' I suddenly felt sick and dizzy and had to quickly sit down on the nearest chair for fear of falling. And what I was thinking was, Sandy went missing and look what happened to him!

Seconds later the front door was pushed open and two strapping young men who looked remarkably like Polly stepped into the room.

'Not a sign of him, Ma,' the taller of the two told her as he nodded towards me. 'We've covered every inch o' the common as far back as the docks but not so much as a sniff of him.'

'I reckon it's time we called the coppers,' the other one now piped up. Polly looked towards me as if for permission, and when I nodded she went at a run into the next room and I heard her babbling down the phone.

A police car screeched to a halt some ten minutes later and Polly admitted two young officers who respectfully removed their helmets as they stepped into the room.

Everyone seemed to be talking at once until one of the policemen raised his hand and said, 'Whoa, one at a time please.' His colleague took out a notebook and pen and Polly told him what she had told me as they both looked on with solemn faces. 'An' there's another strange thing,' she added. 'When me an' Franky got back from the fair, someone had stolen Harold's bike from the back yard. It might be nothin' to do wi' Harold goin' missin', o' course, but it's funny that it should happen on the same evenin', ain't it?'

The policeman nodded.

'And you are the child's mother?' he asked, training his eyes on me when Polly ran to an abrupt stop.

I nodded numbly. Surely I was still at home in bed in the grip of a nightmare? I would wake up in a minute and the events of the last two days would have been nothing more than a bad dream. I screwed my eyes up tight, willing it to be so, but when I opened them again I was still in Polly's small front room and Harold was still unbelievably missing.

The police began to question us. If I was Harold's mother, why had he been at the fair with Polly? How old was he? What colour hair did he have? How tall was he? Did he have a tendency to run off? On and on they went as Polly and I answered them as best we could.

Lastly he asked, 'This bicycle of Harold's: does it have anything unusual about it that we might look out for?'

'It's very colourful,' I answered. 'The mudguards are bright yellow and I bought him a red bell to go on it. The bell is quite distinctive. What I mean is, I've never seen another like it.'

Eventually the young policeman snapped his notebook shut while the other one looked at his watch. 'According to what you've told me, the youngster has been gone for over two hours now, so I think it's time we got a missing child report out to all units. We'll also get them to keep their eyes open for the bicycle. It might be that Harold came back here and went for a ride on it.'

My eyes felt as if they were full of grit as I nodded in reply. His face softening now, he told me, 'Try not to worry too much, Mrs Balfour. Most children that go missing turn up within hours. I've no doubt he's safe and sound somewhere and just lost track of time. Is there anyone you'd like us to contact to come and wait with you while we search for him?'

'M . . . my husband. H . . . he owns the scrap yard down by the docks. He must be working late.' Was it me, or did I imagine a strange look pass between the officers? I thought it must be me, for when he looked back at me the young man's face was straight.

'We'll get someone there straight away to tell him what's happened. Meantime, will you be waiting here?'

'Yes, she will,' Polly answered. 'I ain't lettin' her go back to sit in an empty house while all this is goin' on.'

'Very well, we'll be in touch shortly, and try not to worry.'

I inclined my head, and then they were gone and Polly snapped, 'Elvis, go an' put that kettle on, would you? An' you, Engelbert, go on up an' check if your dad's all right.'

Under any other circumstances I would have been rolling about with laughter at Polly's choice of names for her sons, but at this moment in time nothing in the world could have forced a smile out of me, except seeing Harold stroll in safe and sound.

The two boys, who seemed to be remarkably well mannered, hurried away to do as they were told, and Polly and I settled down to wait for news.

The policemen returned almost an hour later to inform me

that they had gone to the scrap yard to find it in darkness and securely locked up for the night.

'Do you have any idea where else we might find your husband?' one of them asked.

As I shook my head wearily, Hamilton suddenly peered over the policeman's shoulder. Tell him to try the casino in Newcastle, he said.

Choking back a sob, I lowered my head, and the young man turned away, saying, 'We've got every police car in the entire area looking for him, but we have to shoot off now. There's been a report of an explosion in one of the houses on Brampton Hill we have to investigate.'

'*Brampton Hill?*' My head snapped up again as I bounced out of my seat, and without thinking I grabbed hold of his arm. '*Which* house, do you know the address?'

'I believe it is called The Chimneys. Why do you ask?'

Everything was swimming in front of my eyes as I murmured, 'The Chimneys is *my* house! What the hell is happening?'

'Oh, I see . . . In that case you'd better come with us and see what the damage is.'

Polly's hand was tight across her mouth as she followed us to the door, where she dragged me into her arms before saying, 'It will no doubt have been caused by a gas leak or some such. Bye . . . for it to happen on this night of all nights, eh? But don't worry, hinny. If the damage is too bad we can always find you a bed here.'

I followed the policemen out to their car, where they bundled me into the back. It was very late now and pitch dark, but even so I was aware of net curtains up and down the street twitching as we roared past them. I sank back against the seat wondering what else life had in store for me, for at that moment

I felt that things were just about as bad as they could get. It was then that another saying of Gran's sprang into my mind and I had to fight the urge to laugh aloud. Things allus happen in threes! Well, she had certainly got it right this time!

Chapter Twenty-Four

WHEN THE POLICE car drew to a halt outside the house, I stared in disbelief through the window. There were two fire engines there and numerous firemen with their hoses trained towards the upper floor. Where the roof had been was a great gaping hole with flames licking through it. Suddenly my mind raced back in time and I was in my house down in Fellburn with Nardy on the night that Howard Stickle had tried to burn me to death. *No, no!* my mind was screaming. Even he could have nothing to do with this from beyond the grave. But then who could have done it? There were too many bad things happening all at once for it to be coincidental. First Sandy dying, then Harold going missing, and now this!

I tumbled out of the back seat on to the drive and grabbed the arm of the nearest fireman.

'What's happened?' I gabbled, and something about the set of my face must have made him realise that this was my house, for he instantly told me, 'We're not rightly sure yet, ma'am. We'll know more when we've put the fire out and we can get inside for a look around.'

My mouth gaped open in shock. This was becoming more incredible than anything I might have written in my novels.

'H . . . how much damage is there?'

He sighed before answering. 'It looks like it's extensive, I'm afraid. Just thank God you weren't in there when it started, because I'm telling you now, had you been, you might not be standing here now. The police are here – one of them is coming to talk to you now.'

Even as he spoke, a policeman took me by the arm and asked, 'Mrs Balfour?'

'Yes.' I was so shocked that I could barely speak, yet strangely I found that what had happened here was nothing compared to Harold being missing. A house was just bricks and mortar and could be rebuilt, whereas a child was irreplaceable. And still there was no sign of Tommy and I was screaming inside, *Where are you when I need you?*

'Let's get you down to the station, eh? We can't talk here.' I nodded as the policeman led me unresisting towards a nearby police car, and seconds later we were driving down Brampton Hill as visions of my home collapsing flashed in front of my eyes.

It was now almost dawn. I had answered so many questions that my mind had shut off. They had allowed me to rest in one of the offices while I waited for Tommy to arrive, but it was not my husband who came to rescue me but Mike.

When he walked into the small confined room and held his arms out to me I flew into them without a word and buried my face against his great chest.

'There, there.' He soothingly rocked me back and forth as if I was a child. 'I can't leave you alone for a minute without you getting yourself into bother, now can I? What am I going to do with you, eh?'

'Oh Mike, Harold is missing and the house . . .'

'Ssh, I know all about it. But now come on; let's get you away from here, eh? Would you like to come back home with me?'

'I . . .' I had to compose myself before I could reply shakily, 'I think I'd like to go to Gran's if you don't mind. Tommy will go there when he finds out what's happened.'

'Mm, well if he'd come home when he should have he'd have known already.' His voice was heavy with disapproval, but when my face fell yet further he said hastily, 'Sorry. I shouldn't have said that, but you know me by now. Come on; let's get you away from here.'

We walked out of there arm in arm and soon we were standing on Gran's doorstep shivering in the early morning breeze that blew in from the Tyne. I had expected her to still be in bed but she answered the door on the first knock fully clothed saying, 'Come on in, hinny. I've been waitin' for you.'

'How did you know?'

'Huh!' She tossed her head. 'You should know by now what the jungle drums are like hereabouts. You can barely use the lav wi'out everyone knowin'.'

She soon had us seated with steaming mugs of tea in front of us. 'Do the police know you're here, pet?'

'Yes, I made sure they had your address,' Mike answered for me. 'They'll bring you any news on Harold or the house as soon as they have it.'

Gran clucked and shook her head. 'Eeh, that poor little bairn. What do you think has happened to him?'

Mike threw her a warning glance, and she flushed as he said overly loudly, 'The lad will be fine, you'll see. We *have* to stay positive. Positive thinking is a great thing to my mind.'

'Yes, yes, o' course it is.' Her head wagged up and down in agreement. 'I've no doubt he'll walk through that door any time now as if nothin' had happened. But for now, lass, don't you think you ought to go up an' have a lie-down? I bet you've been up all night, ain't you?'

I nodded. Strangely, the tears had dried up and I felt strangely calm, as if I was in a place where no one could reach me.

'Before you do anything, I think I ought to give you a little injection,' Mike said as he watched me thoughtfully. 'I reckon you're in shock, Maisie, and I could give you something to help it.'

'I don't want anything,' I told him dully. There was this huge pain in my chest that seemed to be growing by the minute.

'Then at least do as your gran says and go an' have a lie-down. She'll be here should there be any news an' she'll fetch you in a jiffy.'

I think I surprised them when I rose from my chair and did as I was told without argument. If they had only known it, it was because there was a longing in me to be alone. To be somewhere quiet where I could try to put my thoughts into some sort of order. I went into the spare room and lay down, but I didn't sleep or even attempt to. I just prayed over and over again that Harold would be returned safely to me.

Tommy appeared at about ten o'clock looking ashen and shocked after having visited the house. 'They're saying it was definitely some sort of an explosion on the landing,' I heard him tell Gran and shock coursed through me. 'The forensics and a bomb squad are up there now. But what about Harold? Has there been any news?'

'Not so much as a sausage,' I heard her snap back. 'Though you'd have known that had you been here. I have to say this, be it my place or not: I reckon you ain't been doin' fair by our Maisie just lately. What's got into you, man?'

There was silence for some seconds, and then I heard him

mutter something though I couldn't hear clearly what it was. Slowly I dragged myself downstairs, and when I reached the stairs door I stared at Tommy across the distance that divided us.

I saw colour flame into his cheeks and he spread his hands as he said, 'I . . . I'm so sorry, Maisie. I only just found out what's been going on when I went to the house. How are you coping?'

Ignoring his question, I looked him in the eye and said, 'Where were you when I needed you, Tommy?'

I watched his Adam's apple bob up and down, but before he could answer I turned about and went back to the bedroom, where my vigil continued.

At teatime, Gran came rushing upstairs flapping the evening newspaper at me. 'Eeh, would you just look at this, lass? It's plastered all across the front page. *Local Author's Son Goes Missing*. It don't take the buggers long to clock on to owt that's wrong wi' you, does it?'

For once I didn't mind being in the paper. I wouldn't have minded anything so long as it brought Harold safely back home to me. There was a great empty hole slowly opening up inside me and I just wanted to shut myself away from the world. Tommy had gone back to the house to see if any of our belongings could be salvaged. Meantime I had bathed and was wrapped in one of Gran's faded old candlewick dressing gowns. It was a far cry from the expensive lingerie and nightwear that I had become accustomed to, but at that moment I would happily have worn rags. Nothing mattered, only getting Harold back. Mike had called in twice more during the day and each time he had eyed me silently, as if he was trying to weigh up in his professional opinion how I was coping with things. He had left some pills with Gran but I had refused to take them. I

Rosie Goodwin

wanted to keep my mind clear in case the police brought word
of my son.

It had occurred to me mid-afternoon that I ought to let
Janet know what had happened, but I thought better of it. After
all, he hadn't been missing for that long as yet and I had no wish
to alarm her unnecessarily. The police had assured me that the
majority of children turned up within the first twenty-four
hours of going missing, and I was clinging to this thought like
a lifeline. I had barely spoken two words to Tommy all day
although he had almost bent over backwards to please me. I
could not forgive him for not being there when I had needed
him most, and I wondered now if I ever would. Polly had visited
earlier in the afternoon to see if there was any news, looking like
a ghost of her former self. Father Makin had also put in an
appearance shortly after teatime, but I had left Gran to entertain
him. And now it was nearing dusk and still there was no news
and the first long twenty-four hours was almost up.

Two lots of police officers had called during the day asking
yet more questions and I had calmly answered them all as best I
could. Now I just sat on the edge of the bed staring off into
space and willing Harold to come home. I heard Tommy arrive
back and Gran's voice carried up the stairs as she asked him, 'Did
you manage to get any clothes?'

'Nothing,' I heard him reply. 'If Maisie had been in that
bedroom when the bomb went off she wouldn't have stood a
chance, so I suppose we have that to be thankful for at least.'

Huh! I thought; what does he know anyway? I wished that
I had been in the room, for then I would not be feeling this
pain. This terrible, crippling pain that was threatening to choke
me. But who could hate me enough to plant a bomb in my
home?

'I'll have to go out first thing then an' get her the basics.'

This was from Gran. 'Mary will come with me an' choose her a few bits an' pieces. She certainly ain't up to it! Eeh, I sometimes wonder what we've done to deserve all this, I really do. But then as I've told Maisie afore, trouble seems to find her wherever she goes. I just wonder if she ain't fated for sorrow.'

The police visited us again later that evening to tell us that they were now sure that the explosion at the house had definitely been caused deliberately by a home-made bomb, but seeing as they had no clue yet as to who the suspect might be, they needed to ask some more questions. And so the grilling began again. Could I think of anyone who might have a grudge against me? Did I owe money to anyone? On and on the questions went, most of them going over my head. I was too sick with worry about Harold to care about the house. It could fall to the ground as far as I was concerned, as long as I got my boy back. I was torturing myself with mental images of what might have happened to him. The police were now also thinking that Sandy's disappearance may not have been coincidental and informed us that they were questioning people down at the docks in case anyone might have seen someone with him on the day he had gone missing.

By the time the officers left, I was mentally and physically drained. It was unbelievable that there was someone out there who hated me enough to do these things, and try as I might I could think of no one who might be responsible.

The night dragged by painfully slowly, and with each hour that passed my heart broke a little more. Harold had now been missing for over twenty-four hours and I dared not allow myself to think what this might mean.

Tommy stayed close to my side, as if he was trying to make up for the fact that he had not been there at the time when I had most needed him. Yet strangely, his company meant nothing to me now. I was looking at him through different eyes and had finally accepted that I should never have married him. I had been missing Nardy and had seen Tommy as a port in a storm. Someone to stop the unbearable loneliness. So I supposed in a way that I was as much to blame as he was for our marriage not being a resounding success. I had thought that it would be a case of third time lucky, but yet again I had been proven wrong and now I wondered if I was ever destined to know lasting happiness.

As Tommy and I lay in bed that night side by side, his gentle snores echoed off the walls, but there was no such release for me. My eyes were gritty and smarting through lack of sleep, but until I knew that Harold was safe I could not allow myself to rest. What if he was somewhere calling for me? What if he was injured or . . . I turned my thoughts away from that direction, for I knew that if anything happened to Harold my life would be over too.

Gran brought us a cup of tea early the next morning and frowned when she saw me wide awake.

'You ain't been to sleep, have you?' she scolded as she drew the curtains. 'Your eyes look like two pissholes in the snow. You ain't going to be no good to neither man nor beast if you go on like this. Harold is goin' to need you when he comes home, lass, so you must start to think o' yourself a bit. I'll get Dr Kane to prescribe you somethin' to help you rest when he calls in. An' have you seen what's goin' on outside? There's a row o' reporters a mile long. Happen you'd be best to stay indoors today.'

'I had every intention of doing just that. I'm hardly going to go off gallivanting while Harold is missing, am I? And I don't *want* anything from Dr Kane,' I said obstinately as she handed me my tea.

With a shake of her head she turned and wearily left the room.

It was as I was sitting there propped up against the pillows, sipping at my tea, that a thought occurred to me and I asked, 'Tommy, you aren't in trouble again, are you? With anyone who might be capable of doing this to us?'

'Of course I'm not,' he spluttered indignantly. 'How could you even think that of me?'

'Well, *someone* hated you enough to trash the flat when we lived in London,' I pointed out, but he shook his head vehemently.

It was then that we heard a car pull up outside and soon after someone rapping sharply on the front door. Minutes later Gran ran breathlessly back into the room. 'The police are here to see you again, hinny.'

Swallowing my apprehension, I swung my legs to the side of the bed and dared to ask, 'Have they got any news?'

She shook her head. 'I don't know, lass. They wouldn't tell me nothin'. They just told me they wanted to speak to you.'

I could hear Tommy climbing out of bed behind me as I followed her to the door and we made our way back down the steep narrow staircase in a procession.

A tall man with a large red nose and eyebrows that met in the middle was standing in the middle of Gran's sitting room. When I entered he held out his hand. 'I'm Inspector Blake, Mrs Balfour.' He flashed an identity card in front of my eyes before saying, 'Is it convenient for you to talk? I realise that this is a very distressing time for you.'

'Of course.' I pulled Gran's old dressing gown more tightly about me as I motioned him to a seat and sat down opposite to him.

After clearing his throat he began. 'Given the three incidents that have occurred over the last couple of days we are forced to surmise that someone has it in for you, Mrs Balfour, and it occurred to me that seeing as you are something of a celebrity in the town, someone could have kidnapped Harold and be holding him to ransom.'

My hand flew to my mouth. This hadn't occurred to me before, but I could see that he might well be right.

'Have you had any notes demanding money?'

When I shook my head vigorously he sighed. 'It may be that they haven't had time to send one yet if what we fear is the case. With your permission we will be having an officer stay at the house at all times for the time being. As you must understand, even if our kidnap idea proves to be unfounded, whoever has done these things may well try something else.'

Tommy had come to stand behind me and now he placed his hand protectively on my shoulder as he asked the Inspector, 'Are you saying that Maisie might still be in danger?'

'I'm afraid that we can't rule that possibility out at present.' The Inspector pursed his lips.

Gran sat down heavily in the nearest chair, and now it was me who spoke. 'If that's the case, then I think Tommy and I should go to stay somewhere else. I don't want to put Gran at risk of being hurt.'

'You'll do no such thing,' she sputtered indignantly. 'We're family, an' families should stick together in times o' trouble. Besides, if anyone were to come here tryin' to hurt you, they'd have to get past me, lass. An' I assure you, I'd down the buggers afore I'd let that happen.'

I saw a spark of amusement flash across the Inspector's face. 'I have an officer outside ready to come in to keep watch, and should you receive any communication from anyone concerning Harold's disappearance I wish to be informed immediately.'

This was becoming more bizarre than anything I had ever written in a novel, and I could hardly take in what he was saying.

'I should also warn you, Mrs Balfour, that you could receive a demand for his safe return over the phone rather than in a note. In either case you must inform me straight away. I don't want you to try and handle this yourself. You could be placing yourself in grave danger. Do you quite understand?'

When I nodded numbly he smiled with satisfaction. 'Good, I shall send my officer in then. She will monitor any calls that come in and keep a close eye on the door for notes.'

Tommy saw the Inspector to the door as I sat as if rooted to the spot. When he returned he had a young policewoman with him. She approached me and introduced herself. 'Hello, I'm PC Connor.' I inclined my head and she went on, 'I shall try to stay in the front room as much as I can, Mrs Balfour. I have a clear view of the letterbox from there, but what I would ask is that if you have any incoming calls you will alert me before answering them.'

I noticed that she wasn't the prettiest of girls, but then her plain uniform did her no favours. Her mousy hair was scraped back into an unbecoming bun on the back of her head and her eyes were a dull grey colour. Even so, she seemed to have a nice nature. She smiled and with a nod at us all went discreetly through to the front room, closing the door softly behind her. And so began what was to be another long day.

Chapter Twenty-Five

ARLY IN THE afternoon, Tommy slipped out to check that all was well at the yard. We seemed to have done nothing but drink tea all morning and now my nerves were at breaking point, brought about by lack of sleep and worrying about Harold.

We had received two phone calls, and each time PC Connor had hurried into the room and stood at Gran's side while she answered them. One had turned out to be from Janet, who Gran had phoned earlier in the day, and the other from George. At this stage I would almost have welcomed a ransom note, for the waiting was unbearable. Mary and Gran had also gone out earlier in the morning and had returned with a few clothes for me. I slipped into them without even looking what they were like. I knew I must look a sight but I was beyond caring, and with every hour that passed my spirits sank a little lower. While the police had told me that most missing children turned up safe and well within the first twenty-four hours, they hadn't said what happened beyond that. They had had no need to, and the knowledge was terrifying.

Gran had been upstairs tidying the beds and I noticed when she came back into the room that she looked almost as exhausted as I did. 'Do you fancy a bite to eat, pet?' she asked,

The Sand Dancer

keeping her voice light. I shook my head. I knew that if I tried to swallow anything it would choke me.

'Eeh!' She stood there looking at me, hands on hips. 'You've got to try to eat somethin'. The way you're goin' on they'll be cartin' you off to hospital afore long. What use are you goin' to be to that little lad if you carry on like this, I ask you?'

It was then that Mike strode into the room. Sensing the tense atmosphere he asked, 'So what's to do here, then? You look like a pair of opponents squaring up to each other in a boxing ring.'

Gran's shoulders suddenly sagged and she swiped her hand across her brow. 'Oh, take no notice of us, Mike! I reckon feelin's are runnin' a little high.'

'That's understandable, but you have to stand together at a time like this.'

'Aye, you're right, man. Never a truer word was said; but just look at her, for Christ's sake. She's droppin' on her feet an' I were just tryin' to get a sup o' summat inside her. She ain't slept for over twenty-four hours now an' I'm concerned about the lass.'

As he looked towards me he raised his eyebrows and told me sternly, 'Your gran does have a point you know, Maisie. Why don't you just go up and try to rest for a while? I'll bring you a drink before I go.'

Sensing that it was useless to argue, I slowly made my way towards the stairs door. Once upstairs I curled into a ball on top of the bed feeling more lonely than I had ever felt in my whole life, apart from the dark days following Nardy's death, that was.

Twenty minutes later, Mike tapped at the door and came in carrying a glass of lemonade. 'Come on, get this down you,' he ordered. 'I thought you might have had enough of tea so I brought you a cold drink instead.'

Knowing it would be pointless to argue with him, I sat up in the bed and reluctantly took the glass from his hand. I had had

279

no more than a few sips under his watchful eye when a strange
sort of lethargy began to creep over me.

Staring at the glass suspiciously I snapped accusingly, 'You've
put something in this, haven't you?'

He made no attempt to lie. 'I have. Just a couple of pills,
mind. In a few minutes you'll go out like a light and hopefully
you'll feel a bit better when you wake up.'

Turning my back on him, I slammed the glass on to the
bedside table and lay back down, and just as he had said, within
minutes I was fast asleep. My dreams were vivid and weird. I
could see Harold and he was trying to reach out to me, but
something was stopping him. And there was a noise. It was a
noise I recognised yet couldn't place.

It was dark when I awoke and I went downstairs to find that the
young policewoman who had spent the day with us had now
gone off duty and a policeman had taken her place.

'Ah, there you are, hinny,' Gran greeted me. 'You must be
feelin' a bit better after your rest.'

Ignoring her, I asked, 'Has there been any news?'

Tommy, who was sitting to the side of the empty grate,
looked away as Gran shook her head regretfully. 'Not a peep,
pet. But it's early days yet. You'll have news soon, never you
fear . . . an' guess what? Janet's bringin' the bairn tomorrow. It
seems that James has been posted off on some undercover job
somewhere an' will only be managin' to get home at weekends,
so she's comin' to spend some time with us. That'll be nice,
won't it?'

I nodded miserably. There was something about the dream I
had had that was troubling me, but for the life of me I couldn't
think what it was. It was then that Dusty suddenly walked
straight through the door and stopped abruptly in front of me.

You must think! It's something important. It will lead you to Harold.

I huddled into a ball in a chair and tried and tried to think, but my mind had gone blank and the more I tried to remember what it was that had been so important the further whatever it was I was trying to remember slipped away.

We were all preparing for bed some time later when the phone rang and the young policeman appeared from the front room to stand beside Gran. He nodded at her, and lifting the receiver she said, 'Hello?'

She listened for a second to whoever it was on the other end, and then her face paled as she held the receiver away from her and told me, 'It's somebody for you, lass.'

The policeman was standing against my shoulder now, and when he gave me the nod I took the receiver from Gran.

'How does it feel, eh?' It was a male voice, loaded with menace. 'To have someone you love taken away from you?'

'*Wh . . . at?* Who is this?' I was shaking so much that I feared I would drop the phone, for there was something about the voice that was vaguely familiar. The young policeman was urging me to go on talking, and so I managed to say, '*Please . . .* if you have Harold, I'll pay *anything . . .* only don't hurt him, I beg you. He's just a little boy.'

A harsh laugh sounded in my ear and then the phone went dead in my hand. I stood there staring at it.

'Did you recognise the voice? Mrs Balfour, listen to me, you *must* try . . . Did you recognise the voice?' The young policeman was almost shouting, but I was so deep in shock that I could only gaze blankly back at him with my mouth hanging open. Suddenly taking his radio from his pocket, he began to talk into it, and within minutes the street outside was alive with the sound of sirens and there seemed to be policemen everywhere.

I looked around to see Inspector Blake striding into the room with a grim expression on his face. He stopped directly in front of me. 'You must tell us everything that was said, Mrs Balfour. Did he ask for money?'

'N . . . no.' With a tremendous effort I told him everything word for word, and when I had finished he slammed one hand on the table in frustration.

'Damn and blast. I'd lay odds that whoever that was has the bairn. Are you *quite* sure you didn't recognise the voice? What was the dialect like? Did it sound like someone from around here? A Cockney accent, or perhaps Irish? *Please* think hard, Mrs Balfour. Anything you can remember might help us to find him.'

'It was a northern accent, broad,' I said without hesitation. 'And yes, I *did* think it sounded familiar, but I can't put my finger on where I've heard it before.'

'Did it sound like an old or a young person?'

'Y . . . young, I think . . . but I couldn't be sure.'

'*Blast!*' The Inspector sighed with frustration, then, his expression softening, he told me, 'Don't whip yourself. Try to calm down and happen it will come to you.'

'Happen it will, but not wi' you bloody lot hoverin' over her,' Gran snapped. 'Why don't you all get yourselves away an' if she remembers owt I'll be straight on the phone to you. Can't you see the lass is almost at the end of her tether?'

The Inspector edged towards the door. 'If you do remember anything, no matter how small, tell PC Cook here and we'll be back. Meantime I'm going to post a man at the front and the back of the house just to make sure you're all safe. Good night all.'

Once he had gone I began to pace up and down the confines of the small room going over again and again what the mysterious caller had said. *How does it feel, eh? To have someone you love taken away from you?* Why had he sounded so familiar? There was something . . .

'Look.' Tommy caught my shortened arm and pressed me down into a chair. 'I'm going to get you a stiff drink; you look like you could use one.'

'Make that two, lad,' Gran shouted after him as he went into the front room to fetch the whisky bottle from the sideboard. 'Eeh, what's to become of us, eh?'

If only I knew, I found myself thinking. If only I knew!

Once again I found myself tossing and turning at Tommy's side as the long night slowly gave way to dawn. In the morning Tommy went to the yard to see that all was well. He was also going to call at the house to find out what was happening there. While he was gone, Gran and I heard a commotion at the front door. The young policewoman was back on duty again and it was she that told us, 'There's a taxi outside. It looks like someone's coming here.'

Gran peeped around the net curtain and then cried with delight, 'Eeh, bless my soul, it's Janet!'

She flung the front door open and hurried out to greet her. I stayed where I was. Normally I would have been excited at the prospect of a visit from Janet and the baby, but at the moment the only one I wanted news of was Harold. The papers were still plastered with news of his disappearance, but thankfully the number of reporters who had lined the street was now diminishing and so Gran was happy to step outside again.

PC Connor carried Janet's heavy case in, followed closely by Gran, who was billing and cooing at Jessica, and finally by Janet, whose face was the colour of putty.

'I can't believe it,' she told me as she clasped my hands in hers. 'Has there been any news of me lad? An' how are you bearin' up?'

'Oh, you know . . .' I knew I was being vague but what did she expect me to say? She must have known that I wouldn't be sitting there looking like the end of the world was nigh if there had been news.

When she dropped down beside me and buried her face in her hands I instantly felt guilty. Janet was Harold's grandmother, but I was so locked in my own fear that I had forgotten that for a time. Now I realised that she must be feeling just as awful as I was.

'Shall I go and put the kettle on and make you all a drink?' PC Connor offered, and I nodded at her and raised a smile. She was proving to be a tower of strength and I somehow felt safer knowing she was there.

Minutes later she came bustling back into the room with a laden tray and started to spoon sugar into the cups. Once they were all handed round, Gran placed Jessica in my arms. As I stared down at her, I was sure that she had grown again in the short time since I had last seen her. If anything, she was even more beautiful than I remembered.

'She's changin' wi' every day that passes,' Janet informed me as if she could read my mind. 'An' she's as good as the day is long, bless her. But come on; tell me all that's been happenin'.'

And so Gran and I stumblingly filled her in on everything that had happened, as Janet looked on with her mouth agape.

'Well!' She shook her head in disbelief and we all lapsed into silence. Eventually she said, 'I was wonderin' if you'd mind puttin' me an the little 'un up for a time. I've let James know I was comin' an' seein' as he's been posted up this way somewhere he'll probably put in an appearance.'

'Gladly,' Gran told her. 'But what's he doin' workin' hereabouts?'

'Don't ask me,' Janet sniffed. 'You know he works undercover so I never get to hear what he's doin'. It's all very cloak an' dagger. They sent him up here yesterday, an' I just hope he ain't workin' on a case that's goin' to put him in any danger, that's all.'

The silence settled again and the waiting continued.

It was in the middle of the following morning that someone rapped at the door. PC Connor opened it and took a small package wrapped in brown paper from the postman. She carried it into the middle room and handed it to me.

I took the parcel and slowly turned it over. I did not recognise the handwriting and could think of no one who would address anything to me at Gran's house. It was crudely wrapped and tied with string, and as I began to open it my fingers were shaking. When I had finally managed to pull the paper apart, tears sprang to my eyes as I found myself looking down on a bright red bicycle bell. It was Harold's; I would have recognised it anywhere.

'*Nooo!*' The sound that issued from my lips was like something that might have come from a wounded animal. Whoever had Harold had sent this to torture me, and they had succeeded.

PC Connor took it gently from my hand and instantly began to radio through to the police station as Gran led me to a chair and wrapped me in her arms, muttering, 'Eeh, where is this all goin' to end? May the Blessed Mother have pity on us.'

Harold had been missing for three days when the next call came. I was sitting staring out of the back window across the shared yards when the phone rang. PC Connor appeared as if by magic from her post at the front window and nodded at Gran, who lifted the receiver.

'It's for you,' she told me, her eyes flashing a hidden message.

I gulped deeply before taking it from her hand. Within seconds the same voice was speaking. 'Enjoyin' your wait, are you? Well . . . it won't be long now. What goes round comes round.'

'What do you mean? Who are you? And where is Harold?' I could feel hysteria rising inside me like a tide but I was talking to a dead line. PC Connor tried to take the phone from me but I fought her as I screamed into the receiver, 'Please don't do this . . . I can't stand any more . . .'

'Mrs Balfour. Maisie, please . . . Let me have it.' The police-woman somehow managed to prise the phone out of my hand as tears erupted from my eyes and I began to sob.

'I . . . I can't stand this any longer. What did he mean, *it won't be long now*?' I felt dizzy and sick with fear, and as Gran stood to one side of me and Janet to the other I began to fight them. 'Get off me, do you hear? I want my son. *Where* is my son?' And then the floor was coming up towards me and I must have fainted, for suddenly there was nothing but darkness and I welcomed it.

'Maisie, can you hear me?'

A voice was coming from a long way away but I tried to shut my ears to it. It was nice in the darkness. There was no pain, no fear . . . nothing.

'Maisie, it's me, Mike. Can you hear me?'

My eyes were open now and I heard myself saying, 'He's got Harold. He's going to hurt him, Mike. We have to stop him. But who is he? And why is he doing this? Harold is just a little boy, he's never hurt anyone.'

'I know, hinny, I know. Now try to calm yourself. The police are doing all they can.'

I became aware of Dusty standing behind Mike with his head bent low on to his chest, and as he followed my eyes Mike asked, 'Is that damn horse here again?'

'No, no, it's Dusty.'

'*Dusty?*'

'Yes, Dusty is a donkey. He's Hamilton's friend.'

Mike shook his head in exasperation as he said softly, 'I don't know, Maisie, it's a good job it's me you're talking to otherwise they'd be carting you off to the loony bin. Now come on, try and sit up, and take it steady now.'

When he had me in an upright position, I became aware of Inspector Blake standing at the end of the settee. Coming forward now he asked, 'Was it the same person who phoned before?'

'Y . . . yes, I think so. In fact I'm sure of it.'

'And do you still not recognise the voice? You must think very carefully now, Maisie.'

I screwed my eyes up tight as I again heard the voice in my mind, but try as I would I couldn't place it.

'It's all right.' Mike placed his arm protectively around my shoulder and looked towards the Inspector. 'I think she's had enough for now. I'm going to give her something to make her sleep for a while and maybe when she's a little calmer she'll remember something.'

'I don't want to sleep,' I told him, but even as I spoke he was lifting something from the coffee table and before I knew it he had rolled up my sleeve and I felt a sharp prick in my arm.

'Right, now it's up to bed for you,' he said firmly as he helped me to stand. I went unresisting, suddenly too tired to fight any more.

Even before we had reached the top of the stairs my eyelids were drooping, and within minutes of him laying me on the bed I was fast asleep and once more trapped in nightmares. Harold was there and he was calling for me. The noise that I had heard before was in the background again, but it was louder this time. Much louder, a slapping noise that came and went . . . I was calling to Harold and running towards him, but the faster I ran the further away he seemed to get, and now Dusty was there running alongside me and his voice was urgent as he told me, *You must run faster* . . . I was crying, great gulping sobs that shook my body and slowed me down, but I couldn't seem to stop.

'Maisie . . . wake up. You're having a nightmare!'

My eyes snapped open and I found that I was in the small bedroom at Gran's house. It was dark and Tommy was lying beside me.

'I . . . I was with Harold,' I gasped. 'But I couldn't reach him . . . He . . . he kept getting further away.'

'It's all right.' Tommy's arms were about me now and he was rocking me back and forth, but I pushed him away as I struggled with the memory of the sound I had heard. And then it came to me in a blinding flash.

'It was water!'

'Water?'

'Yes, yes, water. Like a slapping sound. The sound it makes when it hits the side of a boat!'

We were staring at each other now, and both together we said, '*Spring Fever.*'

Tommy swung his legs out of the bed and started to pull his trousers on. 'I'll go down and tell the police. They'll know what to do.'

'*No!*' I was in a panic now. 'If we tell them and they go there, whoever has Harold may hurt him. We have to go alone.'

Tommy paused in the act of doing up the buttons on his shirt. 'Won't it be a bit risky going on our own?'

My chin jutted in determination. 'You can please yourself, but *I'm* going,' I told him firmly. I was already out of bed and slipping my shoes on. Days of not eating or sleeping properly had taken their toll and I felt sick and dizzy, but wild horses would not have stopped me now.

'And just how are we supposed to get out of the house without being seen? They've got officers posted at the front and the back.'

I hadn't thought of that and I chewed on my lip for a moment before saying, 'If we creep out the back way they might not see us in the dark. If they do, we'll just say that we couldn't sleep and needed some fresh air. Where is your car parked?'

'Further down the road. I gave up trying to park outside days ago because of all the blasted reporters.'

'Good. We can slip down the alley and get into it once we're clear of the house.'

Tommy didn't look too happy about the idea but he followed me from the room all the same, probably realising that I meant to go with or without him.

Once on the landing I paused to raise a finger to my lips. I could hear Gran walking about in her room and guessed that she was unable to sleep.

We crept down the staircase like two thieves in the night. Peeping into the middle room, I was pleased to see that it was empty, which meant that the policeman was no doubt in the front room.

Within minutes we were outside in the back yard and I gulped at the damp night air.

'Look, why don't we hop over the wall and go into the alley

through the neighbour's garden,' Tommy whispered. 'That way whoever is watching our gate might not see us.'

I nodded in agreement and Tommy swung his long leg over the small wall that divided the yards. He then helped me to clamber over it, and bending low we crept down the garden like two criminals. Tommy inched the gate open and peeped down the alley to the police car that was parked outside Gran's. Luckily there were no lights here, so it took us only seconds to sneak out. Keeping close to the wall, we made our way to the entry that would lead us back on to the street. And there I dared to breathe again as Tommy fumbled in his pocket for the car keys. We were on our way and I was praying as I had never prayed before: 'Please God, let Harold be there and let him be safe. If you do this one thing for me I swear I will never ask you for anything else.'

I sank down into the seat as Tommy turned the car in the direction of Newcastle. All I could do now was try to quell my impatience and continue praying.

Chapter Twenty-Six

A S WE DROVE TOWARDS the marina where *Spring Fever* was moored, the heavens seemed to open and the rain that had been threatening all day came down in torrents.

Tommy cursed and leaned forward over the steering wheel as the windscreen wipers battled to deal with the downpour. At the same moment there was a crack of thunder and the sky overhead lit up with lightning. The wind was howling around the car and when we finally pulled on to the docks we could see the sea lashing against the quay.

'Damn!' Tommy skidded to a halt and switched off the engine and the lights, and we both looked towards *Spring Fever*. She was thrashing about on the waves, her fenders smashing against the wooden pontoon that ran alongside her, but there was no sign of any life aboard and she was in complete darkness.

'Perhaps we're barking up the wrong tree?' Tommy muttered, but I shook my head. Some gut instinct told me that Harold was close and I had no intention of leaving until I had checked the boat out. Seeing that I was determined, Tommy climbed out of the car, and by the time he had walked around to the passenger door to help me out, his hair was plastered to his scalp.

With our heads bent against the driving rain we ran across the quay. Even in this terrible weather *Spring Fever* still managed to look impressive. Tommy had bought her for the princely sum of £31,000 from Mr Percy Liddle shortly before we were married, and we had honeymooned on her. At thirty-five feet she was one of the biggest yachts in the marina, and though at one time she had been Tommy's pride and joy, since the death of Captain Ned he had hardly set foot on her apart from to sail her up here from London. It seemed a shame, for even I, who had never professed to be much of a sailor, had to concede that she was a magnificent craft.

We hurried past the three ropes that secured her to the cleats on the pontoon. They were tied firmly in figure of eights at her bow, stern and midship, but even so I wondered if they would hold against the ferocity of the storm. Tommy threw a gang-plank up on to her deck and turned to offer me his hand. I stared down at the swirling dark waters below with dismay but Tommy hissed, 'Don't look down, just take my hand, I won't let you fall.'

Taking a great gulp of air, I did as I was told, but my heart was thumping, for I knew that if I were to slip into the raging torrents beneath me I would stand no chance of ever getting out. Before I knew it, though, we were standing on the deck as the rain moulded our clothes to our shivering frames.

'Are you all right?'

I nodded as I tried to compose myself. The boat was rocking alarmingly and every second I expected a gust of wind to take me over the side, but even so I was determined not to leave until we had searched every single inch of her.

'Come on then.' Tommy gritted his teeth and I followed him to a short flight of steps that led down into the saloon. Once inside it and out of the wind, I stood for a moment as my eyes adjusted to the light. It was a wonderful room, all done out in shades of red and gold, and I found myself thinking of how shocked I had been the first time I had seen it. It had put me in mind of Nardy's lovely drawing room and had been nothing at all like what I had expected to find on a boat.

Tommy had located the light and I blinked when he switched it on. As I looked around I swallowed my disappointment, for everywhere was as neat as a new pin, with no sign whatsoever of anyone having been in there. We moved on into the dining area but again everything was as Tommy had left it. The same went for the bedrooms. By now my spirits were low, yet still a little niggling voice told me, 'He's *here*, he's *here* somewhere!' Even as the voice sounded in my mind, Dusty appeared. He was nodding vigorously in agreement, and I pushed past Tommy and raced into the galley. There I ground to a halt and stared about me. I had always been amazed at this room, for there were more labour-saving devices fitted in here than I had had back at The Chimneys. But it wasn't those my eyes were trained on; rather the piles of unwashed pots that seemed to cover every surface. Plates of half-eaten food and mugs of cold tea and coffee were everywhere I looked.

'Someone has been here,' I said dully, and as Tommy came to stand behind me he nodded in agreement. He would never have left the galley in this state. He had always taken a pride in *Spring Fever*. He raced off to check the bathroom, which was fitted not only with a bath but also with a shower, a sink and a toilet. When he rejoined me he said tersely, 'Someone has used that room too. If anyone is still here there's only two other places they could be, and that's either up in the wheelhouse or down in the engine room. Wait there, I'll check the engine room first.'

I stood listening to his footsteps recede and then for some

reason I began to walk towards the stairs that would lead me back up on to the deck. I knew I should have waited for Tommy, but Dusty was beckoning me on and I could feel Harold's presence calling to me.

Out in the driving wind again, I steadied myself as I walked towards the steps that led to the wheelhouse. The windows were in total darkness, but I knew this meant nothing. When I first flung the door open, it appeared that I was alone, but then I suddenly saw a shape huddled on one of the leather seats that stood to one side of the wheel. I ran to the light and clicked it on and in the same instant the shape leapt up and I found myself face to face with the Sand Dancer. He was wearing the balaclava that I had come to associate with him and his voice sent a chill down my spine. 'I wondered how long it would take you to work out where I was.'

It was the same voice that had spoken to me on the phone at Gran's, and my hand flew to my mouth as I stared at him in horrified fascination.

'B . . . but why would you do this to me?' I stammered. 'I . . . I don't even know you.'

'Oh, but you *do*, Mrs Stickle. You *do*.' As he spoke, he slowly pulled the balaclava over his head and I felt my legs buckle with shock, for I found myself staring into Howard Stickle's face. Or at least, a younger version of him.

'Y . . . you're Howard's *son*,' I gasped. 'The one that once kidnapped my poor Sandy and tortured him.'

He nodded his head in agreement and smiled, but his eyes were lit with hatred. 'That's right. But I went a step *better* this time, didn't I? Did you enjoy your flood and the little bang I organised for you at The Chimneys? What a *shame* you weren't in the house at the time I set it off. And Sandy, did he enjoy his swim?'

My head shook from side to side in denial. This was like a nightmare. I was back in the courtroom as the judge passed sentence on Howard, and his words were ringing in my head as he screamed at me: '*What's twelve years? I have a son, he'll see to you, you bloody barmy . . .*'

I wanted to turn and run, but first I must find out what the Sand Dancer had done with Harold.

'Where's my son?' I was standing straight now, and he laughed as he pointed under the wheel. Dropping to my knees, I tugged at a blanket that was lying there, and as it fell to one side there was my beloved boy, trussed and with a gag in his mouth.

Sobbing with relief, I began to pull him towards me, and his eyes snapped open as I pulled the gag from between his cracked dry lips. He heaved but then said weakly, 'Mum . . . yer came for me.'

'Of course I did, dear. And don't worry; you're going to be fine now.' I was tugging at the ropes that bound his wrists, but my hands were shaking so badly that it took me some minutes to untie them. And then he was in my arms, sobbing loudly as I crushed him to me as if I would never let him go.

'You're *mad*. You must be,' I ground out as I stared at Ronnie Stickle over Harold's head.

'Yes. I rather think you might be right.' His lips were set in a straight line now, and to my horror I saw that he was holding a knife in his hand as he advanced on me menacingly. 'But then, you know, my poor father was mad when they found him hanged in prison . . . and it was all because of *you*.'

'No, no, it wasn't.' Still holding Harold tightly to my side I began to inch towards the door, and when I was only a few feet away from it I pushed him in the back and shouted, 'RUN, Harold, RUN!'

The child was stiff from the hours he had spent trussed up, and although he tried to do as he was told I could see that every movement was painful to him. I expected the Sand Dancer to intercept him, but he chuckled and said, 'He can go. It's *you* I want. I only brought him here to get to you. I only ever went out with Betty to get to you! I planted a bomb in your home to kill you! And *now* I'm going to repay you for all the pain you caused my father, you stinking, whoring bitch!'

At that moment flashing lights appeared on the quay and I could faintly hear the sound of sirens above the howling wind and the pounding of the waves. I realised that the police must have spotted Tommy and me leaving the house and followed us, and then everything seemed to happen at once as Ronnie lunged towards me and I turned to run for the door.

The hairs on the back of my neck were standing to attention, and every second I expected to feel a knife plunge into my back. Harold had paused to look back, and as he saw what was happening he screamed, '*MUM!*' and began to run towards me shouting, 'Leave 'er alone, yer bloody great bully! Me Uncle Max will bloody clobber yer for this, you just see if he don't!'

I paused to look back over my shoulder, only to see the knife flashing down towards me. It was then that my foot caught in the blanket that had covered Harold and I felt myself falling. Harold was almost next to me now, and as I fell to the side the knife slashed past my shoulder and plunged into his chest.

I could hear someone screaming as I crawled across the distance that separated us and took my boy in my arms. At that time I had no idea that it was me. The Sand Dancer ran past me, only to collide with Tommy, who was climbing the steps to the wheelhouse, and now they were fighting and I could see fists flying as they fell together on to the deck.

'Harold, oh, my dear.' My tears were dripping down on to his face, and just for a second his eyes flickered open and he flashed me a faint smile.

'I . . . I love yer, Mum,' he muttered, 'Better'n . . . anybody.'

'I love you too.' Blood began to bubble from his lips as I rocked him to and fro, and then there seemed to be policemen everywhere and I heard a loud splash.

'Grab a boat hook before they go under!' I heard someone shout as one of the men dropped to his knees at my side. I was shocked to see that it was James.

'Call an ambulance, and tell them it's urgent,' he screamed over his shoulder. And it was then that the most curious thing happened, for as I stared up I saw Harold float out of his body and walk towards Dusty, who was waiting for him in the doorway.

He smiled at me as he whispered, 'Goodbye, Mum.'

'No, Harold, *please* don't leave me.' But they were walking away, and as I watched, they approached a shaft of bright light that had appeared on the deck.

My attention was pulled back sharply as I felt James put his hand on my arm, and when I looked towards him he shook his head sadly. 'I'm so sorry. I'm afraid he's gone, Maisie.'

I shook my own head in denial as I held my child to me all the more tightly and looked back towards the deck. Harold and Dusty were standing at the bottom of the shaft of light now, and they waved as if they hadn't a care in the world. And then the light slowly began to turn into mist and they were gone.

Hands were dragging Harold away from me and James was leading me out on to the deck, where I saw a huddle of policemen staring down into the churning waters below.

'Wh . . . where's Tommy?'

No one would meet my eye, and I knew in that instant that
Tommy was also gone from me, and I prayed that I might go
too, for I had nothing left to live for.

Chapter Twenty-Seven

I T WAS NOW EARLY in December, and as I stared from the window of St Mary's I saw the first flakes of snow begin to fall. For many months after losing Harold and Tommy I had known nothing. The days and nights as I looked back were just a blank. Sister Mary was now tucking a blanket across my knees as she told me cheerily, 'It will be Christmas before we know it. That's something to look forward to, isn't it now? And you'll be having visitors again today. Mr Bainbridge called this morning to say he would be bringing baby Jessica to see you.'

I nodded numbly. I preferred it when I didn't have visitors, if truth be told. And there had been so many of them over the time I had spent in the mental hospital. Mike and Jane, who looked ready to burst into tears every second of the time they were there. Father Makin, who sat quietly and held my hand as he offered up prayers, Gran, George and Mary, who always ended up weeping before they left the room. Polly, and Betty, who Gran informed me had lost the baby. Somewhere deep down inside I was glad. Had the child been born, there would have been yet another Stickle roaming the earth, and I didn't think I could have coped with that. The poor girl had been forced to face the fact that Ronnie Stickle had only ever bothered with her as a means of finding out my whereabouts, and I could only hope that this would have gone some way towards easing the loss of the child. Now she was free to start a new life.

I knew that I had been admitted to St Mary's after suffering a nervous breakdown shortly after Harold's death. There had followed dark, dark days when I had prayed for death. Over the months the visitors had pieced together what had happened, and I knew that if I had submitted such a story to Bernard Houseman he would have rejected it and told me that it was too unbelievable.

But only this morning the doctor had visited me to tell me that I was now on the mend and might even be well enough to go home in time for Christmas. Huh, what do I care? I could have told him. Christmas will be like any other day. Worse, for now I had no child to share it with, even if I still had a home to go to. The estate agents were under strict instructions to put The Chimneys on the market as soon as it was habitable again. But I didn't say anything. The words stayed trapped inside, just as they had since the night I had lost Harold.

I could vaguely remember being taken back to Gran's that night, where I had been astonished to hear James gently explain to me that the police had been watching Tommy for some time. It appeared that his scrap yard had been nothing more than a front. The containers of metal he had had shipped in had also contained guns and ammunition that he had been smuggling into the country for the IRA. He had become involved with them after running up huge gambling debts in London, which they had encouraged. When Tommy's debts were out of control, they had visited him on *Spring Fever*, where a furious row had erupted, and had resulted in Captain Lee's death when he had tried to defend Tommy. From that moment on they had used this as a way to control him, also threatening what they would do to me and Harold if Tommy didn't comply with their wishes.

As James spoke, everything began to fall into place: Captain Lee's death, Tommy's sudden need to move to Fellburn, the drastic weight loss, the constant need for money. It had been right there under my nose and yet I hadn't seen it.

I sighed as the gentle-natured nun now stood and straightened her habit. 'Right then, if there's nothing you need I'll be away. Ring the bell if you want anything, dear.'

I heard her leave the room as I sat there staring through the window. I had been in a dark, lonely place for a very long time. It didn't trouble me. In fact I would have liked to have stayed there, for anything was better than this great loneliness that seemed to have swallowed me up. Strangely, it had been James's first visit that had started me on the path back to recovery, for the second he had stepped through the door some weeks ago with Jessica in his arms, Hamilton and Begonia had appeared with their little foal between them, and I had felt as if I was coming out of an all-consuming fog. I had seen neither hide nor hair of Hamilton for all the long months I had spent here, and the sight of him had heartened me, for he had been my companion ever since I was a child and when he was absent I felt as if a part of myself was missing. He had been the one who had helped a lonely crippled child to cope with life, and now he was doing the same for the wreck of an adult that I had become.

I rarely thought of Harold, or at least I tried not to. But when I did, I always saw him with Dusty, happy and smiling as they went on their way together. Whenever I stared at the sky I would imagine them there with Nardy in a better place beyond the clouds. I had never seen Dusty since that night either, but I had managed to work out where he had come from. That mangy little donkey who spoke perfect English had really represented what I had wanted my adopted son to be. Well, hopefully, wherever Harold was he was happy, for I saw now that he had been perfect just as he was.

I laid my head against the back of the chair and willed myself to sleep. Sleep was my friend; while I was asleep I didn't have to think. Thinking was too painful.

Sister Mary woke me some time later. 'Your visitors are here, dear, let's tidy you up a bit, eh?' She hurried to the dressing table to fetch my hairbrush, and when she had finished she asked, 'Are you ready?'

I nodded numbly, and she bustled away with her long black habit floating about her. I looked towards a corner of the room and there were Hamilton and Begonia with their foal between them. She was growing now and was like a tiny carbon copy of her mother.

We've decided to call her Sky, Hamilton told me, and I thought this was strangely fitting seeing as the only comfort I got was imagining Harold somewhere up above the clouds.

The door was pushed slowly open and James entered with Jessica in his arms. She too was growing and now had a look of her father about her. James looked well, a far cry from the Mohican I had once known. His black hair now curled on his collar and his dark eyes when they looked into mine were twinkling.

Strangely, James never started his visits by asking how I was, as the other visitors did. He would simply sit at my side and chatter on about everyday things. I knew that I had him to thank for organising the funerals for Harold and Tommy, but as yet I had not been able to bring myself to. I could think of Tommy now without feeling angry, for despite his involvement with the IRA, he *had* tried to save me on that terrible night on *Spring Fever*. That night had led to a multitude of arrests, which I supposed was one blessing and may have saved countless lives. But as James had explained, they were only the tip of the iceberg. The IRA would find another means of bringing weapons into the country now that Tommy was no longer there to do it. I could also vaguely remember the police telling me that the Sand Dancer had drowned too after falling from the yacht with Tommy, but I had no idea what had happened to his remains, nor did I care.

'So,' James said now with a broad smile on his face, 'the doctor has just informed me that you are almost well enough to be discharged, and I got to thinking it might be nice if I took you back to London to the flat for Christmas.'

My eyes widened as I looked at him, and he went on, 'I know you're leasing it to me, but it's still your flat at the end of the day and I don't imagine that you'll want to stay in Fellburn, will you?'

I gulped deeply before slowly shaking my head, and he suggested, 'You could perhaps help Janet out with Jessica while I'm working. She does a grand job, but by her own admittance she's a bit long in the tooth now to be looking after a baby. And this little madam is getting to be a right handful, I don't mind telling you. Don't be fooled by her angelic appearance. She can be a little monster.' He chuckled as he bobbed Jessica up and down on his knee, then quite unexpectedly he gently settled her on to my lap, and suddenly the tears were swelling in my throat as she began to play with my hair with her chubby little fingers.

'There you are, you see.' His face was solemn now. 'She likes you. But don't worry, I don't expect you to be an unpaid babysitter. Once you're feeling stronger, if you feel you want to live in the flat on your own again, I can find somewhere else for

Jessica and me to stay. I just think it will be good for you to keep yourself occupied when you first come home. What do you say?'

As I stared down at that beautiful child, the tears that had been trapped inside suddenly exploded from me like water from a dam, and in a second James had both me and the baby cradled in his arms with his cheek against my hair as he murmured, 'That's it, let it all out now.'

I did just that, and when the tears finally slowed I felt strangely better. I had turned a corner, and when I said quietly, 'Oh, James,' I saw that he too was crying, for they were the first words I had uttered for months.

The nuns were lined up at the door to the home, and as I passed each one they shook my hand warmly. When I came to Sister Mary she wrapped her arms around me and whispered into my hair, 'Have faith, my child. God works in mysterious ways. May peace go with you.'

Peace. The word echoed in my head, for it seemed that this was one thing I had never managed to achieve. But James was not going to allow me to cry today, and taking my elbow he steered me outside to the waiting car and we waved at the nuns over our shoulders.

When we were seated he started the engine and told me, 'We're going to Gran's for lunch and then we'll set off for home later this afternoon if that's all right with you. Janet is already at the flat with Jessica and she can hardly wait to see you.'

I nodded as I swallowed down panic. After the months of being confined in the hospital, everywhere felt enormous and very loud. It was now the week before Christmas, and as we drove into Fellburn I saw that many of the houses we passed had Christmas trees standing to attention in their windows. Most had lights on them that twinkled on to the snowy paths outside, and I found myself thinking back to the previous Christmas and Harold's excitement as he had glimpsed his precious bicycle for the first time. But I could not allow myself to dwell on that memory or I would have to ask James to turn the car around and take me back to the sanctuary of St Mary's.

When we pulled up outside Gran's house, I was shocked to see a small crowd waiting on the pavement for me. There was Gran, George and Mary, with the children spread around them. Mike was there and Polly too, and as the car drew in to the kerb they all ran forward to greet me. I knew in that moment that I still had people who cared about me and I was not truly alone.

Gran hugged me until I thought she would break a rib before ushering me inside saying, 'Come on, hinny. Eeh, it's so lovely to have you home.'

The table inside was loaded with food, and although I wasn't hungry I forced myself to eat something, for I could see that she had gone to a lot of trouble.

Two hours later my case was loaded into the boot and they were once again all standing on the pavement to wave us off.

'You just try an' have a good Christmas,' Gran told me tearfully. 'An' don't forget, there's allus a home for you here, ain't that so, our Georgie?'

George nodded as he too stepped forward to hug me. 'It is so, an' you just remember that, lass. We'll always be here for you.'

I kissed them all before sliding into the car, and then we were on our way and I waved until they were out of sight. I was going home.

Chapter Twenty-Eight

I
t WAS EARLY IN AUGUST the following year. A glorious day
with the sun riding high in a cloudless blue sky. Janet had
moved back into her own home the previous month.

'After all,' she had said, 'too many cooks spoil the broth. Wi'
both of us fussin' over her the little 'un won't know if she's
comin' or goin'.' And so it was now me who cared for Jessica
while James was at work during the day, and I was loving every
minute of it. The months before had not been all plain sailing,
however. There were still dark, dark days when I just wanted to
shut myself away from the world and rant and rave at the
injustice of life. Days when I would have sold my very soul for
just one glimpse of my beloved child. But of course, now that I
had Jessica to run around after that was impossible, so somehow
I managed to force myself to go on, and unbelievably I was
finding that it was getting easier with each month that passed. I
could now think of Harold and smile as I remembered the good
times.

James and I had got on famously ever since the day I had
moved back into the flat. At night when he came home from
work we would bath Jessica and then he would play with her
for a while before she went to bed. Once she was asleep we
would watch television together and share a bottle of wine

while he told me what he had been up to during the day, and at weekends we would take Jessica to the park to feed the ducks or go shopping. Life had fallen into a pattern and I was grateful for it.

Janet called round to the flat mid-morning and we had lunch together as we laughed at Jessica's antics. She was now just over a year old and was a delightful bundle of mischief.

'She'll be walkin' any day now,' Janet commented as she watched her pull herself up by a chair. 'You just mark me words – an' then you'll have your hands full. You'll need eyes in the back o' your head.'

I smiled as I nodded in agreement, and we watched her affectionately as she dropped back down on to her bottom and started to hotch herself across the floor.

'Gran is coming down for the weekend,' I said as I poured a cup of tea. Janet's eyes lit up, and I got the feeling that once Gran arrived, James and I wouldn't get to see too much of her.

When we had finished our drinks, we took Jessica for a stroll in her pushchair, and then Janet set off for home while I headed back to the flat. When the doors to the lift opened in the outer hall I was surprised to see that James was home. Hitching Jessica on to my hip, I entered the flat and asked, 'Why are you home so early then?'

He grinned before retorting, 'Oh well, if it upsets you so much I'll go back to work, shall I?'

I laughed as I placed Jessica on the floor. She crawled across to him and held her arms up to be lifted, which he instantly obliged her with.

'Actually, the boss gave us the rest of the day off and I thought we might take her Ladyship here for a walk, but I see you've already beaten me to it.'

'She's going to need a sleep any time now, but I suppose

we could always take her out again when she wakes up,' I suggested, and he nodded. He followed me into the kitchen and watched as I filled the kettle at the sink. Jessica immediately trailed us in and pulled herself up to stand leaning on a kitchen chair.

'She's really coming on now, isn't she?' James's voice was soft as he stared at his baby daughter. 'And I think I have you to thank for that. You've been so good to her. I don't know how we would have coped without you.'

'You would have coped just fine,' I replied matter-of-factly. 'Janet would have managed.'

'I've no doubt she would, but it wouldn't have been quite the same, would it . . . What I mean is, as her having someone young to care for her.'

I laughed now as I pointed out, 'I would hardly term myself young. Forty is just around the corner for me, I'm afraid.'

'You'll always be young, Maisie. At least you will in my eyes.'

I felt my mouth fall into a gape as I slowly turned to look at him, and now colour flooded into his face as he crossed to stare down into the street from the kitchen window.

It was at that moment that the most incredible thing happened, for Jessica suddenly looked towards me and said quite clearly, '*Mamma.*' Then she loosened her hold on the chair and falteringly took her first steps towards me as James and I stared on incredulously.

I fought back tears of joy as I swept her up into my arms, and feeling ridiculously embarrassed I strode past James with my cheeks burning. 'I'll just go and put her down for her nap. She must be tired by now.'

I could feel his eyes following me as I left the room, and once I had tucked Jessica into her cot I stood for a moment trying to compose myself.

It was then that the nursery door inched open and James beckoned me into the hallway to join him. We stood facing each other until he said gently, 'Did you hear what she called you? I suppose we should make it official, if it's what Jessica wants.'

'Wh . . . what do you mean?'

'What I mean is: I love you, Maisie Balfour. And well you damn know it. I have done ever since the first day I clapped eyes on you. So what do you say? Are you going to make an honest man of me or what?'

I lowered my head and my voice was heavy with tears as I told him, 'I've tried marriage three times now, James, and look how it's turned out. I don't think I want to go down that road again. And anyway, I'm so much older than y—'

'Oh *don't* start that again.' He ran his hand through his hair and turning on his heel strode away to the kitchen, where I found him standing with a bunch of red roses in his hand facing the door.

'Now then, I bought you roses once before when I came to see you in the hospital after that idiot almost did for you, if you remember, but you gave them away to the nurses and married Tommy. Are you going to turn me down again?'

My heart was thumping wildly as I stared numbly back at him.

'All right then. At least answer one question for me. I deserve that much at least, and if the answer isn't what I'm hoping for, then I promise I'll never bother you again . . . Do you have any feelings for me at all?'

My head was up now, and as I gazed into his handsome face it slowly nodded of its own volition.

He took my hands in his and whispered, 'In that case, I have another proposition to put to you. If you don't feel ready to marry me, will you be my love? It's the nineteen eighties. We're not in the dark ages any more and no one cares today if people aren't married. I need a mother for Jessica and she has already chosen you, and I need someone to come home to. Someone that I love. Will *you* be that person, Maisie, and then we'll take it from there?'

'Y . . . you mean we could live in sin?'

His head was back now and he let out a great bellow of a laugh. 'Oh Maisie, you sounded just like Gran then, but yes, that's *exactly* what I'm suggesting.'

When his arms came about me I looked over his shoulder, and there were Hamilton and Begonia standing with Sky between them and they were all smiling and nodding at me. And so I looked back at this wonderful man and what I said was, 'Then the answer is yes, James, I'll be your love, and as you say, we will take it from there.'

His cheeks were wet with tears as he gently took my hand and led me towards the master bedroom. Just before he closed the door I saw Hamilton and his family walking away through the wall, and somehow I knew that I would never see them again. I had the strangest feeling that I would have no need of them any more.

'Goodbye, dear friends,' I whispered. Then I followed James into the room that we would share from now on, and softly closed the door on my past.